SWEET REALITY

REALITY STAR BOOK 2

LAURA HEFFERNAN

EMPRESS BOOKS

THE FALLOUT FROM THIS MADE-FOR-TV STORYLINE MAY BE ALL TOO REAL

Life after TV is looking up: Jen moved to Florida and her themed bakery is prepared to open with a bang. Then a major competitor threatens to put Sweet Reality out of business before they sell their first goodies. She's going to need a smash hit to keep the store afloat.

Then she has a brilliant idea: Jen joins a filmed cruise to convince fellow reality star Tammy Rae to give her the secret recipe for her baking-show-winning cupcakes. Problem is, Tammy Rae watched Jen on *The Fishbowl,* and she thinks Jen faked her relationship with Justin to trick the viewers. To get the key ingredient, Jen must convince Tammy Rae that their love is real—-right when the Network puts it to the ultimate test.

Saving the bakery means nothing if Jen loses Justin. She must find a way to remain true to herself, protect her relationship from her arch-nemesis, and save the bakery-all within the confines of a one-week cruise. Because once the ship docks back in Miami, she's sunk.

BOOKS BY LAURA HEFFERNAN

The Reality Star Series

America's Next Reality Star

Sweet Reality

Reality Wedding

The Oceanic Dreams Series

Time of My Life

The Gamer Girls Series

She's Got Game

Against the Rules

Make Your Move

Push and Pole Series

Poll Dancer

The Accidental Senator

Finding Tranquility

Anna's Guide to Getting Even

PRAISE FOR LAURA HEFFERNAN

SWEET REALITY

"If you like sweet contemporary romances with a reality show theme, then you are going to enjoy Heffernan's Reality Star series...Jen and Justin.are likeable and relatable characters....Heffernan does a wonderful job with character development and painting vivid scenes. There are also some cute and funny moments that makes this book a worthwhile and entertaining read. If reality shows are your guilty pleasure, give Heffernan's *Sweet Reality* a try."

- RT Book Reviews

AMERICA'S NEXT REALITY STAR

"Smart, witty, and really freaking good, *America's Next Reality Star* is a fun read that has you cheering from the first paragraph through the last page. Laura Heffernan spins an entertaining tale, expertly mixing the main character's real life events with the reality show's challenges. With enough drama to not only satisfy fans of reality TV shows, but readers who thrive on a good story with humor and romance, this book is a perfect read." —Kerry Lonsdale, *Wall Street Journal* bestselling author

"Reality TV fans, this is your book! Laura Heffernan captures all the drama and over-the-top craziness in this fun and flirty romance."

—Amy E. Reichert, author of *Love, Luck, and Lemon Pie*

"*America's Next Reality Star* is one sweet, sexy brain-candy read! You won't be sorry you indulged." —Leah Marie Brown

Copyright © 2018 by Laura Heffernan

Cover © 2021 by The Book Studio New Zealand

All rights reserved. No part of this book may be reproduced in any form or by any means without the prior written consent of the Publisher, excepting brief quotes used in reviews.

This book is a work of fiction. Any resemblance to real people, places, or situations is merely a coincidence.

Printed in the United States of America

❀ Created with Vellum

To Mandy

For all the awesome journeys we've shared,
and all the ones to come

ONE

SHOCKING ENTERTAINMENT NEWS ONLINE

RUNAWAY FISHBOWL COUPLE RETURNING TO TV?

by Talky Ted, Nov. 1

During the first season of *The Fishbowl*, Seattle's Jen Reid shocked viewers across the nation by accepting a $50,000 payout to leave the show and allow previously eliminated contestant J-Dawg to take her place.

The brown-haired, blue-eyed former marketing assistant admitted earlier in the show to mounting money problems, including homelessness. Many viewers thought she'd stick around to seek the grand prize. However, after viewers repeatedly nominated her for elimination, Jen wisely decided to take the money and run.

But that wasn't the end. Seconds after Jen announced her decision, her on-again, off-again love interest announced that he, too would leave the show. Despite being what many considered a serious contender for the grand prize, Justin Taylor of the startlingly green eyes and fabulous dimples followed Jen's limo down the driveway. The two shared a thrilling kiss before driving off.

Jen and Justin returned to their respective homes in Seattle and Florida. After the holidays, Jen moved to the Sunshine State where she invested her winnings in a bakery co-owned with Justin's twin sister, Sarah. In May, Justin graduated U. of Miami Law third in his class.

Sixteen months after their famous departure, America's most well-known reality couple may be returning to primetime. The Network recently announced a new show, *Reality Ocean: Caribbean*, which takes a boatload of former reality stars and their guests to the Bahamas, Jamaica, the Cayman Islands, and Mexico. The show begins filming next week.

Jen, Justin, and a spokesperson for the Network refused to comment, leaving this reporter hopeful the hunky blond former law student will be reappearing soon on a television near you.

Related Stories:
Shocking Reality TV Meltdown Gets 20m Hits on YouTube

America's Next Drag Supermodel **winner donates winnings to anti-gay-bashing organization**

Deaf Teen Mother **finale shocking, poignant**

I CRANED MY NECK, seeking any speck of light, but the makers of this blindfold should be proud of their craftsmanship. My roommate Sarah helped me out of her car and led me away, but I hadn't the faintest clue where we were going. Honking cars and street noise suggested we'd driven to somewhere in the city. The cool breeze and taste of salt in the air suggested we'd stopped near the beach, but in Miami, those clues told me little about our actual location.

"Jen, stop. You're peeking." At Sarah's order, I halted.

"I am not peeking. I can't see a thing." I could smell though, so I sniffed the air again, seeking other clues. Beneath the salt, the city odors, and the fabric of the blindfold lingered something else. Something not quite identifiable, but enticing.

"Then why do you keep tilting your head back?" Even with the blindfold, I could perfectly imagine Sarah's hands finding their way to her hips as she glared at me.

"Because I'm *trying* to peek," I admitted. "But I can't see a thing. Also, something smells amazing." The further we walked, the stronger the scent became. Wherever we were, something edible lurked nearby. Something *delicious* and edible.

"I'm glad you mentioned that. Stop here."

A lock *clacked* open, and a wave of cold air hit my face—air conditioning escaping from whatever building we stood in front of. It seemed strange when people used the AC in the fall, but October was oddly stifling in Florida this year. Odd to me, anyway, since this would be my first winter living in the South. Fall in my hometown of Seattle usually brought some clouds, some rain, some temperatures below a hundred degrees. Not in Miami, though.

That's what I got for falling in love with a soon-to-be lawyer. Thanks to state licensing laws, my boyfriend Justin couldn't exactly pick up and move to Seattle as easily as my unemployed, couch-surfing self moved to Florida and found a two-bedroom apartment with his sister.

His sister, who currently was leading me into a place full of enticing aromas. Cinnamon, chocolate, butter, vanilla . . . I couldn't even identify all the components of the amazing smell. While I waited for her to tell me what was going on, I lowered my head and wiped my chin in case I'd started drooling.

It wasn't my birthday, so a surprise party didn't make any sense, but I smelled cake. Justin and I were leaving for a cruise in a few days, but a surprise Tuesday morning bon voyage party seemed out of place. Maybe the cloak-and-dagger routine meant she'd come up with a surprise for our upcoming business venture, opening next year.

When I left *The Fishbowl*, I didn't have any more idea what to do with my life than before I started, but I did have more money. The producers paid a per diem: a cash stipend for every day on the show. After eight weeks on the set, I walked away with almost seventeen hundred dollars. Plus my fifty-thousand-dollar cash prize. Even after taxes, not bad for less than two months' work.

With no job, a boyfriend in Florida, and no place to sleep other than on my friend Brandon's couch, it didn't take long to find the perfect solution: become co-owner and manager of the bakery Sarah planned to open in Miami. My marketing background would help us promote the shop, and I loved talking to people, so the customer service aspect would be a breeze. Plus, being my own boss at least ensured I wouldn't get another crappy mass email if I ever laid myself off.

Starting a business is easier said than done, but while I gained experience working nine-to-five behind the counter of the grocery store's bakery, Sarah came up with the perfect idea: *Sweet Reality*, a bakery offering a variety of desserts inspired by reality shows and contestants. I'd act as the face of the company, hopefully bringing in fans of *The Fishbowl* and similar shows. Sarah had already designed fishbowl-shaped cookies and cupcake flavors inspired by the personalities of several first season contestants.

"Are we doing a secret taste test of a bakery to scope out the competition?" I asked.

"Not exactly. Hold on a sec."

Somewhere, a switch flicked, and light appeared beyond the blindfold. I still couldn't make out any shapes, but we no longer stood in darkness.

Finally, Sarah said, "Okay, take it off."

A sign reading SWEET REALITY hung across the far wall, with little television sets on either side and clapper boards in place of the E's. The sign jumped out from a wall covered with glittering stars, both of the astrological variety and from television.

"OMG, it's our bakery! I love it!"

"Isn't it amazing?" Sarah asked.

"It really is." A framed poster of me and Justin sharing our first kiss, which happened to take place on national television, hung near the front door where passersby could spot it. "Wow, that's a huge picture of us."

We'd had no idea the limousine driver taking me away from the Fishbowl carried a handheld camera, even though it made perfect sense in retrospect. Nothing we'd done during those eight weeks was private, why would our final goodbyes be? They wanted to catch the good stuff, and Justin chasing me down the driveway after I took a cash incentive to leave the show certainly qualified as "good stuff."

The poster brought a smile to my face. That kiss had been pretty good stuff, too.

"You're the draw," Sarah said, breaking into my memories. "We need to bring people into the store, and they want to see you and Justin kissing."

"And you're okay staring at a picture of me and your brother making out all day?"

"I'll be in the back, baking." She winked at me. "Besides, I like to think I played a hand in you two getting together, so why not profit from it?"

I laughed. Sarah and I first met in the bathroom at *The Fishbowl* audition, where we'd bonded instantly. When Justin said she was his twin sister, I'd been ecstatic at the thought of seeing her again after the show. Then, during a surprise family guest appearance on the show, Sarah had helped me and Justin realize we were both being idiots, letting a miscommunication and our fear of getting hurt overwhelm our feelings. We grew closer every day, and she'd become the sister I'd always wanted. No offense to my brother Adam who was lovely, but not quite the same. Sarah never once gave me an atomic wedgie.

"Thanks," I said, "but I think the show also helped a little bit. Not to mention, the two of us."

"Maybe. Anyway, I'm preparing recipes for Opening Day. Come see what I've made."

A row of cupcakes, cookies, brownies, lemon bars, and more filled the counter behind the display cases. My mouth watered in anticipation. "When did you do this? And how? I thought the contractors wouldn't be finished until the fifteenth?"

"They called yesterday to say they finished early. You were at Justin's, and I wanted to whip up a few recipes before bringing you in to see it. Surprise!" Her eyes danced. "We can open as soon as you get back!"

"That's amazing! I can't believe you made all this stuff for me. It looks fantastic. Although I hope you don't expect me to eat everything before I leave."

"No, Justin will help. I'll take a few things over to Mom's later. But also, we can freeze most of this so it's ready for the grand opening. I'm baking and freezing all this week and next."

"*Our grand opening!*" After months of working for this moment, I could almost taste it.

Unable to wait another second, I reached around Sarah and snagged a chocolate cupcake with chocolate-hazelnut frosting. I bit into it, moaning as rich, nutty sweetness exploded across my tongue. "This is fantastic, Sarah. We're going to sell a mill—"

All the color drained from Sarah's face. She started to say something, but choked on her words, sending a chill down my spine.

"What's wrong?"

Soundlessly, she pointed over my shoulder. I spun around, expecting to see the drugstore taking up most of the block across from us, and the silver slats and padlock barring the recently vacant store beside it. A store that no longer sat vacant or empty. Someone had raised the metal slats, the front door stood open, lights filled the front window, and the sidewalk bustled with people going in and out. All within the few minutes since Sarah led me in here.

A sign hung off the storefront, barely visible out of the front corner of our shop. GRAND OPENING! 10% OFF CUPCAKES TODAY ONLY.

No wonder Sarah's face had taken on the color of flour. Patty's Cakes, one of the most popular bakeries in Miami, had set up shop across the street from us. I could almost see our profits racing from our shop to theirs. How could we possibly compete with Patty's? How could we even stay open?

"What the hell is going on?"

Sarah's mouth opened and closed, but no sound came out. Oh, this was bad. So, so bad. The location, the timing, everything.

Patty's Cakes was a legendary shop, as much a fixture of this city as Disney World in Orlando. Well, okay, maybe not quite that much. But they were huge, and amazing cakes filled their windows already. And they'd opened before us.

A line of people already wound down the block and out of sight.

MY MOUTH DROPPED and my hand opened involuntarily, sending chocolate and hazelnut crumbs to the no-longer pristine white-and-silver tiles.

The store across the street sat on a corner, where it would get the pedestrian traffic we needed to bring in. It also sat directly in front of a bus stop. The same bus stop we hoped would bring customers to Sweet Reality, not to our competitor.

Patty's Cakes looked quaint and inviting, with its flowery pink and purple decorations. Worse, it was open *now*, whereas we wouldn't have anything to sell for at least two weeks. Even with the shop all set up, Sarah couldn't exactly throw out the OPEN sign and start selling goods at a moment's notice. The cash register wasn't even online yet, and we'd been counting on the free press from *Real Ocean: Caribbean* to start some buzz once it debuted after Thanksgiving. We couldn't throw away all our plans for a grand opening now.

"How did this happen? Why didn't we know about it?" I asked.

Sarah narrowed her green eyes, and her nostrils flared. "I don't know. They weren't there when I leased this space in June. The storefront wasn't even for rent—it was a cell phone store or something."

"What about when you were setting up, checking on the construction?"

"No! Don't you think I would have mentioned if I'd seen the sign? It's not like I forgot to say, 'Hey, Jen, we're going out of business before we even open!'" Her voice rose with each word, quickly trending toward a frequency only dogs could hear. This wasn't helping anything.

"It's okay. Calm down. I'm sorry. That's not what I meant. Just . . . you didn't see anything?"

"There's been activity over there," she said. "But with shutters over the windows and no sign, I didn't think anything was opening for months. I never thought it might be another bakery. Are they allowed to put a competing store across the street?"

I tapped furiously on my phone. "I don't know, but I'm texting Justin. There are perks to dating a lawyer."

My phone buzzed less than a minute after I hit Send.

It's legal unless you have a non-compete in your lease. I'm on my way. Will be there soon.

Sarah fell into a chair behind the glass cases, burying her face in her arms on the counter. Her shoulders heaved. Not knowing what to do, I patted her shoulder, trying to seem calmer than I felt.

Renovating and redecorating this shop used up most of the last of my *Fishbowl* money. Most of the severance pay from my old job was gone by the time I landed in Miami. If we didn't succeed, I'd be left with nothing. Sarah's baking skills grew more impressive every day; she'd get another job as a pastry chef or in a bakery in a heartbeat. Her former boss would probably pee herself in excitement if Sarah called asking for her job back.

But I'd been laid off a month before going on the show, and I didn't know anyone looking to hire a washed-up reality TV star who once worked in marketing. Justin's temporary job become permanent as soon as his bar exam results came in next week, but he wasn't going to support me. Not that I would ask him to. I needed to make this bakery work so I could support myself long-term.

"It's going to be okay," I said. Even to my ear, it sounded unconvincing. "We've got a unique hook, right? It's not just a bakery, it's Sweet Reality. People who eat here get baked goods to remind them of their favorite TV personalities. *Delicious* baked goods."

"What if it's not enough? They've got name recognition. We can't compete with that."

"Of course we can! They only make cakes and cupcakes. We make everything. Besides, you've got great recipes."

She didn't answer, absorbed by the scene outside. There wasn't much we could do until Justin showed up with more information, so I went into the kitchen for a broom to sweep up the mess of crumbs I'd made. If possible, it smelled even better in here than in the main room. Following my nose, I quickly found the source: four giant cupcakes, much bigger than the samples sitting by the display cases.

Strawberries peeked over the top of each white dome, and the bowl in the sink held the remnants of what turned out to be whipped cream, not vanilla icing. She'd made strawberry short-cake cupcakes! Judging from the little white cake bits on the counter beside the plate, the strawberries weren't only on top: Sarah stuffed these babies. It was just like her to hide the best treats for last, to completely floor me after I finished raving about everything else she'd made.

If I wasn't careful, I'd gain three hundred pounds working here. Unless Sweet Reality turned enough profit to buy me a whole new wardrobe in the next few months, I should talk to Justin about signing up for a joint gym membership before Sarah and I opened. Or maybe I should walk to and from work every day instead of taking the bus.

I promptly abandoned my plan to find a broom. We could clean up later. Instead, I ripped the wrapper off one of these amazing cakes, grabbed another with my free hand, and backed into the swinging door leading to the main room.

"Look what I found." I called.

Sarah stood at the front of the shop, peering out the window and nibbling her thumbnail. "You got a broom?"

"Better! Why didn't you tell me you'd hidden strawberry shortcakes back there? They look amazing!"

Sarah whirled around, her face stricken. I bit into the first cake, holding the second out to her.

"Wait!" She said at the same moment.

Too late. My teeth sank through the whipped cream and vanilla cake, closing in on the sweet, sticky strawberry filling. I savored the flavors in my mouth for a moment, eyes closed. Then my tooth hit something hard. A foreign object flew down my throat. I choked. The other cupcake tumbled to the ground, exploding at my feet.

"Oh, shit!" Sarah said. She ran toward me. "Are you okay?"

Unable to answer, I coughed and spit. Something hard lodged in my throat. Tears poured down my cheeks.

"Water," I croaked. "I think I just lost a filling."

Spinning around, I tore for the sink, one hand over my mouth to catch the crumbs spewing everywhere. Running my tongue around my mouth, I didn't find any holes, so my dental work remained intact. What I choked on was a mystery.

What the fuck did Sarah put in these things? How did strawberries and cake get so hard? And why would anyone put them in food if they did?

When I reached the sink I leaned over, hacking until I feared a lung might come up. Something shot out of my mouth, clattering against the sink. I shut my eyes, sagging against the counter for support.

Sarah appeared at my side. "Jen! Can you breathe? Talk to me."

"I don't think those are going to be a bestseller," I said when I finally got control of myself. "One of them cut me. My mouth tastes like metal."

I was reaching for the faucet to get some water when Sarah's hand closed over mine, staying it. Her green eyes were huge. "Listen to me. Did you swallow the ring?"

Did I what the huh?

I stared at her for what felt like a full minute. "The… ring?"

"My grandmother's diamond ring. I hid it in your cupcake. Where did it go?"

TWO

CELEBS MAGAZINE
RUNAWAY FISHBOWL COUPLE RETURNING TO TV?

by Anna Gomez, Nov. 4

The couple sits on the couch, holding hands against the cushion. It's a sweet scene, made more touching by the way Justin occasionally rubs the back of Jen's hand with one thumb or she rests her head on his shoulder. To anyone who doubted this "showmance," the love in the room is palpable.

My first question for them is what everyone in America must be wondering: What's it like transitioning from TV "love" to a real relationship?

"Any relationship has a honeymoon period at first," Justin says. "But now we've more or less settled into a routine."

"We're focused on developing full lives, apart and together." Jen adds. "Justin's sister welcomed me into her circle of friends. I started a new dinner club, I still host board game nights, and Justin and I are determined to beat every mystery escape room in Florida."

"Next year, we're planning a week-long vacation to Boston to beat a questing place there," Justin says, flashing those irresistible dimples. "We're not so different from any other couple. We just have a cool 'How We Met' story."

It's fun to see them so lively, but board games and escape rooms aren't what readers care about. Finally, I ask the twenty-five-thousand-dollar question: What's next for this couple? Are wedding bells in their future?

Jen ignores the second half of my question. "There's a lot of hard work ahead for us. Justin's getting his bar exam results any day. He's excited to work full time as a lawyer after all these years of studying."

"Jen and my sister are opening a bakery." Justin chimes in. Undeniable pride shines from his eyes. "It's called Sweet Reality, with recipes inspired by several people I think you'll recognize. It's going to be a hit."

Read more

Related Stories:

Runaway *Fishbowl* Couple Returning to TV?

You won't believe what this former *Fishbowl* star has been up to

Contract Negotiations Stalled for *Suddenly Single in Seattle's* second season

---

As Sarah's question sank in, realization slowly dawned. The hard object in the cupcake. The clattering when I spit what should've been strawberries and cake into the sink. The four cupcakes set apart from all the rest. The romantic dinner Justin planned for this evening. He was going to propose!

And I'd ruined it. Dread replaced my growing excitement. Because I hadn't swallowed the ring at all.

Without speaking, I pointed down the sink. Desperately, I grabbed the whipped cream bowl, praying the ring landed in it. Nothing but whipped cream.

"Oh, fuck," I said. "I'm so sorry, Sarah. I didn't know."

For a heart-stopping moment, she didn't answer, shoving her arm down the garbage disposal. I winced, remembering this article I once read that garbage disposals in some states were illegal due to domestic disputes. Even knowing the machine wouldn't spontaneously start on its own, I squeezed my eyes shut.

Finally, she sighed, pulled her arm out, and pulled her phone out of a pocket in her apron. "I'll call a plumber. But you need to get out of here before Justin shows up. Go wait in the front and act like you're watching Patty's Cakes."

"What are you going to do?"

Sarah raced around, flipping on the oven, filling a cupcake tin with batter from the fridge. "I'm going to burn the fuck out of some cupcakes so Justin doesn't know you're the one who ruined his surprise. I just hope he doesn't get here too long before the smoke alarm goes off."

"You're a real friend," I said.

"I know. Now get out." Her broad smile took the bite off her words. Unlike her twin, Sarah didn't have dimples, but her green eyes crinkled when she smiled. "My future sister-in-law deserves a dream proposal."

Her words sent a thrill through me. Her sister-in-law! Justin's wife! Mrs. Jennifer . . . Well, Mrs. Jennifer Reid, actually. But still. Justin and I were getting married! Or we would've been, if I hadn't choked on the ring. The antique, irreplaceable ring.

Oh, hell. I'd ruined my own marriage proposal.

Grabbing the broom and a rag, I thanked Sarah again and trudged to the front room. The few crumbs I'd originally gone to sweep up now resembled a Jackson Pollock painting on our floor. Not wanting Justin to wander into a war zone, I scrambled to clean up the scattered crumbs, strawberries, and frosting.

By the time I finished and returned the broom to the kitchen, I'd nearly forgotten about the line of people waiting to buy baked goods from our competitor. I couldn't stand and watch. What a mess. Instead, I pulled my tablet out of my bag and sat on a stool behind the counter, reading article after article on Patty's Cakes. Keep your friends close and your enemies closer.

A few mentioned plans to start at least one surprise new location. Other than a blog posted half an hour ago, none hinted they'd be opening across the street from us. Not a single article I found mentioned the competition at all, because no one presented real competition for Patty's Cakes in the area. They dominated the cake and cupcake market.

Sarah joined me a few minutes later, wrapping one arm around my shoulders. "It'll be okay."

I only wished her words made me feel better. What if the ring couldn't be recovered, and Justin never forgave me?

Twenty minutes later, the front door opened, bringing in a blast of hot air from outside and my boyfriend. As always, being near him lifted my spirits. No problem seemed insurmountable when the two of us put our heads together. Not even the slight problem of him giving money to the enemy, as evidenced by the pink cardboard box in his hands, "Patty's Cakes" emblazoned on the top.

"Hold on there a minute," Sarah said. "You're not coming in here with that."

Ignoring her, Justin greeted me with a kiss, sending tingles down to my toes. "Hey, beautiful."

"Hi. Kiss me like that, and you can shop anywhere you want," I said.

"No you can't," Sarah said.

Justin peered at my tear-stained face. "Were you crying?"

"Just stress. I'm fine now," I said.

He pulled me close, running one hand up and down my arm. "Don't worry. We'll figure this out."

If only he knew what truly bothered me. But telling him how I ruined his surprise proposal would kill him, so I kissed his cheek and murmured something unintelligible. Hopefully he'd reach the logical conclusion that I was upset about the imminent demise of our fledgling business.

Before he asked too many questions, Sarah said, "Seriously, what's going on? Why are you consorting with the enemy?"

"Calm down. How can we prepare to take out the competition without seeing what they do? Knowledge is power. This isn't betrayal; it's recon."

Genius. My boyfriend, the genius. I kissed him again. "Good call."

Sarah dropped her hostility like a Halloween mask. "Okay, fine. Tell us what you found out."

Justin opened the box, revealing three cupcakes, which he gave to Sarah to cut up into pieces for sharing. "First, they're not only selling cakes and cupcakes anymore."

"What?"

"They've expanded their line," he said. "They're selling cannoli, cookies, brownies . . . all kinds of stuff."

"All the same stuff we make." If Sarah's face fell any further, her chin would hit the floor. I suspected my expression mirrored hers.

"Well, the good news is, their cookies aren't shaped like fishbowls, so yours are cooler. Also, they're selling them freaking cheap. No way they can stay in business at those prices."

If he thought this news would perk me up, he had another think coming. "That's a marketing ploy. It's called a loss leader. They sell the cookies below cost to bring customers into the store. Once they're inside, everyone buys the stuff that's marked up more. That was our entire plan with the ninety-nine-cent fishbowl cookies."

"Well, crap," Sarah said. "So much for your marketing expertise."

"Hey. It was a good plan. It's not my fault they also took Marketing 101. I couldn't have predicted this."

"No one could have known this would happen," Justin said. "Let's all calm down and put our heads together. We'll find a solution."

Sarah handed us each a small plate of cupcake bites and fell into a chair. "Good luck with that. These are amazing."

First, I tried a carrot cupcake with vanilla frosting. It turned to glue in my mouth, but I didn't know if I should blame the bakery or the gaping pit of despair in my stomach.

Justin spit his bite out onto the plate. "Ugh. Do your customers a favor and use cream cheese frosting. That's terrible."

"We're offering options," I said. "The Birdie is carrot cake with cream cheese frosting, but we also do one with vanilla. Options are part of our hook. It costs almost nothing to make two types of frosting, especially when we use both for other things."

"I appreciate the loyalty, guys, but this is delicious. Trust me," Sarah said. "At least, if you don't hate carrot cake. And this chocolate? It's like an orgasm in my mouth. A painful, miserable orgasm."

With my stomach flip-flopping all over the place, I couldn't eat any more. It didn't even matter whether our cupcakes tasted better than these if we couldn't bring anyone into the store to try them because they all lined up across the street.

"What else can you tell us?" I asked Justin.

"I was the youngest person in the store by about thirty years. They're more elegant, catering to the mothers and the grand-mothers. The reality TV schtick you guys created may help bring in the Millennials."

"Millennials are broke," I said. "Remember? Lots of student loan debt, no jobs?"

Justin shuddered. "Don't remind me."

"Broke people are sad, and sad people like baked goods," Sarah said. "What we need is to wow the customers. Justin, these are all fairly basic: chocolate, vanilla, carrot cake. What else did they have?"

He shrugged. "All the usual stuff: vanilla with vanilla frost-ing, chocolate with chocolate, vanilla with chocolate, etc. I didn't see anything that holds a candle to your raspberry lemon cupcakes with almond frosting."

"Okay, now we're getting somewhere," I said. "We can

promote the heck out of those. Sarah, what other special recipes do you have?"

Before she could reply, the fire alarm went off.

Sarah shrieked, so convincingly she'd either forgotten about "accidentally" burning the cupcakes or she should've been the twin to appear on TV. She tore into the kitchen, blond hair streaming behind her. I followed on her heels before skidding to a halt inside the door.

Thick, black smoke billowed out of the oven, stinging my eyes. The stench of burning sugar made me gag. Coughing, I raced past Sarah to open the back door.

What a friend. She didn't need to *actually* burn the cupcakes to tell Justin she'd done it. But now he witnessed the glorious wreckage as she flipped the entire pan upside-down over the sink.

Justin stayed in the doorway, his eyes swiveling from the smoke now rising from the sink to the bowl of strawberries on the counter. "What happened?"

"I got so wound up by Patty's Cakes, I must've spaced on setting a timer. I completely forgot these were in the oven." She yelled over the still screeching alarm.

Grabbing a towel from a drawer near the stove, I waved the black clouds toward the open door, praying no reporters lurked in the alley. The last thing we needed was a reviewer on the way to check out Patty's Cakes to see me and Sarah nearly burning down our kitchen.

The alarm stopped, silence blanketing the kitchen.

Justin's face looked much like Sarah's when she'd seen me spit the ring into the sink. Barely moving his face, he whispered. "What were you making?"

Sarah's eyes widened so much I would've laughed if the entire morning hadn't been so wretched. She clapped her hands over her mouth. "Oh, shit. Justin, I'm sorry."

"Hey, Jen, could you go up front while I talk to my sister?"

I started to go before remembering it wasn't in my nature not to ask questions. "What's up?"

"It's nothing," he said. "Just . . . need to talk about Mom for a minute. Sarah's staying with her while we go out tonight, remember?"

I nodded. "Oh, right."

"These cupcakes were for her," Sarah added, not convincingly. "I feel terrible."

Justin's face crumpled. This illusion made me feel like the worst person in the world. If Sarah couldn't get the ring out of the sink, I'd tell him the truth. For now, I needed to get out of there before I burst into tears.

"Actually, if you guys don't need me here, I'm going to head home," I said. "With this new store opening, I need to tweak our marketing plan, and I'll work better where it's quiet. Okay?"

Justin nodded, relief flooding his features. "Take my car. Sarah can give me a ride to your place before dinner."

Something silver flashed through the air. I reached up cupped hands to make the catch, unable to speak. His keys. Holy shit, he must love me more than I thought.

I'd never driven in my life before moving to Florida. Although he'd been giving me driving lessons for almost six months, all lessons since took place in Sarah's beat-up old Toyota. He must desperately want me out of the store to hand over the keys when he wasn't missing a couple of limbs.

The fact that Justin trusted me with his car stunned me even more than the news that he was about to propose. I stood there, the metal cold against my palm, afraid that if I moved he'd change his mind.

Sarah gasped. "You don't even let *me* drive your car!"

"You're a terrible driver. It's only a couple of miles." To me, he said, "I'll see you later."

Before he changed his mind, I kissed him goodbye and left.

The whole way home, I prayed they would find the ring. Sinks have traps, right? In the movies, people are always opening sinks and finding stuff caught in them. We hadn't turned the water on at all after I spit out the cupcake. If we found the ring, I'd always help the needy. I'd give leftover cupcakes to the homeless. We'd donate a percentage of our profits to charity. But we couldn't lose Justin's grandmother's engagement ring. It would kill him.

The moment the front door of our apartment closed behind me, I got to work, reading reviews and market research. Trying not to think about Justin, the ring, and the disaster I'd inadvertently caused. After about an hour, I gave up.

By the time Sarah arrived, I was walking in a continuous loop through the living room and kitchen, wondering how much an antique diamond ring cost. How many cupcakes would I personally need to sell to repay Justin?

Before the door even closed behind her, Sarah said, "We got the ring."

I stopped mid-pace, flopping onto to the couch with relief. "Oh, thank you, thank you, thank you. I didn't know what to do if I lost it."

"I'm an idiot. I should've waited to bake the cupcakes until after you left."

"You couldn't have known I'd wander into the kitchen and shove whatever I found into my mouth."

Sarah raised her eyebrows and gave me a stern look. When I hung my head, she giggled and collapsed onto the couch next to me.

"Hey, where's Justin? Is he coming to pick me up for dinner?"

"No, we got a call from Mom on the way here. He's going over there now instead of waiting until later." Their mother beat cancer twice when they were kids, and it went into remission for more than ten years. Unfortunately, it recently reappeared with a vengeance. After their father broke his back at work, Sarah and I spent a lot of time caring for both parents over the summer while Justin studied for the Florida State Bar Exam. Now that he was back at work, the two of them shared duties. I pitched in as needed.

"Oh, no. What happened?"

"I'm sure it's nothing, but since he's going to be gone all week, he wanted to check on them. Asked me to tell you he's sorry about dinner and he'll call you in the morning. I'm supposed to take the ring to be cleaned and give it to Justin in a few days. If you want, I'll take it now and grab sushi for dinner on the way home."

"Sounds great." The full impact of her words sunk in. "Wait, the ring is here, with you? Can I see it?"

"You're kidding, right?"

Instead of replying, I tried to gauge whether she might possibly show me. Of *course* I wanted to see my future engagement ring. But also, of course Justin should be the one to give it to me. The set of her jaw suggested the futility of pushing her. I arranged my features in a way I hoped said, *I'm definitely kidding if you're not going to show it to me.*

Sarah said, "You're not even supposed to *know* about the ring. Justin would kill me if I told him you found it. If I actually let you see it before he proposes, he will dig up my corpse, resuscitate me, and kill me again. No way. Nuh-uh. You're not even coming to the jeweler's with me."

I let out a fake, huffy sigh. "Fiiiiiine."

"Weren't you supposed to be working on the bakery? Did you get anything done this afternoon?"

"Absolutely!" Momentarily rejuvenated with the idea of saving Sweet Reality, I grabbed some pages I'd printed when I first got home. "First, we can do plenty of business with catering. Younger brides love cupcakes for their weddings, because they can order different kinds and give their guests options."

"That's a good point," Sarah said. "But Patty's Cakes already does cupcake towers."

"They do, but they're still appealing more to the Mom set.

Graduations, birthday parties, etc. We're going to bring in the Millennials. The Network's target demographic is our audience, and that's who we'll advertise to. Start practicing superhero-themed cakes and stuff. Blue cakes for girls, pink cakes for boys, gender-neutral cakes, coming-out cakes. We support everyone."

"Okay, I like that."

"There's more," I said. "People like variety. They like choice. This goes back to what Justin said earlier. Patty's Cakes makes the basics, and they do it well. Their products taste delicious. But our niche can be a rotation of baked goods with unique flavor profiles. What new recipes have you been working on?"

"Well, I came up with a s'mores cupcake, which isn't totally unique, but Patty's Cakes doesn't make one. Justin found a picture of their menu on Yelp after you left."

"That's good. I'll come up with a name to tie it into one of the survivalist shows. Something like, 'S'more clothes, please?'" The name referenced a popular show that dropped people into the wilderness naked and gave them two weeks to find their way to civilization.

Sarah giggled. "I love it. I thought about coming up with some kind of Ariana-based cupcake, but I'm not allowed to actually poison people."

She named my arch-nemesis from *The Fishbowl*, the snake who repeatedly tried to come between me and Justin, who said and did whatever she thought necessary to keep us apart. My hackles rose just thinking about her. If I got to choose, I'd never lay eyes on her again—on or off the television. No one confirmed whether she'd be on the cruise, and I spent three nights tossing and turning before Justin convinced me everything would work out.

I said, "Ariana would probably demand a royalty for using her name. I hear she trademarked it last year."

"Of course she did." Sarah sighed, shaking her head. "Whatevs. Anyway, I've been trying to recreate those coconut cupcakes for ages, but they're never quite right."

While Justin locked himself away to study for the bar after I moved here, Sarah and I entertained ourselves every Tuesday night with *Totally '80s Celebrity Bake-off*. The show pitted former child stars against each other, creating and selling baked goods at charity events. One of the contestants, a former pop star named Tammy Rae, won the finale with cupcakes every single judge and guest raved over. People went for seconds and thirds. But no one knew what she put in them. Tammy Rae made a big show of emptying out the kitchen before adding whatever her "special" ingredient was, and not a hint leaked to the media in the months since.

The solution to our problem hit me while scrolling through the DVR around lunchtime. Sarah and I discussed the recipe endlessly over the summer, and she thought she figured out most of it, but we still needed the last ingredient. Now, the reminder of the show-winning recipe gave me an opportunity to feel useful, and I leapt at it. Maybe I couldn't decorate cakes or make up recipes on my own, but Tammy Rae was rumored to be part of the cast of *Real Ocean: Caribbean*, which Justin and I started filming next week. I could talk her into helping us.

"You keep working on it," I said. "Next week, I'll convince Tammy Rae to give us her secret ingredient. Then we'll offer something no one else can compete with: the cupcakes that won *Totally 80s Bake-off*. We'll get a ton of business. She's more legendary now than when she was a pop star."

The cruise Justin and I were taking next week wasn't only a much-needed vacation, although I couldn't wait to help him relax during the final countdown to his bar exam results. We both needed some time away together to relax after an exhausting summer. How could we refuse a free cruise? Especially after the Network agreed to pay to rush our passports. Plus, Sarah and I got added publicity for Sweet Reality. Win, win, win.

Win, win, win, win, if I got Tammy Rae's recipe while on the ship. Sure, I didn't know her, or have any real idea how to ask, but . . . I couldn't let doubts get in my way now. We needed this.

As if she read my mind, Sarah asked, "What if she won't give it to you?"

"I'll find a way. I promise." We had no other choice. Our livelihood depended on me getting this recipe. No matter what it took, I'd get Tammy Rae to give up her secret ingredient. Sarah and Sweet Reality were counting on me.

THREE

QUEEN KELLY'S VOICE
WELCOME TO REALITY CRUISES!

Sunday edition

Today, we set sail from the beautiful port of Miami, Florida, on a ship packed with America's favorite reality stars from shows such as *The Fishbowl*, *America's Next Drag Supermodel*, *Deaf Teen Mother*, *The Marrying Kind*, and more. Settle in, unpack, and enjoy a beverage atop one of our glorious lookout decks as we move away from Florida into the vast wide ocean. After dinner, you'll have the opportunity to attend meet-and-greets and Q&A sessions with the stars, watch a movie from the comfort of our outdoor hot tubs, attend a comedy show, and more. The casino opens at 5:00 PM.

Tomorrow, enjoy a full day at sea. The buffet's open 24 hours, as are the cafes throughout the Lido Deck. Get to know the people you've seen on TV. Attend our *Reality Star Bake-off*, where stars fight for bragging rights over the best baked goods at sea. Contact Leanna before 8:00 PM Sunday if you're interested in participating or judging.

On Tuesday, we'll arrive in the Bahamas. Reality stars and civilians alike will have from 7:00 AM – 5:00 PM to explore the island. Check out various excursions like zip-lining, snorkeling, kayaking, etc. Those of you with scuba certifications can rent gear onboard, and someone will meet you at the disembarkation point.

Wednesday's itinerary involves a stop in Ocho Rios, Jamaica. There's something for everyone on this island, from rich local culture to water sports to gorgeous sightseeing to magnificent excursions.

After leaving Jamaica, we'll sail directly to Grand Cayman in the Cayman Islands. Tour the Tortuga Rum Factory and get samples of some of the highest quality rum in the world. Not a drinker? No problem. Grand Cayman also offers snorkeling, swimming with stingrays, and more!

On Friday, the Queen Kelly arrives in Cozumel, Mexico. Tour ancient ruins on horseback, enjoy deep discounts at our shopping area, or kick back and enjoy tacos and margaritas under the sun.

Enjoy another activity-filled day at sea on Saturday before the ship returns to Miami. We'll be docking at midnight to allow you to make the most of your last day onboard. Keep an eye out for daily schedules with more information.

Inside this Edition:

FOUR DAYS LATER, Sarah delivered me and Justin to the docks for our trip. Between Justin's parents' needs, his work schedule, and the time Sarah and I'd spent working on new recipes, I'd barely seen my boyfriend since the disaster at the bakery. I didn't know if Sarah returned the ring, if Justin brought it with him on the cruise, or if he'd prefer to wait and propose when we weren't on camera. It wasn't like I could ask him. Instead, I tried to push it out of my mind and focus on enjoying our trip. And getting Tammy Rae's secret recipe.

We barely stepped onto the curb separating the boarding area from the parking lot when a barrel of energy slammed into me.

"Jen!"

"Ed!" Finding my footing, I threw my arms around *The Fishbowl*'s runner-up and my good friend, Eduardo Silva. He grinned down at me unabashedly. From his lean, muscular frame to his longish dark hair and warm brown eyes always gleaming with mischief, Ed melted hearts all over America during our summer on television. And pretty much anywhere he went.

He greeted Justin briefly before turning to me. "It's marvelous to see you. How the hell have you two been? Can you believe this monstrosity?"

The ship towered above us, nearly as long as an entire city block and casting about a mile of shade over Miami's docks. At least ten rows of windows stretched upward from the ground to the upper decks. To my left, rows of balconies hung off the rear of the ship. The front extended beyond the edges of my peripheral vision. Strains of music reached my ears, so high above us we couldn't make out anything but the faintest melody. The brochure told me to expect outdoor activities on the upper decks, including three pools and a water slide, but I couldn't crane my neck far enough to see the top. We could spend the entire week exploring.

How did something so enormous float? It must weigh a million tons.

On either side of us, thousands of people streamed up gangways onto the ship. Before us, a third gangway led into the belly of the beast. Er, led into the ship waiting to take me, Justin, our friends, and a bunch of former reality stars on a fabulous vacation.

"How many levels does this thing have?" I asked.

Sounding like a page from the brochure we'd spent hours poring over when we first got the call, Justin responded. "Fifteen. Seven or eight floors of cabins, two floors of shopping in the middle levels, a casino, a gym, a running track, a miniature golf course, and the kids' area for families. The Lido Deck has two buffets—"

"There's a Lido Deck? Like on *The Love Boat*?"

"All cruise ships have a Lido Deck," Ed replied. "That's where the entertainment is. On this ship, there's a twenty-four-hour pizza place, a deli, and the pools, plus some other stuff."

"Okay, we get it. It's bloody amazing," Sarah grumbled. "Rub it in, why don't you? This will be the most awesome vacation adventure ever, and I don't get to come with you."

"You could've come," Justin said. "As long as you paid for it."

"Right. Let me dig into my buckets of cash." Sarah rolled her eyes at him. "It's fine. I've got plenty to do at the bakery before our grand opening. I need to make Patty's Cakes regret ever setting up shop across from us."

"Don't be too sad you're not coming," Ed said. "Hiking all over the ship will be the most exhausting 'vacation' I've ever been on. I'm going to need to hit the spa every day for a foot massage."

Sarah rubbed her thumb and forefinger together. "Hear this? World's smallest violin playing a sad song for you."

Laughing, Ed pulled her into a hug. "Good to see you, too. I wish you could come with."

"Me, too!" I said, joining in.

Sarah kissed both our cheeks before pulling away and

handed me a small, clear plastic container. "You're the best, both of you. I gotta go before they tow my car. Love you all, I'll see you next Sunday. Bring me alcohol, and try not to get into any trouble. Especially you, Ed."

He winked at her, and Justin pulled her aside, supposedly to talk about their mother for a minute before dropping our suitcases with the porter. I suspected he had another reason for this conversation, which made me grin far more than I should at the prospect of having my luggage checked.

This excitement would not be contained. Nearly two years ago, I'd been so sure my ex-boyfriend planned to propose right before finding out he was married. I'd been excited, but the thought of spending my life with someone as perfect as marrying Justin. He was my other half, the absolute best partner for me.

Sarah winked at me over his shoulder, her way of telling me she'd slipped him the ring. I shifted my weight from one foot to the other, wishing I could share my excitement with someone, but got distracted by the massive ocean liner casting shadows over the dock. More specifically, by the lifeboats.

Eyeing the orange rubber vessels lining the sides, I turned to Ed. "Do you think they brought enough lifeboats?"

"Yes. Also, this isn't the *Titanic*. We're not gonna sink. We have communications devices to call for help. And you, Jen, have your very own hunky stud in Justin to save you if anything goes wrong. Relax. Take your Dramamine."

I rooted around in my carry-on for a moment before giving up. "My Dramamine must be in my big suitcase . . . which I probably shouldn't have given to him to check. At least not without putting this Tupperware in first. The carry-on is about to burst."

Ed gestured at the container Sarah handed me before leaving. "What's that for?"

"So I can bring her one of Tammy Rae's cupcakes. They're doing a tasting after the bake-off tomorrow, remember?"

One of the onboard events pitted reality stars against each other in a baking competition, which Ed apparently forgot to sign up for. Hopefully, he wasn't going to wing it. My friend created excellent meals for everyone while we were in the Fishbowl, but his laissez-faire attitude to cooking wouldn't produce the same delicious results in baked goods.

Instead of competing against Ed, I signed up to judge with Justin. Partially as a way of getting on Tammy Rae's good side, and partially because rumors said everyone involved got to sample her winning cupcakes after the event. I needed to be in the right place to snag one. Well, two. One for me, one for Sarah. Then I could verify whether these things tasted as good as the inter-webs claimed and butter Tammy Rae up by raving about what a baking genius she was before begging for a favor.

Where was Tammy Rae? Hopefully she hadn't changed her mind and canceled at the last minute. According to E-Entertainment News Online, she'd mysteriously pulled out of *Celebrity Poker Match* a few years back, despite being a favorite to win. I scanned the docks, looking for her.

With luck, the recipe would be in my hand and I'd be lounging by the pool before the ship arrived in our first port. But one thing at a time. First, Justin and I needed to thoroughly explore and "enjoy" our cabin. Our glorious *private* cabin where we wouldn't have to worry about my boyfriend's sister or his somewhat creepy roommate hearing us through the paper-thin walls of our respective apartments. Or well, at least we wouldn't know the people on the other side of our walls, so it wouldn't matter what they heard.

Ed's voice called me away from those thoughts, back to our conversation.

"What?" I asked.

"I said, calm down. Justin will be back soon, Tammy Rae will arrive before the ship leaves, and your suitcase, with Dramamine, will be delivered to your cabin sooner rather than later."

"Why didn't I take seasick pills before leaving home?" I moaned. "Why am I doing this?"

"You mean, freaking out over nothing? I couldn't tell you." Ed hugged me. "Really, Jen, you'll be fine. I've cruised before. You won't feel a thing."

Finally, Justin walked toward us, sans luggage. I found myself relaxing as he put an arm around my waist and squeezed. I kissed him.

"Ugh. Lovebirds!" Ed moaned. "Get a room!"

"Hey, Ed, isn't your boyfriend around here?" Justin asked with a grin. "Why don't you go find him?"

Ed met his boyfriend Connor, formerly known to me only as Curly Beard, while filming *The Fishbowl*. Although the Network strictly prohibited staff from socializing with the contestants, they still found a way to make a connection. More importantly, they'd managed to keep it going ever since. The Network promoted Connor from production assistant to camera operator, and Ed recently moved from Boston to Los Angeles to be with him while pursuing a stand-up comedy career. I couldn't have been happier for them.

"He's doing some pre-boarding filming. I'm not allowed," he said to Justin. "Besides, someone had to keep your belle here from having a panic attack. Did you know she gets seasick?"

Justin tilted his head at me the way he did when he didn't want to say he thought I wasn't being one hundred percent truthful. "You never mentioned that. You do?"

"I don't know. When I was in high school, I threw up on the swan boats at the local fair."

"Wasn't that right after you bought tacos out of some guy's van? Because I'm not sure that was the boat's fault."

This was the problem with dating someone long enough for them to hear all your stories. "Maybe…"

"You'll be *fine!*" Ed said. "Now, let's go before they take off without us."

"Depart," I said. "Or set sail."

"Whatever." Ed took off for the ship, luggage in tow.

"What's really wrong?" Justin asked.

He gazed into my eyes until I realized I'd been freaking out over nothing. "I don't know. I've been on edge all week. Partially it's the bakery. What if Sarah can't come up with new recipes? What if Tammy Rae hates me?"

"You are a resourceful, brilliant woman. You can be very persuasive. Plus, Sarah's a genius in the kitchen. Even if Tammy Rae says no, the two of you will come up with something."

I sighed. "You're right, I'm sorry. I'm being stupid. I don't know why I'm so jittery."

Behind me, someone walked by wearing a t-shirt showing a woman with long, dark hair, pouting out from the inside of a clear fishbowl. And suddenly, I realized exactly why I felt so on edge: Ariana. The one person who could always make me act like my brain took a vacation without my body. No one confirmed whether she'd be onboard. I couldn't relax until we set sail without her.

Justin followed my gaze and understanding flashed across his face. Instead of commenting, he squeezed my hand and gestured grandly toward the ship. "Shall we?"

We rolled our carry-ons through the special check-in point reserved for VIPs. After presenting ID and going through the metal detectors, Justin and I headed up the gangway. My head swiveled to catch every speck of activity. To our right, I spotted one of the stars of *The Marrying Kind*, a popular dating show. When I turned to talk to Justin, over his shoulder, I spotted Tabby Rangoon, winner of last year's *America's Next Drag Super-model*. I'd missed her season while locked in the Fishbowl, but many people had been excited to see a forty-something queen beat out all the twenty-year-olds vying for the crown.

The interior of the ship was more extravagant than any hotel I'd ever visited, with marble floors in the entrance, gold paneling on the stairs, and huge glass elevators giving us a view of every-thing on the way up. Colored lights alternated on and off, flooding the entryway with dancing pink, blue, and purple beams. As the elevator traveled upward, I spotted a coffee shop, the purser's desk, a row of designer shops in the background, and a sign advertising a live show in the theater later.

"Is that a real casino? I thought Ed was joking." I pointed through the window at the edges of a neon sign.

Justin consulted a sheaf of papers in his hand. "It is. There's a casino on the fifth floor, nightclubs on the sixth and twelfth, and a five-star restaurant overlooking the ocean on the fifteenth. They serve romantic dinners, by reservation only. We should go there one night."

For the zillionth time, I thought about how lucky I was to find this guy. Popping onto my toes, I leaned in for a quick kiss. "That sounds amazing."

The elevator dinged to a stop, and we exited on the ninth floor. My feet sank into the plush carpet filling the room. No dancing lights here, thankfully, but the public areas of the ship gave me visions of the most lavish room I'd ever stayed in. Even nicer than the place my ex-boyfriend took me for my birthday a few weeks before I found out about his wife.

Consulting the packet holding my keycard and ship map, I headed to the right. Justin called me back before I moved three steps.

"Where are you going?"

Pointing at the sign, I said, "Room E622 is this way."

"I'm sure it is, but Room E615 is over here."

"What's in Room E615?"

"We are."

"No, we're not. We're in Room E622." At Justin's expression, the suitcase handle clattered out of my hand onto the faux marble floor. "Wait, what? We're not in the same room?"

We met in the center of the hallway to compare notes. Since we were a couple who met on *The Fishbowl*, and the Network paid for the cruise, we assumed we'd share a cabin. Neither of us thought to compare our room assignments.

Disappointment flooded me. "How can we not be sharing? Are we each stuck in single rooms? Can we share a twin bed?"

He shook his head. "Somehow, I doubt it. If so, there would be no reason for us not to share."

"No sex for a week?" I didn't try to hide my disappointment. Especially since the only night we'd spent together the past few days, Justin fell asleep while Sarah and I worked in the kitchen past midnight. I'd expected to make up for lost time on this cruise. All week long.

"That's not possible." He looked like he'd just been told we only had a week to live. "They wouldn't do that to us. Would they?"

"They probably would," I said glumly. After being constantly locked out of my college dorm room by a roommate who thoroughly embraced the hookup—and waking up more than once in the middle of the night to a show—I couldn't kick my roommate out of our cabin. Justin and I would have to find another solution.

"Well, if they do, we can always sneak off to a janitor's closet or something. They probably don't have any doors that lock you in after sixty seconds onboard, right?"

I laughed at the reminder of the changing rooms in the Fishbowl. One of the first nights on the set, my friend Rachel snuck in there with another competitor, and they got stuck. It took over an hour for the producers to let them out. "All we need is an empty cabin. Maybe Ed can sweet talk Connor into helping us come up with something."

"You think if there's a secret sex area, they're not going to hog it?"

Damn. He had a point.

I said, "Ok, fine. I hear there are giant hammocks in the spa area. Ever have sex in a hammock?"

"Not in front of thousands of people. Besides, we'd probably fall out." Justin shook his head. "This has to be a mistake. I'll go down to main level and talk to the producers."

"What if they did it on purpose?"

"Then we'll find another way to steal some time alone. We're not going to spend a week on a cruise ship completely apart. Anyway, how much time would we have spent in the cabin, with so much ship to explore? We'll be fine. Don't worry."

"Thanks." With a sigh, I kissed him and turned down the hall behind me.

Alone and significantly less excited than I'd been a few minutes earlier, I continued to my room, eyes following the patterned carpet. When I reached my cabin, the door stood cracked, so I nudged it open with my hip and called into the interior. After a moment, a familiar voice responded, and my spirits lifted a tiny bit.

"Hel-loooo?"

"Rachel?" I barreled into the room, jumping into a tackle hug. We hadn't gotten off to the best start in *The Fishbowl*, but as the show progressed, the Midwestern cheerleader became a good friend and one of my most respected competitors. "Rachel! It's so good to see you!"

"Hello, roomie! How are you?"

With her dancing brown eyes and shoulder-length wavy blond hair, Rachel looked exactly the same as I remembered. Her tan hadn't even faded over the winter, leading me to strongly suspect she'd gotten it from a bottle. If only I'd thought of that. By the end of this week, I'd either still be ghostly white or turn eggplant purple. My fair skin knew no in-between shades. It even bypassed the normal reds usually associated with sunburns.

"Don't think I'm not glad you're here, but I'm bummed not to be sharing a room with Justin. Do you know what happened?"

"The Network split us all into single-gender rooms to avoid hanky-panky."

"Hanky-panky?"

She blushed. "That's what my grammy used to say, and I'm

sticking with it. Anyway, they don't want us hanging out in our cabins too much, so we're stuck sharing. Tiny spaces, with roommates."

Until she mentioned it, I hadn't paid much attention to the size of the cabin. Behind her, two sets of bunk beds dominated a room about the size of my bedroom at home. Twin bunk beds, naturally. Lovely. Any remaining dreams for a romantic getaway cruise with my boyfriend skidded to a halt.

Heavy curtains along the starboard wall suggested a much larger window than the one-foot porthole ensconced in the far wall. A flat screen TV hung in one corner over a mini-fridge, across from a wooden chair and built-in desk. The room service menu, cruise newsletter, and telephone took up the entire surface.

"It's small, but cozy. We'll be fine. Except for the part where I should be sharing with Justin." I wrinkled my nose at her. "Ugh. Any idea who else we're sharing with?"

She shrugged. "Ed said it should be no more than two people from each show per room, so you lucked out with me. If Ariana's onboard, she should be sleeping elsewhere."

"Have you seen her yet?"

"Nope. And no word if she's coming. Ed didn't know."

"Yeah, I asked him, too. Even offered to bring Connor cookies if he'd tell me, so I know they weren't holding out on me."

Rachel glanced at her watch before answering. "I'm going up to the deck to watch the ship cast off. I'll meet you here when it's time to meet at the muster stations."

"The mustard stations?"

"No, silly." Her tinkling laughter never failed to make me smile. "*Muster* stations are where we learn what to do in the event of an emergency. Like an evacuation station. But don't worry. The boat's not going to sink or anything."

Again, I envisioned Leo and Kate floating on a wooden door among the wreckage of the *Titanic*. Unsinkable, my ass. Of course, if Justin and I found ourselves in the same situation, I knew to secure my life jacket underneath to make room. Thank you, *Mythbusters*.

Before I responded to Rachel, my phone buzzed with a text from Justin confirming that the cabin assignments weren't a mix-up. I texted back, promising to meet him at the muster station in about half an hour, after I unpacked and gave my first confessional interview. Rachel left me alone to unpack. Her clothes already took up more than half the closet, so hopefully whoever our other two roommates were, at least one of them was a nudist. Had the cast of *Terrified in the Jungle* been invited?

A few minutes later, I navigated my way down the halls to the elevators, scanning for familiar faces among the crowd and seeking out the nearest emergency exits.

When I reached the hallway housing the elevator bank, I stopped dead in my tracks. *She* stood in front of me. The last person I wanted to run into, here or anywhere else.

Ariana. Even more impossibly thin than the day I left the Fishbowl, somehow looking taller, every bit as beautiful, and probably with a voodoo doll of me stashed in her suitcase. After the way she'd lied and schemed to get me off *The Fishbowl* so she could steal Justin, not any part of me was remotely happy to find her here on the ship. As long as no one confirmed her presence on the cruise, I'd stupidly allowed myself to believe she decided not to come. On a free Caribbean cruise.

She stood regal as ever, with her shoulders back and her nose in the air. Silky black hair streamed down her back. She crossed her arms over her enormous fake breasts, glaring at the elevators as if their slow arrival were a personal insult.

Into her phone, she spoke very slowly, as if explaining something to a three-year-old. "Is everyone who works there an idiot? Let me talk to your supervisor. I can't possibly spend a week on vacation with only a five-thousand-dollar daily limit on my debit card."

I snorted at the thought of not being able to exist on "only" five grand a day, when food and shelter was covered. Unfortunately, the sound drew her attention to me. She sneered.

Of all the times to run into her, I wished I hadn't been alone. If Justin stood beside me, he'd squeeze my hand reassuringly and say something like, "Hey, it's okay. You won, remember? You can't avoid her all week, so you might as well be polite."

Ugh. I hated when he was right. Or, I mean, when I was right, talking to myself.

At least no one around witnessed this first encounter with my nemesis. Maybe. I peeked at the corners of the ceiling, searching for cameras. A vase on a table by the wall could have concealed a camera, but there was no non-obvious way to check. The mirror above the vase could have been two-way, but since it appeared to be older than me, I doubted it.

The Network had been vague about what type of show we signed up for. Justin and I got all excited about a romantic getaway and a free cruise and didn't push for answers. The forms we signed involved waiving a lot of rights, but very little facts about what we were getting into. That wasn't a huge surprise. Before going on *The Fishbowl*, I'd known only it was a competition-based reality show offering a cash prize. No one mentioned a prize or a competition when soliciting us for this show.

The producers promised to explain everything else in a meeting after embarkation. It didn't escape my notice that we couldn't quit after finding out what we agreed to, but whatever. Life's full of surprises, right?

Justin and I figured, after our last experience, we could handle whatever the Network threw at us, but as soon as I spotted Ariana, butterflies beat out a symphony in my belly.

I could do this. *Be the bigger person, Jen.*

"Hello, Ariana," I said, hoping I didn't sound completely appalled.

"We'll discuss this later," she said into the phone, waiting exactly long enough before greeting me to make me fidget. Her brown eyes narrowed to slits before she spoke. "Jen."

Once I got over the disappointment of running into Ariana, I spotted a stroller parked about a foot away from her. A rainbow-colored teddy bear peeked out of a pocket on the back. No one else stood near enough to be keeping an eye on the infant. Before I could ask, the elevator dinged, and Justin appeared in the open doors. My shoulders straightened immediately when he walked to my side and kissed me before acknowledging her. *Take that, Ariana!*

"Hi, Ariana," he said. "Nice to see you again. And you brought a baby?"

She beamed up at him. "Why yes, I did! Would you like to meet my son?"

Both of us blinked at her. She hadn't been pregnant when we were on *The Fishbowl*. At least not judging from her concave stomach, skintight clothing, and daily alcohol intake. How did she get pregnant, give birth, and return to her usual size two self in only sixteen months? Without anyone in the media catching on?

She laughed, a piercing sound I'd convinced myself annoyed me more in memory than real life. Wrong. "Naturally, I named him after his father. I'd like you both to meet my son, Justin Jr."

FOUR

JENNIFER IN THE GUPPY GABBER, SUNDAY:

It's great to see my old Fishies all back in one place! Well, most of them. No one's changed a bit. Not even the ones I wish would. At least J-Dawg isn't here, right?

But it's all good. This is a huge ship, and there's plenty of stuff to do. I'm on a mission: Sarah and I need to find out Tammy Rae's secret ingredient so we can recreate her cupcakes for our bakery. Plus, Justin's been working super hard, worried about his parents, and we haven't taken a real vacation since the show, so we're going to enjoy ourselves. We're very excited about this trip.

Ariana will not ruin this week for us.

My stomach lurched, sending me a reminder of the *huevos rancheros* I'd devoured for breakfast. I couldn't believe this was happening. No way. No. Justin swore they only kissed a little, even after Ariana told me they slept together. He promised—

She burst out laughing. "My God, your face, Jen! You're too easy."

I glanced from her to Justin, who stood rigidly beside me, fists clenched at his sides. His posture told me he slowly counted to ten before speaking. Or possibly to a thousand.

"What are you talking about?" I asked.

"Me and Justin! I wish you could see the way you're glaring at him. Don't you trust your man more than that?"

I turned to my boyfriend, but Hurricane Ariana already inflicted her damage.

"I'm going to my cabin," Justin said before I could say anything else.

"Are you okay?"

The tick in his jaw answered me before he spoke: he was pissed, and not only at Ariana. "I need a minute alone. I'll meet you for the emergency briefing after I unpack. I'm sorry."

Helplessly, I watched him storm around the corner and out of sight, wondering if I should follow. Once again, Ariana was sowing seeds of doubt about our relationship, and we hadn't left the dock yet. How would I make it through an entire week without her poison infecting us?

With a forced smile, I stomped on the sprouting seeds of doubt. "Of course I trust *my boyfriend*. It's you I don't trust farther than I can throw you. Did you really kidnap someone's baby to freak me out? That's low, even for you."

"The stroller belongs to Madison, who asked me to watch it while she dealt with some issue in her cabin. There isn't a baby in here. C'mon. You shouldn't make things so easy on me." She nodded over my shoulder, where presumably Madison approached, carrying a toddler on one hip. She seemed vaguely familiar, but I couldn't swear where I'd seen her before. Maybe she'd been on some family quiz show or something a few years ago. She walked beside a gray-haired woman I guessed must be the child's grandmother.

Ariana said, "Oh, noes! Justin seemed mad at you. I hope he

can take a joke. Surely he's not concerned you lost faith in him so easily?"

I refused to rise to her bait a second time. Instead, I turned to our new arrivals. Madison was probably a couple of years out of high school, with shoulder-length brown hair and a smattering of freckles covering her open face. She towered over me and Ariana. I opened my mouth to introduce myself, but closed it when Madison walked by without so much has a glance in my direction. The older woman followed her into the elevator.

"Whatevs," Ariana said. "I need to go find my date."

Smirking, she pushed the stroller in front of the other two women, angling it to block the doors. As if I'd get into an enclosed space with a rattlesnake. She leaned over to punch the Close Doors button while I debated my next move.

I could go after Justin, apologize again, and hope he understood that I couldn't control my facial expressions sometimes. Or I could keep walking, give him some time to think, and take a moment to let go of my frustration toward Ariana before apologizing. Option B seemed more conducive to having an adult conversation. Chasing him now could cause a fight, and I wanted to have fun on this trip.

In the Fishbowl, Ariana always managed to get the better of me. No matter what she said or did, I always turned into the bad guy. I resolved not to let that happen on the ship. At least, not anymore.

Turning, I took the stairs two at a time to our assigned muster station. My rage propelled me quickly down the short flights, leaving me plenty of time to find and enter the confessional before the meeting.

On *The Fishbowl*, they'd called this part of the show "the School Room." Here, signs identified it as the Guppy Gabber. Apparently, I'd always be considered some form of sea life by the Network. And one of their employees spent way too much time coming up with bad puns. The room looked much the same as the one I remembered: small, a single chair in the middle, with a mirror on one wall, speakers in the ceiling, and bright lights in my face.

After giving my interview, the loudspeakers asked everyone to report to their muster stations wearing their life jackets. Which I wasn't wearing. With a sigh, I trotted up the stairs to my cabin, ignoring the elevator bank completely.

Bonus: If I spent all week avoiding being alone in an elevator with my archenemy, my ass would be rock hard by the end. And hey, Ariana brought a date. What was he like? Presumably not a reality show watcher or an Internet user, after the video of her meltdown went viral last summer. But good for her. Maybe now that she got one dig in, she'd leave me and Justin alone.

When I finally made it to the muster station a second time, life vest on but uninflated, I found Justin frowning into his phone.

"Hey," I said. "I'm sorry about before. I know you didn't sleep with her. She surprised me. As usual."

"Jen, we went over all this in the Fishbowl. She's a fan favorite." He shook his head. "If you want to get positive publicity from this cruise, you've got to either learn how not to let her get to you, or start avoiding her at all costs. I know it sucks, but there's nothing we can do about it."

"You're right. I should've prepared myself better. We knew she might be here. I promise, I'm working on it. And I will avoid talking to her whenever possible."

"It's fine." He returned to poking at his phone, still frowning. Not exactly the demeanor of someone who forgives his girlfriend for like acting a jealous dumbass.

"Justin? If it's fine, why won't you look at me?"

He set the phone down and slid one arm around me, pulling me against him. "I'm sorry. It really is fine. I wanted to call my mom one last time before we sailed, but something's wrong with my phone. I charged it fully before we left, and it's down to thirteen percent already." He slid the device into his pocket. "It doesn't matter. We're here to have fun. Even if we're sleeping in separate rooms. I'll plug it in when we go to the cabin and if that doesn't fix it, I can worry about a new phone when we get home."

"We'll have a great vacation, even in separate rooms." I leaned over, sealing the promise with a kiss.

Someone slid into the seats across from us. Before checking, I said a prayer it wasn't Ariana with her fake baby. For once, the fates were listening. When our kiss ended, Ed and Rachel sat across from us.

"Get a room," Ed said.

"We tried," Justin said. "The Network separated us."

"Ah, yes, they did. Sorry about that." Ed's unabashed grin didn't seem the slightest bit remorseful.

"Does the production crew get their own rooms?" Rachel asked. "That's not the expression of a man who's been separated from his boyfriend for the next week."

He waved one hand. "No, he's stuck sharing, too. Justin and I are rooming with some guy who's here as a date. Hairiest bro I've ever met, and I've dated some bears. He seems okay, though. I'm guessing he didn't know he wouldn't get laid on this trip, either."

"You're not serious! No sex for anyone?" I asked.

"Don't bet on it." He winked at me. "It's a big ship, right? Lots of nooks and crannies."

"Speaking of sex, where is Connor?" Rachel asked. "That man is sex on legs."

"Over there." Ed nodded at a muscular, redheaded man on the other side of the room.

Never in a million years would I have recognized him without the long, curly beard that inspired my nickname during filming. Connor stood with the other Network staff, wearing a camera bag, clean-shaven, and better looking than ever.

"What happened to the beard?" Justin asked. "That thing was legendary."

Before Ed could respond, a whistle blew, reminding us why

we gathered. A crew member went through a quick safety demonstration, doing nothing to assure me the ship wasn't going to sink. But at least I knew where to go if we hit an iceberg. I sent up a silent prayer of thanks for my years on the high school diving team, which left me a fairly decent swimmer. I might survive if disaster struck. Depending on the water temperature.

At the end of the presentation, the Network asked all passengers who were part of *Real Ocean: Caribbean* to remain behind. The crowd thinned considerably.

Ariana sat across the room with Madison and the older woman, the baby stroller against the far wall. A lot of other familiar faces filled the room, but I didn't see anyone else from *The Fishbowl.* No Mike, no J-Dawg. I smiled at the realization— most of my allies were here. I hoped the difference in numbers would convince Ariana to behave if basic human decency wasn't enough.

Under the table, Ed nudged my leg with his. "Relax. Those daggers could take out innocent bystanders."

"Sorry. Also, you suck for not telling me she was going to be here."

He laughed. "I had no idea. Connor refused to tell me anything. If you hadn't texted me, I might not have known you two would be here."

The room fell silent, and suddenly, our old production assistant Leanna stood in the middle of the room, hands up. She'd grown out her black spikes since I last saw her, her hair now in twin braids with a peacock blue streak in one. Matching eyeliner rimmed her oval eyes. "Hello, everyone! How are you doing today?"

An enthusiastic cheer went around the room. So enthusiastic, I wondered when the ship opened the bar.

Leanna smiled and waited for the cheer to die down. "We've got about a hundred stars here from several reality shows airing in the past fifteen years or so. Some of you also brought friends and family. Try to remember, not everyone here is a TV star. There are also some fans onboard. They could ask for autographs or pictures. It's up to you how much you want to interact. However, these are your fans, and they're the bread and butter of the Network. We ask you to be polite, even when you don't want to chat or be photographed."

Across the room, Ariana tossed her hair. She lived for being photographed. Meanwhile, I made a mental note never to leave my cabin again without makeup.

"The bar at the rear of the Lido Deck is for reality stars and their guests only. No members of the public are allowed in. Similarly, you guys are only allowed at the main pool on the Lido Deck for official fan interactions. This helps everyone. The larger buffet on the starboard side of the ship is for civilians only. The smaller buffet on the port side is for stars. You're allowed to bring a guest or two, but if things get out of control, we'll take away the privilege. To make this work, there has to be some separation."

My phone vibrated with a group text from Ed.

I'm taking bets on how long it takes before Rachel makes it to the right buffet without going to the wrong one first.

Rachel stuck her tongue out at him. I chuckled, but kept my attention focused on Leanna's explanation of what we'd be doing all week.

"There are cameras throughout the ship in all the public areas. We're going for a *Real World* style show here. The Real Vacations of Reality Stars, if you will. All the fans have signed waivers, so don't assume conversations with them won't be recorded or used. Be yourself, have fun, but know we're watching."

Of course they were. Watching, recording, editing. Creating drama. The things I did for a free vacation.

"For those of you who didn't read the cruise brochure, we've got four days in port and two full days at sea. When you're onboard, make sure to visit the confessionals located inside the spa on the sixteenth level and on the fifth level, near the photo displays. Sign up for excursions with the concierge on the fourth level before Tuesday if you haven't done it already. The Network is picking up excursion costs for the contestants, but not your guests."

Maybe it was better Sarah hadn't joined us, after all. As a budding small business owner, her tiny budget didn't allow much for extras. I'd feel terrible ditching her at every port to go on excursions she couldn't join while she wandered around alone.

"You will all find comped alcohol at the Reality Bar, which is located at the rear of the Lido Deck, and in the Randy and Simon dining rooms. We're going to hand out wristbands. You may get charged at other bars, and we won't reimburse you, so don't get lazy. The Paula dining room is off-limits. We've set that one aside for the civilians."

I chuckled at the names of the dining rooms. When my mom took a cruise last winter, she'd eaten in rooms named after famous renaissance painters—or possibly the Ninja Turtles.

"One more thing. You can download the Queen Cruises app for your phones and use it to message other people while we're at sea. The ship's Wi-Fi lets you run this one app at no cost. However, we've instructed the ship's crew not to allow any more web access for the duration. We're here to make a show, not to sit around on Twitter. If there's an emergency, come talk to me for a temporary authorization."

Justin grinned and leaned over to whisper in my ear. "At least I can send you dirty messages when we're sleeping in separate rooms."

Blushing, I kissed his cheek. Across the table, Rachel waggled her eyebrows at us, but she was smiling.

"Any questions?" Leanna asked. No one responded. "Okay, then. Welcome to the *Real Ocean: Caribbean!*"

My suitcase still hadn't been delivered by the time Leanna released everyone, so I went to find the infirmary for some Dramamine. Justin and Rachel promised to meet me on the Lido Deck after stopping to check out the onboard gym and the running track ringing a mini-golf course the upper deck.

The infirmary took up about two hundred square feet, with two tiny patient areas and a tiny, gray-walled waiting room that would've been extremely depressing if not for the dazzling ocean view. A smiling brunette with an Australian accent directed me into one of the patient areas. The other door stood closed. After a few minutes, I possessed a pack of seasickness pills and a not-unexpected desire for mai tais.

On my way out, I glanced at the other door, which still sat firmly shut. It seemed early in the week for injuries or illness. We hadn't left the port yet.

A voice traveled through the door, and my spine stiffened. I knew that voice as well as my own, even if I hadn't spoken with the owner less than an hour ago. I spent every day for eight weeks stuck listening to it, and then the same piercing voice invaded my living room after I returned home. I watched the viral YouTube video of her meltdown with my best friend Brandon at least a thousand times. Ariana.

The devil on my shoulder told me to step closer, put my ear to the door, find out what she was doing in there. My more moral side suggested the voice might not belong to her, and even horrible people deserved medical privacy. Then again, she wouldn't hesitate a second before doing the same to me. But did I want to sink to her level?

Before I finished my internal debate, the door from the outside opened and a woman entered carrying a small child, his foot bleeding. The receptionist rushed them past me into the room I vacated, calling for a doctor, so I took my cue to exit.

Feeling less queasy from the pills already (despite the doctor's certainty my discomfort was all in my head), I jogged toward the stairs, shoving Ariana out of my mind. I couldn't wait to find my friends. Plus an alcoholic beverage or three.

It turned out, the Lido Deck held four bars, spread across at least a quarter mile of ship. After seeing the huge crowd of people waiting at the railings for cast off, I headed in the opposite direction. At the rear of the ship, I found a bar overlooking a kidney-shaped pool about half the size of the one at the Fishbowl (and beyond it, the sidewalks of Miami). The location promised glorious ocean views once we got out to sea. I texted my friends a note where to find me.

With a ship this big and not sharing a room with Justin, my cell phone became a lifeline. Not even knowing the producers would read every word I wrote put a damper on my excitement over the onboard messaging app.

Settling onto my stool, I ordered a mai tai and turned to look out over the sea. With my back to the dock, the view was stunning. Glittering blue waves expanded out as far as the eye could see. I couldn't wait until water surrounded us in all directions, with not a hint of land to be seen.

Someone settled into the stool beside me. A female voice ordered a cosmopolitan. Definitely not Justin, so no reason to move yet.

I recognized her voice, but couldn't place it. Half the people on this trip appeared on my television at some point over the last twenty years, so naturally most of them would sound or look familiar, or both. I didn't pay attention to the woman seated next to me until she spoke again.

"You know, Jen, I was hoping to get a chance to talk to you."

"Excuse me?" I swiveled to meet her gaze. Then I fell off my stool.

Long, swishy red hair. Giant sunglasses covering eyes that last viewed me with thinly veiled pity. A swimsuit revealing almost as much as the lingerie she'd been wearing when we first met.

Danielle Rossellini. My ex-boyfriend's wife.

FIVE

MORE FROM THE GUPPY GABBER, SUNDAY

Jen: *Oh, of course this would happen. Why do I let the producers surprise me anymore?*

Justin: *Lived in Florida my whole life, never took a cruise. What's wrong with me? All you can eat, lots of booze, no textbooks, plus Jen. This is the best vacation ever.*

Ed: *Hello, America. I'm back and ready for more fabulous drama! I can't wait to see what the show has cooked up for us. Mystery? Love? Deception? No one knows! Isn't this awesome?*
. . . . Except for the sleeping situation. What's up with that? Why am I in bunk beds with Justin and some strange dude? This isn't summer camp. Although, come to think of it, when I was fifteen, summer camp with Johnny blew my mind. And other things. Oops. Can I say that? Hi, Johnny!

Justin: *I can't speak for our roommate, but my bunk bed unfortunately won't be used to recreate Ed's child summer camp experience. I wish Jen and I were in our own room.*

Ariana: *Okay, fine, whatever, the baby joke wasn't funny. I just wanted to break the ice and address the elephant in the room. No one gets me around here. Why do I subject myself to this?*

When my butt slid off the stool and slammed into the deck, I prayed for the ground to open up and swallow me. No such luck. I'd be watching this scene on YouTube for the rest of my life. My fall would be a viral gif before the first episode finished airing.

"Are you okay?" Danielle asked.

She reached one hand down to help me, but I ignored it and pulled myself up. "What do you care? I'm nothing but a home-wrecking liar, right?" I quoted directly from the interview she'd given to Talky Ted, the tabloid "reporter" who apparently never found any real news to talk about. He'd taken quite an interest in me, Justin, and Ariana during our summer on *The Fishbowl* and never quite moved on.

To my surprise, she turned pink. "I never should've said those things."

The only thing more surprising than Dominic's wife appearing on this ship in the first place was hearing her words, which sounded suspiciously like an apology. I must've broken my ears in the fall.

"Come again?"

"I'm glad to find you alone," she repeated. "I've been hoping for an opportunity to talk to you."

"Oh yeah? Calling me a slut and a home wrecker online and on TV wasn't enough for you? You needed to insult me to my face?"

After *The Fishbowl* announced the cast, Danielle thrust herself into the spotlight, garnering not only some high-profile interviews but also her own reality show. It hadn't been renewed after the first season, and until she sat next to me, I'd completely forgotten the show existed.

I didn't need this conversation, especially so soon after my run-in with Ariana. I started to leave, but Danielle put one hand on my arm. The pleading in her eyes surprised me. How good an actress was she?

"Don't go, please. I only came on this cruise because I knew you'd never agree to meet me face-to-face."

"Fine." I stopped and crossed my arms, waiting. "What do you want to say?"

She lit a cigarette, taking a long drag before blowing the smoke out over the pool.

"Are we allowed to smoke onboard?"

"Nope," she said. "But the Network can't show me smoking, so I'm securing us a private conversation before someone tells me to put it out. Let's walk away from the bar."

I followed her to the far railing, not speaking. To quell my nerves, I sipped my mai tai. Then I waited for her to fill the silence.

"You know Dominic and I are divorced now, right?"

"I think Ed mentioned it when your show aired, but I forgot. I'm sorry to hear that." Kind of. Not really. But it seemed like the right thing to say.

"Don't be. I'm not." She waved one hand, keeping the smoke away from me. "Still when I found out my husband was cheating on me, it hurt."

"Imagine how I felt," I said dryly.

"I know, I know," she said. "I handled things badly. The more I trashed you, the more attention I got. Getting support from outraged fans on social media made me feel better. The pain lessened. The Network set me up with *Suddenly Single in Seattle*, and the whole thing spun my head. I don't know how you managed to stay so down-to-earth."

"I was living off the grid. We didn't get any news in the

house. No Internet. I didn't know anything about the rest of the world until I left. Plus, our show aired mostly live. By the time I got home after leaving the show, most of the buzz about me had died down," I said. "Besides, you went attention-seeking. Justin and I aren't trying to make the news these days. We just want to live our lives and be happy."

"That's all I wanted, too. But I went about it all wrong. I imagine you didn't watch my show?"

"My best friend tried to talk me into sitting through the first episode or so, but after seeing the ads, it hurt too much. Especially when they kept airing the dramatization of me finding you with Dom."

"Oh, yeah." She laughed. "That woman was the worst actress I'd ever seen in my life."

"It was Ariana," I said. "She starred in *The Fishbowl* with us."

"Was it?" Danielle blinked at me. "Small world, I guess. I didn't recognize her in the wig she was wearing."

"Whatever. I couldn't watch the show, and I'm not sorry I missed it."

"I understand. And I'm sorry. I never should've agreed to do it in the first place. In one of the later episodes, I apologized for everything. I did another interview where I retracted all the nasty things I said about you. You'll never believe Shocking Entertainment News Online didn't post my change of heart on their homepage."

I grinned at her, willing to play nice now but also making a mental note to find the article when we got home. "No, I guess they wouldn't have. Thanks for letting me know."

She glanced over one shoulder. Following her gaze, I spotted a couple of people walking toward us. Their headsets and clipboards identified them as members of the production staff.

"We're running out of time," Danielle said, dropping her cigarette into her now-empty cup. "Let's get a big hug on tape for the viewers."

She opened her arms, and I fell into them, marveling at how

much she'd changed since our first meeting. Then again, finding out your husband is cheating because his mistress walked in on the two of you about to have sex would come as a shock to anyone. Danielle was as much a victim of this as me. Originally, anyway. I supposed I couldn't blame her for reacting badly.

I pulled away, and she brushed a lock of hair from my cheek. She leaned in, kissing my cheek. I opened my mouth to remind her about personal bubbles.

Her breath touched my ear, so light I could've imagined it. "Keep smiling, okay?" I nodded, and she moved to the other cheek, European-style. "Dominic's onboard. Ariana brought him as her date."

THE CHILL RUNNING down my spine had nothing to do with the cool sea breeze. Shock waves hit me, intense enough to freeze my smile in place.

"Wh-h-wh-ow?"

Danielle confirmed with a glance that the producers moved away and lit another cigarette. Genius. I vowed to take up smoking ASAP.

"I don't know why or how. His lawyer emailed me last night to let me know he'd be here," she said. "It was too late to do anything before departure, but I wanted to catch you as soon as we got onboard."

"Thanks. I wish I'd known early enough to think about canceling the trip."

Would I have? Probably not, all things considered, but now I'd never know.

"No need," she said airily. "Our divorce agreement requires him to remain at least twenty-five feet from me at all times. His lawyers upgraded me to one of the balcony suites near the top of the ship. And you and I are about to become best friends, so he can't get too close to you."

What an amazing offer.

An amazing, unbelievable, much-too-good-to-be-true offer.

"Why would you do that for me?" I asked.

She counted her response on her fingers, a stream of smoke punctuating each sentence. "One, because Dom screwed me over, too, and I'm not about to help him play kissy face with the girl he cheated on me with. Two, you were young when you met him, and I'm thirty-five years old. I can't blame you for my marital problems anymore. Three, like I said, I feel bad. I was an unforgivable ass last year. Consider this my way of making it up to you." Then she added, "Besides, I'm in a generous mood. His job doesn't pay shit, but my lawyer got me half of the trust his parents left him, so I'm living well. Let me spread the joy."

The producers reappeared across the deck. They were good. I hadn't yet spotted the cameras out here, but they must be set up somewhere. Danielle dropped her second butt into the cup and deposited the whole thing in the nearby trash can, where it hopefully wouldn't start a fire. Just what I needed on Day One of this new show: Jen Reid, the Pyromaniac's Assistant.

Justin and Rachel appeared at the top of the stairs, so I left Danielle to make excuses to the producers and went to fill my friends in.

"Wow, hello drama," Rachel said. "You have a knack for stumbling into it."

"But I don't want drama," I grumbled. "Why did I sign up for this?"

"Do you really need a list?" Justin asked.

"No, that was rhetorical."

Justin sighed, raking his hand through his hair. "It's all about the ratings. You know that. The Network wants more viewers. And the people who watch this type of show like to see love triangles. Or a love square, apparently. The best thing we can do is avoid Dominic and Ariana."

"I'll drink to that," I said.

"Me, too!" Rachel said. "As soon as I find a mudslide. Why

are we standing around talking? Free drinks at the bar, remember? And did you know there are poker tables downstairs? I'll catch you later."

We stopped by the bar so they could pick up drinks. I ordered another mai tai, having downed most of mine while talking to Danielle. Rachel went off to play cards, leaving strict instructions not to bother her unless she didn't reappear in time for the meet-and-greet. With one eye on Danielle to ensure I didn't stray from her limited protection, I led Justin to the railing.

He put one arm around my waist, and I leaned against him. As I took in the view and breathed in the salty air, the tension slid out of my upper back and neck.

"Alone at last," he said, raising his glass.

"To a fabulous vacation where we're surrounded by frenemies and not allowed to sleep in the same room!" I gave him a rueful smile to take the edge off my comment.

"Don't worry about that," he said. "I'll talk to Ed. If anyone knows where to get some secret nookie, it's him and Connor."

"How about some not-so-secret nookie?" I pulled him toward me for a kiss.

On the show, we'd been so concerned about keeping our relationship private, about not having our first kiss on camera, and it turned out to all be for nothing. At the airport on the way home, every newsstand offered a wall of newspapers and magazines plastered with a picture of us, taken in the driveway of the Fishbowl, bodies locked together.

After getting over my embarrassment, I'd bought three. Then I signed a fourth for the cashier.

How many people are lucky enough to have their first kiss with their true love caught on camera? I'd also asked the show for a larger copy and framed it, before Sarah got the idea for the bakery.

After doing our best to give America a good show, Justin and

I stared out over the glittering blue water, watching the shoreline get further and further away. Despite my earlier concerns, the motion of the ship didn't bother me one bit. Either the pills they gave me helped, or my nervous stomach related more to fear of seeing Ariana than any motion the ship might make.

After our rough morning, Justin and I decided to eat in relative privacy up on deck rather than joining the others in the dining room. When we finished, the producers had scheduled us for a Q&A session with fans of the show. We separated briefly to shower, change into regular clothes, and for me to reapply my makeup, then met again in the auditorium.

The enormous room sat mostly empty, leaving me both nervous about speaking in front of a large audience and concerned that no one would show up. Sure, I'd done television, but in TV, if no one watches, you read about it later. We couldn't see out through the cameras to the empty living rooms. Heckling also was never an issue on the first show. What if the "fans" secretly hated us? What if everyone who showed up wanted Justin to pick Ariana? My palms sweat.

Bright lights already pointed at the raised stage, which held a long conference table. With those shining in my eyes, at least I'd never know if no one else showed up. A quick scan showed Rachel, Ed, and Ariana already sitting on the stage. Danielle was nowhere to be found, which meant Dominic might wander in at any second.

That kind of thinking wouldn't get me anywhere. The only way to enjoy the week was to stop glancing over my shoulder every five seconds. Dominic would show, or he wouldn't, and Justin and I would enjoy ourselves either way. I straightened my shoulders, took a deep breath, and plastered a smile on my face.

"Are you okay?" Justin asked. "You're a bit green."

"Sorry," I said. "These events make me nervous. I'm glad I have you by my side."

Hand-in-hand, we approached the stage and settled into the

two open seats on the far end, next to Ariana. A glossy stack of my favorite photograph sat between two pens, one green and the other blue. We were apparently signing joint autographs.

"Look at that," Justin said, pointing. "Jen and Justin. Justin and Jen. Always together. If I hadn't chased after you, no one would remember my name."

"That's not true!" I said. "Plenty of people cheered you on. Most of them fifteen to forty-year-old women. You had lots of fans."

"No, I didn't," he said. "Not like Rachel or Ariana or Ed. People watched to see who I'd pick."

"Well, people only watched me because they thought I was a home-wrecking liar. At least you had more fans than I did."

He laughed. "When you put it that way, I'm surprised anyone wanted to watch either of us."

"We're like Nutella. Better combined than chocolate or hazelnuts on their own."

"Mmmm, Nutella." Leaning over, he kissed my cheek. "Thanks. Things are always better when I'm with you."

"I think so, too," Leanna said behind us. "That's why there aren't any solo pictures of either of you. Make sure to talk to fans together, sign together. You're a team. Got it?"

"Got it," Justin said.

He still seemed a bit uncomfortable, but the A/C being pumped into the rest of the theater wasn't making it to the stage. Plus, being reduced to one-half of a couple rather than one full person was a bit degrading. It didn't bother me, but I understood his frustration. There was just nothing we could do about it.

"We're the best team I've ever been part of," I said.

He leaned over and pressed his lips against mine. Tingles went down my spine. We were a very good team, indeed.

Beside me, Ariana said my name, so quietly I thought I imagined it. Then I heard it again. "Hey, Jen?"

Reluctantly, I broke the kiss, forcing myself to smile pleasantly for the cameras and the crowd. "Yeah?"

"I wanted to say I'm sorry about before." She leaned around me and raised her voice. "You, too, Justin. Running into you brought up all these old emotions from the show, but I'm trying to turn over a new leaf. I should've resisted the temptation to mess with you. I'm sorry."

Those mai tais must've been super strong, because it sounded like Ariana was apologizing to me. Or the show cast a very convincing identical actress. Key word: actress.

It's another one of her tricks.

When *The Fishbowl* announced the cast last year, Brandon and I streamed all of Ariana's movies. She played many bit parts, all of which seemed to be cast due to her boobage. None of which were well-acted. She'd done a bit better with some of her lies on the show, but still. She couldn't possibly be sincere.

Beside me, Justin spoke. "Thanks, Ariana. I hope we can all start over."

I resisted the urge to grunt and roll my eyes. The cameras captured everything. She must know that, and she probably counted on me to snub her. No such luck. Besides, I'd won, right? I walked away from the show with the second-largest cash prize (technically giving me second place, although the show named Ed the official runner-up, since he lost to Rachel in the finale). Plus I wound up with Justin. She got nothing but an offer for a minor role in the new Bond movie, pulled when someone more famous became available at the last minute.

I forced the corners of my lips upward into an expression that hopefully looked sincerer than it felt. "I understand. Let's start this cruise with a clean slate."

"That would be lovely," she said.

She'd yet to mention bringing my ex onboard, and I suddenly wondered if Danielle made the whole thing up. Maybe my hostilities were aimed at the wrong target. After all, Dominic's ex-wife had hated me as much as Ariana, and she'd already trashed me all over the media. But would she lie about a retraction I could easily find myself?

At the other end of the row, Ed gazed out at the audience, smiling and waving effortlessly. His Brazilian good looks made him a standout in any crowd, but he was completely in his element here in front of adoring fans. The quick wit that kept me laughing in the Fishbowl no matter what Ariana did or what the producers threw at us served him well on stage. In Los Angeles, Ed found himself rocketing through the local club scene. He'd even scored an audition for a series of guest spots on the *Tonight Show*.

Scanning the crowd, I noticed several people carrying signs. When I spotted one saying Justin + Jen 4-Eva, I waved. Fans of Justin, Ed, and Rachel all got waves, too. I pretended not to see signs saying, Ariana Is the Better Woman and Long Live J-Dawg!

Then I spotted my face on a poster board, surrounded by a heart drawn in green marker. My favorite color, and my assigned contestant color on the show. The sign wasn't too strange in and of itself (after being on TV, I mean. It would've been weird if someone did it when I was in college), but I kept returning to the image, trying to figure out why it caught my attention.

Finally, I realized: the picture on the poster wasn't a promo shot from the show. It wasn't a screen cap, either, or one of the photos from my public Facebook page or official Twitter account. The sign displayed a picture taken of me in the early morning, head resting on a pillow, gazing lovingly up at the man who'd taken it.

The man who cheated on me. Whose wife turned me into a villain, making it impossible for me to win viewer loyalty—which was key to remaining on *The Fishbowl* from one week to the next. The man with no business being on this cruise in this first place, since he did not qualify as a "reality star" by any stretch of the imagination. The man holding the sign? My ex-boyfriend, Dominic.

Even after learning Ariana brought him as her date, seeing him sent a shock wave through me. And what on earth was he doing holding a sign with *my* face if the two of them came here as a couple?

Justin leaned over, nodding in the direction of my gaze. "Hey, Jen. I think my roommate's got a crush on you."

SIX

STILL MORE FROM THE GUPPY GABBER, SUNDAY:

Danielle: *Hello, fans! I'm so excited to be above the Queen Kelly this week. I met the delightful Jen from* The Fishbowl *by the pool this morning. I take back everything I said about her on the show. Did you know the drinks are only free for the reality stars, not their guests? Suck it, Dominic!*

Rachel: *I don't trust Danielle farther than I can throw her. She may seem sweet as pie, but I'll be watching her. But, hey, I won fifty bucks playing Texas Hold 'Em. Woo-hoo!*

Danielle: **sips drink* Did I mention this drink is free? Free free free free free free free free free free free free free free free free free free free free free free free free. In case it's not clear my alliances have shifted, I'm 100 percent Team Jen and Justin. Yay young love!*

Like a deer in headlights, I froze, glaring at Dominic. He stood tall, meeting my eyes squarely. The last time I'd seen him, he'd been naked, dragging me down his hallway to get me out of the house before his wife spotted me. He'd grown a beard, cut his dark, curly hair, but otherwise hadn't changed.

"What's wrong?" Justin whispered. "You look like you've seen a ghost."

"It's my ex-boyfriend," I replied. "Danielle warned me that he paid for the cruise, but I didn't want to believe it until I spotted him. And why is he holding a sign with my face on it when he's here with Ariana?"

Before Justin replied, the cruise director came out on stage to introduce all of us. He recapped our season, with pictures flashing on a screen I hadn't paid attention to on the wall behind us. I cringed at some of the highlights, like me climbing up the bathroom wall to catch Ariana in a lie, but glowed at the sighs passing through the crowd at the replay of Justin running down the driveway after me and our kiss. He squeezed my hand under the table.

Every picture of Justin in the entire slideshow included me, Ariana, or both. The longer the show played, the worse I felt. The two of us overshadowed his identity without realizing it. The Network played up the love triangle for the drama, and Justin as a person disappeared into the show. He'd forever be defined by the moment he left the show.

Members of the cruise staff stood in the rows holding microphones. When the introduction finished, we said hello to the audience. Then the cruise director opened up the floor for questions.

"This question is for Jen and Justin." A woman about my mom's age went first. "The two of you lived in the house together, with all the scheming and lies. Jen thought Justin was using her to stay on the show. Justin, you thought the same thing. It took you eight weeks to learn to be honest with each other. Do you find that you still have problems with communication and trust, after returning to your regular lives?"

Justin's face grew red. The woman couldn't have planned a more perfectly worded question to push his buttons. Heck, for all we knew, maybe they did.

"Not at all," I said. "The show was a different environment. We all wanted to win the money, but alliances still formed. Ed and Rachel supported me every step of the way, and so did Birdie, who unfortunately wasn't able to make it this week. I let my doubts shake me because my ex-boyfriend cheated on me before the show started. I didn't trust my instincts after being so wrong about someone I thought loved me."

"And the other thing," Justin said, "is that when you're trapped in a house with someone for several weeks, you get to know them. Until the show pulled the stunt with the 'serious boyfriend' at the end, I never doubted Jen or her feelings for me. I was just focused more on winning the show than starting a relationship in front of fifteen million strangers."

He referred to a mini-challenge near the end of the season, when we competed to bring a loved one to visit us on the show. When I found out Dominic waited in a nearby hotel in case I won, I'd refused to participate. Thankfully, Justin won, and when Sarah came into the house, she helped us work through the misunderstanding.

Justin's eyes lingered on my face, his pupils dilated. A warm fuzzy feeling started low in my belly. That expression in his green eyes, combined with his dimples, usually led us straight to the bedroom. Where we couldn't go any time soon, darn it. Stupid Network. Instead, I rubbed his thigh under the table. He pressed his leg up against mine, and I shivered.

He continued, "I always intended to call her the second I got eliminated. I knew she was something special, as soon as we met."

Awww. Leaning over, I kissed him. The crowd cheered.

We got stuck answering three more questions about our relationship before the audience moved on, directing their attention to the rest of the panel. Justin was right: neither of us had any identity on our own. Every question went "to Jen and Justin" or "to Justin and Jen." We existed in this reality only as a couple.

Ed talked about the difficulty of coming out on the show and his move to Los Angeles to work as a gay rights activist/comedian. He did not mention his relationship with one of the crew members. Not a single member of the audience asked him about sneaking off to have sex during the show (which I knew for a fact he did, unlike me and Justin) or whether his relationship was a sham for ratings. Lucky.

Rachel explained her plans to open a cheerleading camp for underprivileged kids with her grand prize money. No one asked how I spent my fifty thousand. Perhaps I'd have gotten some questions about it if I spread rumors about spending all the cash on my boyfriend. Or on the two of us buying a house together. For almost an hour, I sorely missed having my own identity.

Then the cruise director announced the last question. To my horror, my ex stood up. When we'd been dating, I thought Dominic the most handsome guy in the world, with his bronze skin, curly dark hair, and always-smiling brown eyes. Now, my stomach churned at the sight of him. When one of the crew members handed him a microphone, I groaned internally.

"This question is for Jen. Do you believe in second chances? Do you think the two of us could ever be together again?"

A chill ran down my spine. Ariana's date, my ass. She'd brought him for one reason and one reason only: to torment me. So much for turning over a new leaf.

I took a long moment to collect myself before answering. Justin squeezed my hand under the table. "Everyone, I'd like to introduce you to my ex-boyfriend, who you may remember from several conversations on *The Fishbowl* about how he forgot to mention being married."

The resulting boos throughout the audience made me feel

better. But when they died down, the cruise director turned to me. "Jen? The question?"

Right. Here I'd been hoping to ignore my ex and move on to another question instead of answering him.

"First: No, Dominic and I could never be together again. I'm in love with Justin." I paused to gaze at my boyfriend. The love shining out of his eyes nearly made me forget the rest of the question. He kissed me briefly, and I returned my attention to the crowd. "Generally, I don't think it would be fair to say no one is ever entitled to a second chance. People make mistakes, and forgiveness is part of being human. But even if I hadn't moved on, you are the last person I would ever go out with again. I can forgive a lot, but I won't tolerate cheating—and I shouldn't have to."

Dominic opened his mouth, but the audience burst out in applause, and the person holding the microphone swept away down the aisle. I was happy enough not to be able to hear his words. Even at this distance, I could see my ex mouthing, "I love you."

I resisted the urge to stick my tongue out at him.

Instead, I turned to Ariana and whispered under the cover of the clapping. "If you're so sorry, what's he doing here?"

"My agent set it up," she whispered back. "He didn't tell me until few days ago, after it was too late to cancel. Trust me, the last thing I wanted was to spend the entire cruise watching Justin *and* my fake date drool all over you."

That was the most sincere-sounding thing she'd ever said to me, but I still didn't trust her. The whole story seemed too pat, too well rehearsed. What possible reason would she have for bringing Dominic along on the cruise if she wasn't trying to stir things up?

The director thanked everyone for coming, and we waited while the audience cleared the aisles. To my horror, Dominic stayed behind as the rows of seats emptied, then approached the stairs at the side of the stage.

"Everything okay?" Justin asked, pulling me toward him. "Great final answer, by the way."

"Thanks. Don't look, but Dominic is walking this way," I said. "Is there another exit?"

"I don't know, but don't worry about him. We're a team, remember? We can deal with this guy. Although I may throttle whoever set up the room assignments."

"Seriously." I rolled my eyes. "Can you stay somewhere else?"

"Not without spending a lot of money we don't have right now. But how much time are we really going to spend in the room? I'll be fine. And if he gets out of line, we'll sic Ed on him. No problem."

"What am I doing?" Ed asked.

We explained the situation, but before I finished, I realized Dominic had vanished from the side of the stage. Did security take him away?

A swish of long, dark hair caught my eye. On the far side of the theater, Ariana walked up the aisle toward the doors with Dominic. His arm wrapped around her waist, almost as if he were supporting her, and she leaned her head on his shoulder.

Ariana said she turned over a new leaf. She claimed she didn't invite Dominic on the cruise, and he wasn't really a date. But then why was he here? Dominic said he wanted me back. Both were demonstrated liars. And now they walked off together, arm-in-arm, appearing like any other devoted couple. What was going on?

And why did I care?

SEVEN

QUEEN KELLY'S VOICE
ROW, ROW, ROW YOUR BOAT

Monday edition

Welcome to our first full day at sea. We've got a day packed with activities, from miniature golf on the eighteenth deck to the Hairy Back Contest by the pool to arts and crafts in the kids only area. The gym on the fourth floor is open all day, as is the attached spa.

Mid-morning, drop by the theater for a Q&A and autograph session with Danielle Rossellini, the star of last year's breakout hit, *Suddenly Single in Seattle.*

After lunch, four of our reality stars face off to create the perfect dessert for our host, *America's Totally 80s Bake-Off*'s Tammy Rae! Former contestants from other shows will be on hand to judge.

Meet us on the Lido Deck at 1:00 PM. Stick around after the winners are announced for a sample of Tammy Rae's show-winning chocolate coconut cupcakes recipe. You definitely won't want to miss these, but there's a limited supply, so don't be late.

Inside this Edition:

Our other roommates apparently either missed the boat or paid for upgrades to better rooms, because Rachel and I found ourselves alone in our cabin. We didn't mind. Already, Rachel's excess clothes and accessories littered the top of both bunk beds. Two more bodies wouldn't have fit.

The next morning, I armed for battle before heading to the dining room for breakfast. My new white-and-purple sundress flattered my coloring perfectly. White wedge sandals helped me stand tall. Well, tall-*er*. At five-foot-four, I'd never stand super tall without stilts. A slathering of sunblock gave me the coconut odor I would forever associate with all things *The Fishbowl*. I took twice my usual amount of time with my hair and makeup, despite knowing twenty seconds in the winds on the Lido Deck would render my newly created curls flaccid. When I finally told Rachel I was ready to go to breakfast, I felt like a million bucks.

She emerged from the bathroom wearing a green bikini and flip-flops. "You don't look like you're heading to the pool. And you're not holding a fruity beverage. I see no umbrellas."

"Isn't it early for alcohol?"

"We're on vacation! It's five o'clock somewhere."

"Okay, true, but I need your help," I said.

"Are there cabana boys involved?"

I thought about it for a minute. "Probably not. But there is one evil bitch, and your old friend needs backup. Ariana is probably at this very moment trying to convince Justin to dump me and go out with her instead."

"Well, that's a waste of breath. Didn't she bring a date?"

"Remember the guy from the Q&A? The one who asked me about second chances?"

"Oh, right." Rachel said. "Never mind, then. That girl is clearly on a mission."

"Exactly. She told me her agent set it up and she didn't know, but why would I believe her? This is the girl who lied about having an art history degree for no apparent reason. Nothing she says can be trusted."

"Ugh. What a mess. But seriously, Jen, don't worry. Justin loves you," Rachel said. "Don't let your insecurities ruin a good thing. Go. Be awesome. I'm sure he won't pay any attention to her. It's a huge ship."

"But . . . come with me?" I puffed out my lower lip and gazed up at her with sad, round eyes.

Rachel sighed heavily. "Fine. But you owe me a fruity, boozy beverage later."

"Did I mention they have mimosas in the dining room?"

"No, you did not! Let me grab a cover-up. I need to do my makeup before facing this witch."

Justin messaged me that he'd been seated at a table for eight by the window on the starboard side. I let him know Rachel and I would be meeting him shortly.

At dinner the night before, the waiter had explained that on a regular cruise, guests were seated randomly at large tables, regardless of the number of people in their party. New diners were taken to any table with space for them unless they asked for a private table. That meant most passengers would be seated with strangers unless they requested otherwise. The idea was that it promoted interaction among passengers from all over the world.

The producers had asked the waitstaff to continue this practice for our trip, even though it would leave about half the tables in this dining room unused for the duration. Great. I wouldn't have minded being randomly seated with a nice retired couple from Idaho or something, but the fans had been funneled to another dining room. Sitting at a random table with two friends and five empty seats virtually guaranteed that Ariana and Dominic would be joining us, along with everyone's best friend, Murphy's Law.

When I turned toward the stairs instead of the elevator, Rachel stopped. "What are you doing?"

"Taking the stairs."

"Well, yes, I see that. Why?"

I dropped my voice in case anyone was listening. "I can't stand the possibility of being trapped in an elevator with Dominic or Ariana. Or worse both. Not even with you beside me."

She lifted one foot, revealing perfectly polished, cherry-red toenails and three-inch wedges on her sandals. "You can't possibly expect me to take the stairs in these."

Reality TV makes for strange bedfellows, but you really got to know someone when locked in a house with them for eight weeks. I wracked my brain, trying to recall a story she'd once told me. "Didn't you help deliver a calf on your way to prom, in a floor-length mermaid gown and six-inch stilettos? Right before being crowned queen?"

Her gaze dropped to the ground. "That story may have been embellished for the sake of the viewers."

I crossed my arms and waited, not speaking, as her lips twitched. We could have been in the dining room already.

Finally, she met my eyes. A giggled escaped. "They were *five-inch* stilettos. Darn you and your perfect memory."

I followed her down the stairs, listening to her faked grumbles every step of the way and hoping we didn't run into Ariana or Dominic on the way to the dining room.

For once, my luck held out. Ed and Connor waited at the

table with Justin already. I dropped into the empty seat at Justin's right and rested my head on his shoulder.

"I missed you last night," I said. "Rachel doesn't snore. It was too quiet."

She snorted. "I may not snore, but it sure wasn't quiet in our room."

I flushed, and Justin kissed my forehead.

"Told you I'm not the one who snores." he said, lifting my chin until our lips met.

The strain of the last twenty-four hours vanished. I moved my hand to his thigh, and a thrill went through me when he tensed beneath my palm. Five minutes. I'd have given anything for a mere five minutes alone with him. Maybe we could sneak into a bathroom or something. They couldn't have cameras everywhere.

Across the table, Ed cleared his throat. "Get a room."

"We're trying." I grumbled, my lips still attached to Justin's. "The Network said no."

"Sorry, Jen, but I can't hear you with that lawyer on your face."

With an exaggerated groan, I moved back to my seat. My hand remained on Justin's thigh. He squeezed it under the table, and I smiled at the promise in that touch. We'd find some alone time, sooner or later.

Less than five minutes after we sat down, the hostess brought Danielle to join us.

"No way," Ed said. "You can't sit with us."

"What is this? Some movie about high school?"

Apparently, he'd seen her show. I hadn't gotten a chance to talk to him about Danielle after the Q&A, so he had no idea we'd worked things out. I'd much rather sit and eat with Danielle than Ariana and Dominic. Or her rude friend, Marilyn or whoever.

"It's okay," I said. "Danielle and I have a lot in common. We're going to be BFFs."

He shot me a questioning look.

"Really," I said. Danielle shot me a grateful look, and I continued. "Dominic's not allowed within twenty-five feet of her. And since I don't want to see him, either, letting Danielle sit with us is the best way to have a peaceful breakfast."

"Dude's not a total wanker," Ed said. "If he hadn't lied and cheated on you and come to help Ariana steal your man, I might actually like him."

Rachel snorted.

Justin said, "I doubt she came all this way just to break us up. As if she could."

Although I wouldn't put anything past Ariana, now wasn't the time to argue. The look he shot me made me face grow warm. I raised our clasped hands to my lips, my eyes never leaving his.

Ed cleared his throat. "Let's change the subject before the lovebirds make us too uncomfortable. Connor and I aren't allowed to make out in public, and we're getting peanut butter and jelly over here. Please let us enjoy our breakfast before he has to start working, and I have to go schmooze the fans."

"Let me stay, and I'll tell you a secret," Danielle said. Ed motioned for her to continue. "The hot chocolate in the dining room is ten times better than what they serve upstairs. Even without booze. Down here, they make it with milk instead of water."

Ed waved the waiter over and ordered five, signaling that all was forgiven.

Danielle said, "Did you see the improv show last night?"

Talking comedy was the best possible way to Ed's heart. Before our beverages even arrived, the two of them were chatting like old friends about the show I'd missed the night before and the stand-up contest Ed would be hosting on the main deck later in the week. Seeing everyone get along put my mind at ease.

Craning my neck, I scoured the room for Tammy Rae, hoping

to get a chance to say hello before the bake-off. Finally, I spotted her on the other side of the room, being led toward us. Under the table, I crossed my fingers, silently begging the waiter to bring her to one of our empty seats.

Tammy Rae (never Tammy, although I didn't know if Rae was her last name, part of her first name, or an affectation) fronted an all-girls pop band from 1984 to 1988. At nineteen, she quit the band to go to college, and mostly vanished until the cast of *Totally 80s Bake-off* went live a couple of years ago.

Nearly twenty years after the height of her fame, Tammy Rae still sported her trademark long blonde hair and big blue eyes, although at some point, she ditched the perm. A wise choice, indeed. She looked much older than I expected, which shouldn't have surprised me since she'd been famous before I was born. From what I could see, her music videos must've been filmed either wearing platform heels or using special camera angles to increase her height. Her head bobbed along only a few inches above the waiter's elbow. Perhaps I should've worn flats; even I would tower over this woman.

To my chagrin, the waiter sat her beside Ariana and Dominic at a table across the room. I hadn't noticed them sitting there until the waiter swerved away from us, winding his way toward the far windows. That made it impossible for me to go introduce myself to Tammy Rae, like I'd planned. The idea was to befriend her, butter her up, find out what she wanted in exchange for the secret ingredient, then figure out how to give it to her.

Unfortunately, if Ariana suspected I wanted information from Tammy Rae, the poor woman would probably find herself locked in a closet for the rest of the trip. Still, I kept one eye on the table, searching for my opening, while half-heartedly partici-pating in conversation about everyone's plans for the day.

Justin, always a good sport, told animated tales from his final semester in law school, knowing I'd heard the stories and didn't need to listen to laugh at the right places. In response to my grateful look, he leaned over and kissed my cheek. I lingered over breakfast as long as possible, trying not to obviously stare but also never letting Tammy Rae out of my sight. Ed and Connor gave up waiting for me and went to find the pool. Rachel and Danielle soon followed, with a promise to message me their location once they got settled.

Eventually, two glasses of water and a pot of hot cocoa caught up with me. The ship's layout turned me around twice on the way to the restroom, which for some reason wasn't connected to the dining room. By the time I found my way back, Tammy Rae's table sat empty. Dominic and Ariana were gone, but so was she.

My shoulders slumped. I'd missed my chance.

THERE WASN'T much time to dwell on missing Tammy Rae at breakfast. Leanna swept me, Justin, and the other judges to the salon for hair and makeup before the baking competition started. Then she isolated us from the contestants by banishing everyone to an empty seating area. It didn't seem prudent to remind her that one of the contestants was my close friend and Justin's cabinmate. Avoiding Ed now after we ate breakfast with him seemed illogical to me, but it wasn't worth arguing.

Not that it mattered. We'd agreed to judge because Sweet Reality needed the publicity. Ed loved cooking but had zero experience as a baker; he was doing the contest more to increase visibility and entertain the audience than to win the actual prize —dinner for two at one of the private onboard restaurants. Justin, Ed, and I all knew he wasn't likely to win, and that was fine. Voting for my friend's creation if it wasn't amazing would only convince people I didn't know what delicious baked goods tasted like. Not exactly the impression I wanted to convey right before inviting people to purchase food from my bakery.

It was bad enough that the audition video of me burning cookies still got hits on YouTube. No one cared how many times

I made cookies while on the show, or how good they turned out. None of my prior baking experience, or the fact that the oven knob came off in my hand, made a difference. All that mattered was, the first time I filmed myself baking, I set off the fire alarm while talking about how much I liked making cookies. After *The Fishbowl* became available on Netflix, that clip went viral. Someone auto-tuned it.

Which, okay, that video totally cracked me up when Brandon showed me. I may have saved it on my phone to watch whenever I needed a laugh.

Once the sun set, our waiting area would house a nightclub. A bar lined one wall, and a dance floor sat in the middle. Neon strips in several colors crisscrossed the floor. There was no TV in the lounge, but the other judges scattered around the room. The windows provided glorious ocean views with no sun, wind, or rain. If other people knew this spot existed, they'd pack in like sardines every day.

Justin wound his way through the room to a spot near the rear window. I went to grab a couple of waters someone set out on the bar before going to join him. He stood stiffly, brow furrowed. When I held out his water, he took it and set it on a nearby table with a mumbled, "thanks," his eyes never leaving the water.

I wrapped my arms around his waist, planting a soft kiss on the back of his neck before leaning into him. "Everything okay? I know the view is glorious, but it hasn't changed much since we spent two hours looking at it last night after dinner."

He sighed and turned in my arms, kissing the top of my head gently. "I'm sorry. I'm worried about my mom. She's not much older than Tammy Rae, you know. And Tammy Rae is vibrant, larger-than-life, running around making reality shows on a cruise ship. Mom's confined to a bed, so full of tubes and medication she barely remembers me."

My heart went out to him. "I'm so, so–"

He placed one finger against my lips. "Shh. You know how I am with public sympathy. Say something else."

"Want to go have sex behind the bar before the bake-off starts?"

"Yes!"

"Sadly, we can't," I said. "Anyway, do you want to beg Internet time off the producers so we can email Sarah for an update?"

"Thanks, but no. Sarah would get upset if she knew I was worrying instead of relaxing out here." He sighed. "I wanted to wait until we got home to tell you this, but Sarah and I think it's time to move Mom into full-time hospice care. I wish we didn't have to, but caring for her is really taking a toll, and ever since Dad broke his back, he's not much help. He needs surgery. It could be months before he's back on his feet."

I started to tell him again how sorry I am that he's going through all this, but stopped myself. "We'll work everything out when we get home."

He smiled at me. "Thanks. I'm trying not to worry about them. But my phone's battery still isn't charging, which means I can't call Sarah while we're in the ports like I promised."

"You can use my phone."

"I love you." He kissed me briefly before returning to the view. In the distance, a few splashes reminded me we weren't alone out here in this ocean. A bird swooped out of the sky, plucking a fish from the ocean and veering away from the ship.

Still staring out the window, Justin smoothed his fingers over the pocket of his cargo shorts. He'd been doing that a lot the past few days. Maybe it was a subconscious gesture, but it always took my thoughts back to that day in the shop.

WAS he carrying the ring around with him on the ship? When would he pull it out? Before the bake-off? After? What did it mean if he didn't propose at all this week? Was the botched proposal a bad omen? Or was he just looking for the right moment?

It killed me that I couldn't ask what he thought about this very important topic. But I didn't want to ruin whatever surprise he planned. Not a second time.

"If anything goes wrong, the producers will tell us. I gave Sarah the emergency number for the ship."

"I know. That's not all of it." He hesitated, biting his lip. "I told you the bar results are being posted Friday?"

It was Monday, meaning he had four long days to worry before finding out his fate. Between his mom being sick, his failed proposal, and waiting for the results, his moodiness and distraction suddenly made perfect sense.

Leaning over, I kissed his cheek. "I'm sure you passed. You're super smart, and no one could've studied more than you. Try not to worry about it."

He pulled me close, murmuring a thank you into my hair.

What Justin really needed was to rest and relax for a week. He wouldn't say it, but he also worried about whether the bakery would turn a profit. Our financial future had been a concern even before we found out about Patty's Cakes. Justin wouldn't rest and relax until I hurried up and got Tammy Rae's secret ingredient.

EIGHT

JEN IN THE GUPPY GABBER, MONDAY:

Things between me and Justin are great. Absolutely fantastic. Couldn't be better. He's just stressed out about work and his family and the bakery. Don't worry about him. We're here to cut loose and relax. Judging the bake-off is a great way to get started. I can't wait to see what everyone comes up with!

And I can't wait to try Tammy Rae's special cupcakes. I hope they live up to the hype.

About half an hour later one of the production assistants, a tall woman with short, curly brown hair framing her heart-shaped face appeared. She introduced herself as Janine and led us to the Lido Deck for the competition. I tried to assure her that we didn't require an escort to go to the place we'd already visited about eleven times, but she insisted she'd get fired for letting us walk alone.

When we get to the pool area for the contest, people

swarmed the deck. Having someone to lead me through the crowd suddenly seemed much better. Janine took us to Leanna, who pointed out a row of judges' tables for us. Three tables. Tiny, one-person tables. One for Danielle, who hadn't mentioned she was also judging, one for Wyatt from Season 2 of *The Marrying Kind*, and one marked "Jen and Justin."

"Wait a minute. Why do we only have one chair?" Justin asked.

"Well, since the two of you are a couple, you're acting as one judge." Leanna said.

The two of us exchanged a look. "You mean, my vote's only worth half as much as the other judges?" Justin asked.

"Look, the two of you together are a huge draw. Everyone loves Justin and Jen, the couple who ran away from the Fishbowl together. Apart, you're not as exciting. It's like the Q&A. More people come out to see the two of you. Sorry, but also, not sorry at all."

With each word she spoke, my boyfriend's face reddened more. He didn't like losing his identity, and if we shared one chair, no one would see him with me perched in his lap.

"Is it really necessary to give us only one chair?" I asked. "I mean, even if we have to talk before voting, can't we each have our own place to sit? That way, Justin can eat without dropping crumbs in my hair."

Leanna sighed. "I don't understand why this is such a big deal. You two still like each other, right? But, whatever. If you can find another chair, you can have it. I don't have time to deal with this."

Justin left to grab a chair from one of the giant stacks less than twenty feet away, which told me the Network was just trying to stir up trouble. Clearly, they had enough chairs. Ah, ratings.

I started to say something to Leanna, but she'd already moved away, on to finish the setup. I stuck my tongue out at her back. Mature, I know.

The other contestants stood behind a second row of tables lined up beside the pool: Ed; the girl whose stroller Ariana was watching the first day; a thirty-something guy I didn't recognize; and Tabby Rangoon. She stood out at the table as the only one wearing six-inch heels and a flaming red wig. Plus, who could forget an Asian drag queen named Tabby Rangoon? Not me. I found myself hoping her creation would be deep-fried, with cream cheese filling. My mouth watered as I thought about it.

Originally, I considered signing up for the contest to gain publicity for the bakery, but didn't want Tammy Rae to bring up my audition video. Besides, Sarah was the baker in our little organization: my "old family cookie recipe" came preprinted on the bag of chocolate chips. But it had been used by several generations of Reid women, dating to whenever Nestle started printing recipes on their bags.

The judges' smaller arced around the deep end of the pool, and beach chairs filled the rest of the patio area. To my surprise, I spotted Ariana on one of those chairs, sunning herself.

Finding her lying out tanning came as no surprise; she spent half her time on *The Fishbowl* doing exactly that. No, what struck me as odd was her skirt, which reached nearly to her knees. I also didn't understand why she'd be at a bake-off in the first place when she wasn't participating. From the look of her, she hadn't eaten a bite in months.

A baby's cry split the air, and I realized Ariana had been sitting with her friend from the elevator. Hopefully, Tammy Rae would remind me of her name before I had to talk to her. At least Ariana hadn't come to see us. If she knew Justin and I were judging, I hoped she wore something under her skirt. I wouldn't put it past her to pull a Lindsay Lohan on my boyfriend.

To my surprise, the older woman rose when the contestants were announced, her hands flying through the air with each word from Tammy Rae. Finally, I recognized the young girl as Madison, star of *Deaf Teen Mother*. The show was about to enter its second season. That explained both why she brought a baby on a cruise and why she ignored me in the elevator. She probably saw me and Ariana talking and didn't want to interrupt. She couldn't have known I'd been about to introduce myself. Ariana stayed with the baby, whose name I didn't know, while Madison joined the competition and introduced herself to the audience.

The guy I didn't recognize turned out to be Braden, from Season 3 of *The Marrying Kind*. He'd made history by changing his mind after the final episode, dumping the girl he originally chose and proposing to someone else halfway through the reunion episode. He and his bride, Amanda Something, were scheduled to get married on the air sometime next year. According to Ed, we'd probably all be invited, just to fill the seat with, as he called it, "Reality Royalty."

Tammy Rae explained the rules: Each contestant had been allowed into the kitchens individually earlier to "shop" for ingredients. Now, they'd get access to a hot plate, a toaster oven, and a microwave. They would get one hour to create a delicious dessert for the three judging teams.

I glanced at Justin when Tammy Rae referred to us as a "judging team" rather than as two separate judges, and he raised an eyebrow at me. The Networks ploy didn't really bother me, since they were footing the bill, but I understood his frustration. I nudged his knee with mine under the table, and he kissed my cheek. Someone in the audience "awwed," and I blushed. More than a year after our show ended, I'd forgotten how it felt to be constantly on display until we arrived onboard.

Tammy Rae further explained that, when she called time, we'd taste each of the final products and judge them, one at a time. Each creation would receive a score on a scale of one to ten, and the entry with the highest overall score won a bottle of champagne from the ship's gift shop, plus dinner for two at one of the fancy restaurants onboard. Ed smiled when she announced the prize. The reality star cruisers were allowed in those restaurants, but only if we wanted to pay for the dinners, and most of us didn't. Not when they offered free food all over the ship, including in our cabins via twenty-four-hour room service.

While the contestants measured, stirred, and worked the crowd, Justin pulled me close, his hands moving up and down my sides. His lips tickled the side of my neck, sending chills down my spine, before resting against my earlobe. "Hmmm. Maybe sharing a chair wasn't such a bad idea, after all. Come closer."

With a happy sigh, I leaned against him, still mostly sitting on my chair. "It's too late now. You ruined our chance."

"I know. I'm dumb. It's just that the idea of being only half a person bugged me. It's like we don't exist as individuals outside of this relationship. I'm no one without you."

"Without me, you're still Justin Taylor, loving son, world's best twin brother, and devastatingly handsome lawyer-to-be."

"This doesn't bug you at all? I'd have thought you'd be pissed."

I shrugged. "Maybe I should be, but this week is just a tiny slice of our life together. It's not real. When we go home, none of this matters. The Network is just trying to add drama to get better ratings. I'm trying not to let them profit at the expense of our relationship."

"This is why you're the smart one," he said.

His words from before came back to me, and I realized what frustrated him. "This isn't about the chair, right? You're still worried about your parents? And the bar results?"

He nodded, keeping one eye on Tammy Rae for our cue to pay attention. When he spoke, his voice was low. "I'm trying not to worry, but what if I don't pass? I'll have to wait until February to take the test again, and I'll probably get fired. Mom and Dad are living off their savings and Mom's disability until Dad's worker's comp settlement comes in. How can I help if I lose my income?"

My heart went out to him. He had a lot on his mind. Keeping everything inside must be taking a huge toll on him. An overwhelming rush of love hit me. I moved closer, letting my breasts brush against his bicep as I pressed my lips into his neck. From the way his breath caught, he definitely felt the same jolt of electricity I did at the contact. If we didn't find some alone time soon, our libidos were going to explode when we finally made it home.

"You're not going to get fired," I said quietly. "Your bosses love you. If you don't pass, they'll give you another chance. Besides, you're a genius, remember? You got a twenty-three hundred on your SATs. The Florida State Bar Exam is nothing to you."

He smiled against my ear. "I'm sorry. I didn't mean to ruin the day with this stuff. Want to take off?"

"Abandon the contest?"

"Well, Ed's over there baking away, and Dominic's never around, so the cabin should be empty." His voice trailed off, and he wiggled his eyebrows at me suggestively.

For a long moment, I was tempted. We hadn't seen each other in days before the trip, and wouldn't be alone again until Sunday. Alas, duty called. We could have all the sex we wanted back in Florida, on Justin's comfortable king-sized mattress, rather than a twin bunk bed.

I chuckled and kissed his cheek. "Nice try, Romeo. I need to get this recipe, which means I can't piss Tammy Rae off by abandoning my post. Besides, I have to taste these coconut wonders before I spend all week sucking up to her. What if they're gross?"

"The ones Sarah made weren't half bad."

"True, but we can't build a business on 'not half bad.' We watched the finale a hundred times this week to figure out what she was doing, but our cupcakes still aren't as light and fluffy as the ones everyone raved over on the show."

"Did you ever consider that the whole thing was over-hyped for TV?"

"Of course not. That never happens." I rolled my eyes at him. "We know it could be a red herring. But since we're here, I need a cupcake. And hopefully a recipe. If I don't get it, I have to do the floors for the next month to make up for leaving Sarah right before our grand opening."

The cupcakes in question sat on a platter about five feet from the judge's table, little bits of chocolatey goodness piled high with coconut frosting and sprinkled with toasted coconut. With all the chlorine and sunscreen in the air, I couldn't get a whiff of the promise they held, but they looked exactly like what I'd seen on television.

Hopefully, when I bit into it, I'd find moist, fluffy chocolate cake and coconut filling. Every time Sarah tried to make something similar, it fell apart, or it turned out too dense. It could be a matter of proportion, but Tammy Rae had gone on and on about her "secret ingredient" while she made the cupcakes, going so far as to cover the camera when she added something from a brown paper bag to the mixing bowl before adding the rest of the dry ingredients. That bag held the key to the cupcakes' texture. And I was determined to find out her secret, by whatever means necessary.

"Okay!" Tammy Rae said from the deck in front of the pool. "Let's see what our contestants came up with. Contestant number 1? What did you make for us?"

Tabby stepped forward. "This dessert was inspired by my favorite movie in high school. Tammy Rae, I'm sure you're familiar with *The Breakfast Club*."

My mom loved that movie; she watched it every rainy weekend when I was a kid. I never really saw the appeal. Then again, most of the jokes went right over my head. Tammy Rae was much closer to my mother's age than mine.

"Absolutely, Tabby! Who doesn't love the Brat Pack?" Tammy Rae said.

"Exactly. Remember the scene where they eat lunch?"

"Do I? Actually, we've got a surprise for you. If you turn toward the big screen over the pool, we've brought the clip so our judges and contestants can witness your inspiration firsthand."

On the screen, a chick about my age with dark, shaggy hair sat at a table in a room filled with books. She was supposed to be in high school? My mouth dropped in horror when she pulled out two pieces of bread, smothered them with Pixie Stix, added breakfast cereal, then put it together and ate it. Beside me, Justin shuddered. What the hell had we gotten ourselves into? I didn't want to eat that.

"I went with an interpretation. This is bread pudding, made with a Coca-Cola caramel reduction, Cap'N Crunch base, and sugar sprinkles. I used white and wheat bread, like in the movie." That didn't sound completely horrible. But then she said, "I present to you–The Basket Case!"

The name of the dish did not make me feel any better. Would anyone notice if I dropped it into the pool?

"For those of you who don't know," Tammy Rae said, "This character is referred to in the movie as 'the basket case.' We don't think you have to be crazy to eat it. Well, probably not."

They both laughed while I congratulated myself on my strong stomach. The plate set before us looked like normal bread pudding. The dessert wasn't my favorite, but eating it wouldn't kill me. Probably.

I pushed it toward Justin. "You first."

"Oh, no," he said. "Ladies first. Absolutely."

Tentatively, I leaned forward and sniffed.

"What do you think, Jen?" Tammy Rae asked.

"It smells normal!" The crowd cheered, so I prodded it gently with my fork. "It's nice and soft."

"Moment of truth. What does it taste like?"

Slightly emboldened by the smell, I forced myself to take a bite. Cinnamon and caramel filled my mouth. The cereal, which I expected to be appalling, added a nice crunch. The sauce tasted like regular caramel—I'd never have guessed she used soda to make it.

"I'm very sorry, Tammy Rae, but you're going to have to bring Justin his own piece, because I'm not sharing this. It's delicious!"

The crowd went wild. Justin leaned around me and grabbed the plate, popping the entire rest of the piece into his mouth in one bite. Unable to speak, he raised both his hands, giving it two thumbs up.

"Looks like our *Fishbowl* judges love the Basket Case!" Tammy Rae shouted. "Now, what did contestant number two make for us?"

Ed stepped forward. "As Jen and Justin well know, I'm one hell of a chef. However, I don't have a ton of experience with baking. I prefer acting on instinct, not having to measure precisely or worry about ratios. So, I let the muse guide me through this recipe. Here we have, Ed's Apple Crema Brownies: apple butter brownies made with a hand-whipped caramel-scented whipped cream."

The thing sitting on the plate in front of me was not brown. As a lifelong brownie connoisseur, I immediately recognized this as a problem. "Ed? Why is this brownie yellow?"

He waved one hand. "Come on, Jen. You know 'brownie' is a figure of speech."

Right. Next he'd be telling me "chocolate chip cookie" could be interpreted by adding things like ham or motor oil. I lifted the plate, then let it thud onto the table.

"Justin, you're first this time. No arguing. And I see you trying to run." Tammy Rae chortled.

My boyfriend stopped trying to scoot his chair away from the judge's table. At least he had the good grace to blush at Tammy Rae's words. The crowd laughed. Leaning forward, he pressed his fork against the top of the "brownie." It slid smoothly through the whipped cream, then stopped. He pressed harder. Nothing happened.

"Out of curiosity, what's in this?"

At the table beside us, a judge with dark brown hair and

glasses knocked carefully on the top of the brownie. At the table to the right, a plate clattered loudly to the floor. "Oh, no!" Wyatt said. "I seem to have . . . destroyed mine?"

He leaned down to pick up the plate, but when he straightened, the brownie remained in one piece. Being dropped three feet onto a hard surface didn't even dent it. I resisted the urge to see if it left a hole in the deck.

"It's normal brownie stuff," Ed said. "Oil and flour and eggs and sugar and stuff. Taste it. I'm sure it's great."

Still looking doubtful, Justin picked up the brownie. He moved it toward his mouth in exaggerated slow motion.

"Do you need me to make airplane noises?" Ed asked.

Tammy Rae laughed. Above us, a yell split the air. I turned to see something yellow whizzing toward us. Before I could move or say anything, Justin lurched forward, dropping the brownie onto the deck and knocking me onto the floor.

NINE

MORE FROM THE GUPPY GABBER, MONDAY:

Ed: *I want to make sure we're all totes clear that my brownies did NOT knock Justin over. Total fluke, and not my fault at all.*

Ariana: *I bet Jen pinched Justin to make him drop her. It's exactly the kind of thing she'd do to move attention away from the competition, on to her. No one paid any attention to Madison, after she worked so hard on those cupcakes.*

Braden: *Dude, what is wrong with that Ariana girl?*

Danielle: *Does anyone want this brownie?*

Landing on the same spot on my butt twice in two days left me wincing. What happened? Justin wouldn't throw me on the ground on purpose.

He sat doubled over in pain, eyes squeezed shut.

"Are you okay?" I asked, still lying on the deck. Tammy Rae rushed over to see what happened.

"Fuck, that hurt." He sat up and reached one hand to me. "Something hit me. A bird?"

Nearby, a small golf ball rolled under Wyatt's chair. The yellow blur I spotted before I fell.

Danielle pointed. "Hey guys? I think a ball escaped the mini-golf course."

Tammy Rae addressed the crowd. "We're going to take a quick break, everyone. Sorry for the delay."

Following Danielle's finger, I found an older woman leaning over the railing of the deck above us, waving her club. "Are you okay, son?"

Grabbing the ball, Justin and I moved toward her. "Did you lose something?"

"Oh my heavens! I hit Justin," the woman said. "I'm so sorry. My friends will never believe this."

"It's no problem." He raised the ball. "Catch?"

"Wait! Will you sign the ball for me?"

He flashed his dimples at her. "Sure. Give Janine your room number, and I'll have someone bring it to you later."

The woman blew him a kiss and vanished from the railing.

Justin's smile faded the second she disappeared. He winced, rubbing his shoulder. "Man, that hurts. Can you check it out for me?"

"I thought you were fine?" I asked.

"What was I going to say to a sweet old lady, that she maimed me? It would break her heart. I'm sure I'll live. But, damn." He winced.

"Turn around." Lifting his shirt, I immediate spotted the point of impact–a big red welt on his left shoulder blade. "That's going to leave a bruise. You should put some ice on it or something."

"I'll be fine."

Janine appeared at our side. "Sorry, Justin, but you have to go to the infirmary and get a doctor to sign off. Legal's rules."

He sighed. "Right now? Can't I finish the competition?"

"No, you can't, and you really need to go now. We can't finish the contest as long as you're standing here."

"Well, crap. I'm sorry, Jen," Justin said.

"It's okay. I'm going with you."

He cupped my face, gazing deeply into my eyes. My heart fluttered. "Don't even think about it."

"You're wounded. I'm not ditching you."

"Yes, you are," he said. "Tammy Rae will be pissed if you leave. You have to finish the competition. Besides, if you leave now, you'll never get to taste those cupcakes."

"I could have Ed bring me one?"

"You trust Ed with baked goods?"

"Good point. Thanks." Popping onto my toes, I kissed him lightly. He pulled me in, sending a thrill down my spine. By the time Tammy Rae cleared her throat behind us, I'd nearly forgotten where we were.

Justin let me go, his ears tinged a bright pink. "Sorry, everyone. I'm headed to get checked out. But, Jen, I think this is a sign not to eat Ed's brownies."

Ed moved beside me, the two of us watching Justin's back move toward the elevators. "Do you think I should go with him? I mean, I didn't win, right?"

"If this were a doorstop-making competition," Danielle said, "I'd give you ten out of ten."

Tammy Rae dismissed Ed, and he trotted off down the deck after my boyfriend. The crowd clapped politely.

The remaining two contestants presented regular desserts of the type I expected when signing up for this deal. Braden created a pie using a chocolate cookie-crumb crust and a chocolate pudding filling with chocolate-hazelnut spread on the top. It may not have been the fanciest or prettiest dessert I'd ever seen, but it smelled awesome, and all the ingredients tasted good separately. Were we awarding points on what would be easiest to throw together while drunk, Braden would've won hands down.

Madison approached the table last, her interpreter translator as her hands flew through the air. "This is my grandmother's recipe. Chocolate cupcakes with a caramelized banana filling and whipped peanut butter frosting. She called it 'The Elvis.'"

Before Madison finished giving the description, I wanted to snatch the cake from her hand and devour it. I asked Tammy Rae to give me two so I could take one to Justin, but neither lasted more than about five seconds. Madison's creation was by far the most delicious thing I'd ever eaten. Moist, chocolate cake. Caramelized bananas sounded weird, but added interesting texture and a smoky sweetness. Add in the nutty creaminess of the frosting, and all I wanted was to abandon the coconut cupcake plan and beg Madison to tell us what she'd put in these instead. Too bad I'd need Ariana to translate. If she agreed to do it at all, she'd probably tell me the cakes were made with shards of glass and dog poop or something.

Once all the scores were tallied, Tammy Rae read the results. "In fourth place, well, this isn't much of a surprise. You maim a judge with your creation, you usually don't win. I learned that lesson on my first episode of *Totally 80s Bake-off*, when one of my co-competitors accidentally stabbed a judge in the arm while slicing a lemon meringue pie. We're still not sure how he managed it."

The crowd gasped, then nervous titters waved around the deck.

"I'm kidding, guys!" Tammy Rae said. "Well, sort of. The judge was fine. In third place, with a total score of twenty-seven, is Braden with his chocolate-hazelnut pie. Well done, Braden!"

He smiled and waved, while I wondered how much longer I needed to wait before finding Justin. Or if he and Ed would come back once he got an ice pack and some painkillers. They'd probably make him sign another waiver.

"In second place," Tammy Rae said, "with a total score of thirty-five points, is Tabby Rangoon's 'The Basket Case!' Congratulations, Tabby! The producers have awarded you this bottle of champagne for your efforts. And the winner is Madison from *Deaf Teen Mother!*"

The crowd erupted, several people leaping to their feet. A flash of confusion crossed Madison's face, but she broke out into a smile when her interpreter finished translating Tammy Rae's words.

On the table to my left, I noticed Danielle hadn't finished her cupcake, and I thought about popping it into my mouth while no one was looking. She caught my gaze, and shook her head, drawing one finger across her throat like a knife.

"I'm serious about my baked goods, girl," she said. "Don't try it. I'm saving the rest for later."

Finally, after a round of pictures with all the winners, Tammy Rae gestured to the table full of cupcakes now starting to droop in the sun. I promptly forgot the baked goods already sitting in my belly and raced for the table.

Halfway there, I tripped. Catching myself, I spotted a teddy bear lying on the deck. The same rainbow-colored stuffed animal I'd seen peeking out of the bottom of Madison's stroller that first day by the elevator. She must have dropped it. My quest for the perfect cupcake would have to wait a minute.

Scanning the deck, I spotted Madison and Ariana headed toward the elevators.

"Madison!" I yelled. The interpreter must not have heard me over the crowd, because neither she nor Madison turned their heads. I tried again, shouting for Ariana instead.

The three women stopped, and I waved the bear over my head. Madison thanked me profusely while Ariana snorted at the ground. Whatever. A moment later, the bear was back in the arms of its rightful owner, and I made it back to the cupcake table before the other guests ate them all.

With a sigh of relief, one cupcake went straight into the

plastic container in my bag. Silently, I thanked Justin for going to the infirmary, giving me an excuse to take an extra. Then I found a shaded corner of the deck area and sat down to examine my prize.

The cupcake looked perfectly normal. It didn't weigh a ton like Ed's "brownie," it was the right color for what was supposed to be in it, it wasn't made primarily from pre-packaged junk food, and it didn't have a scary eighties movie introduction. Melted frosting ran down one side. Had this been entered in the contest, the presentation put it in a distant second place so far, but the melting wasn't Tammy Rae's fault. She hadn't planned for a mid-contest interruption.

For a moment, panic seized me. What if I hated it, and I'd dragged Justin on this trip for nothing? Left Sarah all alone to prepare the store and watch their mother for no good reason? But the tiny cake looked good, it smelled good, and it won the grand prize on a baking show, so I swallowed my fears and took a bite.

To my surprise, the cupcake delivered fully on its promise. The cake itself was light, chocolatey, and moist. The filling exploded with coconut flavor. The frosting carried a hint of almond or something, and the toasted coconut gave the texture a nice contrast. Had Tammy Rae's cupcake been in the competition, it would've won, hands down. I sat back, patting my stomach with a satisfied smile.

Now I needed to convince Tammy Rae to tell me what she put in it.

After the bake-off, Tammy Rae stayed on the main deck, handing out cupcakes and posing for pictures with the fans. Although part of me knew I should check on Justin, I stayed, sitting with Danielle on a nearby chaise and waiting for my window to approach Tammy Rae. I'd come here with a purpose.

I couldn't let one Taylor twin down because of the other: Both would be pissed. Besides, maybe some time in the infirmary would help him get over his frustration with being only half of "Jen and Justin."

Remembering what he'd said earlier made me fume. I wasn't the one who insisted we share one judge spot. I wasn't the one who set up the Q&A with pictures of both of us instead of the individual head shots they gave Ariana, Ed, and Rachel. I wasn't the one who chased him down the driveway, which is what started all the hype in the first place.

I'd been perfectly happy to go home to Seattle, wait for him to get eliminated, and then sit by the phone like a normal person. Or . . . find Ed on Instagram, get him to get contact info from Connor, and then send an email. Whatever.

Now I worried that, after all the Network's focus on turning us into one pair instead of two individuals, he'd changed his mind about proposing at all. Was that why he hadn't done it yet? We'd been together almost constantly since Sunday morning, and he hadn't dropped a single hint.

"Okay, so, I have to admit, those cupcakes are amazing," Danielle said, interrupting my thoughts. "When you first mentioned this plan, I thought you were nuts, but now I get it."

"Yeah, they're awesome. I'm glad. Sarah's got her heart set on adding this cupcake to our menu."

"What else?"

The question threw me off-guard. "What do you mean?"

"I mean, it's a reality-show inspired bakery, right? So, what's my cupcake?"

"Until about three days ago, we'd have called you the arsenic and old lace or possibly the viper," I said. "Silent, yet deadly."

She snorted. "I guess I deserve that. And now?"

"I'm not the baker, that's Sarah. But I'm thinking something like—The Firecracker. Red, white, and blue, possibly. Maybe something with a dash of cayenne pepper. We've already got a cake inspired by my friend Birdie, who's also a redhead, so carrot cake is out for you. But we'll come up with something."

"What about you?"

"I'm the all-American girl, at the moment. Sarah's doing yellow cake with chocolate frosting and cookie dough centers for me. And we've got fishbowl-shaped sugar cookies, Pavé de BumBum, which is an Ed-inspired play on the *Pavé de Bombom* popular in Brazil, plus all the usual bakery stuff," I said. "Our name is Sweet Reality, so that's the hook, but we've got a lot of old classics. You can walk in and order a regular chocolate chip cookie. It just might be called 'the Rachel.'"

"Did I hear my name?" My friend approached, carrying a mudslide in one hand and a leftover cupcake in the other. "These things are amazing. What's in them?"

"That's what I'm trying to find out." Across the deck, Tammy Rae's fans finally disbanded. She stood gazing out over the railing. "I'm going in. Wish me luck."

"You don't need luck," Rachel said. "Be your awesome self."

I smiled gratefully at her as Danielle wished me more traditional luck. The two of them agreed to meet me at the dining room later.

Beyond the railing, the ocean spread in all directions as far as the eye could see. I leaned against the metal barrier, about a foot from Tammy Rae. Close enough to talk, not close enough to look like a stalker.

"Beautiful view," I said.

"Yeah," she said. "The ocean is so vast. Like, I totally knew water covered huge sections of the earth, but being out here, part of it, with no land anywhere, is totally mind-blowing. Just, the utter vastness of it, you know? It's, like . . . so vast!"

"It's awesome," I said, trying not to roll my eyes. "Like those cupcakes."

"You mean Madison's? Those weren't bad."

"Madison's cupcakes were good, and totally deserving of the

win, but no, I meant yours. I snagged one off the table after the show." She looked at me over her sunglasses. "Okay, two."

"I'm glad you enjoyed them. I'm very proud of my recipe."

"*Totally 80s Bake-Off* was my favorite show last season. I didn't have a job for a while, so my roommate and I watched reruns almost every day. We were rooting for you from Day 1."

"Oh, yeah? I'd have thought I was too old for your demographic."

"My mom's a huge fan. She listened to your music all the time. It stuck with me." I started to sing a few bars of one of her big hits before remembering I didn't want this woman to hate me.

"That's good to hear. You want me to sign something for your mom? I got more pictures on the table over there. Or you could buy a CD from the gift shop."

"That would be great," I said, wondering if anyone still owned CD players outside of old cars. "She'd love it. But I was hoping, you'd be willing to give me a hint as to your secret ingredient. I'm starting a bakery with my roommate–Justin's sister, actually. The grand opening is in a couple of weeks. She's a baker, and we're doing an entire reality-themed shop. We love the concept of your cupcake, but we haven't managed to recreate it yet."

The more I talked, the more Tammy Rae's expression hardened until I suspected a grave error of judgment. Maybe I should've taken the picture or bought her dumb CD before asking for a favor, but what did people do with signed pictures? My mom would get a kick out of my stories of going on a cruise with one of her favorite high school celebrities, but did she need a piece of paper with Tammy Rae's name on it?

Then Tammy Rae spoke, and the problem had nothing to do with my mom or autographs at all. "Let me give you some advice, kid. I've been around the block a few times. That'll serve you much better than my recipe."

I bristled at her condescending tone. Advice, I did not need.

A recipe, that's what I needed. Plus, kid? A twenty-six-year-old starting a business is not a "kid." But in the interests of maintaining a pleasant interaction, I bit my tongue. "Thanks."

"Never mix business with pleasure. You bought into this bakery, why? Because you're sleeping with the brother?"

"It's not like that. Justin and I have been together more than a year. We're committed to each other."

She waved one hand. "Yeah, yeah, yeah. You're super in love. I saw the show. Where's the ring?"

Involuntarily, my right hand went to the empty spot on my left ring finger. Tammy Rae's eagle eyes followed. "That's what I thought. What happens to the business if you break up?"

"We won't break up." The words "I'm getting a ring" teetered on the tip of my tongue, but after the last couple of days, I wondered if Justin reconsidered.

"Famous last words," she said. "That means you don't know, right?"

Only my need to establish camaraderie and trust with her allowed me to suppress my desire to tell her to mind her own damn business. "We have a contract. If the relationship between me and Sarah, my partner, goes downhill, she can buy me out. It doesn't specifically say she can exercise the clause if Justin and I break up, but we both know that's a possibility."

"Do you get your full investment back?"

"With five percent interest if she exercises the clause within the first year. After that, there's a formula. The total depends on how the business is doing. Plus half the profits until she finishes buying me out."

She looked impressed. "Well done. Who wrote it?"

"Justin, but my best friend back home is also a lawyer. He read it over before I signed."

"Well, I'll give you one thing," Tammy Rae said. "You're better at business than I expected. How are you at baking?"

"I make a mean chocolate chip cookie, notwithstanding anything people may or may not have seen on YouTube."

She laughed. "Yeah, I saw your auto-tune. Don't sweat it. You made an entertaining video, and that's what an audition video needs to be."

"Thanks. Sarah's the baker. I'm onboard for marketing, day-to-day operations, and overall management so she's free to bake and develop new recipes. That's why I'm here. Your recipe sounds amazing, but we haven't been able to duplicate it. The difference has to be your secret ingredient. We thought if maybe I could convince you to tell me what it is—you don't need to give the proportions, we can figure it out ourselves—"

"What's in it for me?"

I blinked at her. Sarah and I talked about paying her, of course, but after the direction the conversation took, it seemed odd for Tammy Rae to ask. "We'll pay you five hundred dollars. There's cash in my cabin, and a nondisclosure agreement."

"That's it?"

My heart sank. "What do you want for it?"

She rubbed her chin, tapping one long fingernail against her teeth. "Honestly, sweetheart, I'm not sure you've got anything to offer me. Money? I've got plenty saved. Notoriety? Check. I was the lead singer in an all-girls eighties-hair band. How much more notoriety do I need?"

"Why did you do *Totally 80s Bake-off* if you didn't need the money or the fame?"

She shrugged. "Same reason I came here. I was bored. Will giving you the recipe entertain me?"

I didn't have the slightest idea how to answer that. "We're willing to put up a display in the store with the cupcakes, with your name, or a picture. We could sell your CDs if you wanted. You could do a signing at our grand opening."

Tammy Rae stood, patting me on the shoulder as if I were a small child. "You're sweet, but I think I've gotten all I need from this conversation. Have a good night."

She sauntered off down the deck, leaving me alone to watch her go. The woman did reality shows because she was bored?

And she'd give me her recipe only if I could make life more interesting for her?

I leapt to my feet, yelling at her back. The wind swallowed my words, carrying them out to sea, but it didn't matter. Determination raised my chin, lifted my spirits. I could do this.

"Challenge accepted!"

TEN

QUEEN KELLY'S VOICE
THE BAHAMAS WELCOME YOU

Tuesday edition

Welcome to the beautiful Bahamas! Our ship will arrive offshore at approximately three o'clock in the morning, ship time. Passengers will awaken to gorgeous views and plenty of options for things to do!

Start with breakfast before hopping a catamaran to transport you to the mainland or go straight to the beach to start a full day's activities.

All water sports are available here: snorkeling, paddle boarding, floats, kayaks, banana boat rides, aqua chairs, and more. If you prefer to hang out on the beach, rent a clamshell to enjoy the shore with your sweetheart.

Our TV fans can join *Suddenly Single in Seattle's* Danielle and *Deaf Teen Mother* Madison on a glass-bottomed boat ride around the island. The more adventurous among you can follow *The Fishbowl's* Ariana and *America's Next Drag*

Model's Tabby Rangoon on a dune buggy ride through the jungle, or go zip-lining with *Totally 80s Bake-off Winner* Tammy Rae and *The Fishbowl*'s favorite duo, Jen and Justin. We've even got a shuffleboard tournament and a Q&A session here on the ship for those of you who aren't up traveling to the mainland.

No matter what level of adventure you're up for, we've planned an awesome day full of interacting with the stars while experiencing the very best the Bahamas have to offer.

Inside this Edition:

THE NEXT MORNING, Justin and I disembarked at eight o'clock, dressed for adventure in the Bahamas. We'd signed up for zip-lining to give me a chance to talk to Tammy Rae again; apparently, she was into extreme sports. I counted myself fortunate the ship hadn't offered parasailing, hang gliding, or other activities more likely to make me break my neck. Zip-lining sounded like fun and probably wouldn't result in bodily injury.

In their infinite wisdom, the Network insisted each excursion group be accompanied by at least one member of the production staff to film us. However, since we were zip-lining, Leanna decided at the last minute to send two: one for each platform. No need to miss a single second of potential drama due to logistics.

To my delight, Connor was assigned to our trip, bringing Ed along with him. The Network preferred they keep their relationship reasonably discreet in public, but no one thought twice about Ed announcing at the last minute that he'd be taking one of the open spots on our excursion. It was, as he said, his prerogative to change his mind several times a day about anything and everything.

On the other side of the platform, our guide Ryan explained how to hook our harnesses onto the line, wait for the go-ahead signal from someone on the other side, and push off. Trepidation filled me.

"We're hooking ourselves up?" I asked. "You don't do it for us?"

"We give you the hooks and show you how to do it. You've got two lines attaching your harness. As long as you follow directions, you'll be fine," Ryan said. "Really, a seven-year-old did it yesterday."

Once we took turns hooking the two clips over the line, facing in opposite directions, I felt much better. Scientifically speaking, this should work.

The line disappeared into the distance, but Ryan assured us that a megaphone waited at the other end. We would call "all clear" when we landed, and the next person would go. He also said the line angled downhill, so lighter participants could sail into the next platform without getting stuck.

Spectacular scenery unfolded below us. While everything in Seattle would be brown and dead this time of year, tropical plants dotted the landscape with color. In the distance, dazzling white beaches stretched as far as the eye could see, separating the island from the glittering turquoise water in the distance. When I squinted, I pretended I saw our ship, but we were far enough inland that the speck I spotted could've been anything.

Usually, Justin was the one making everyone sure everyone else paid attention when someone gave us instructions. Instead, as the guide spoke, Justin kept his gaze firmly planted on his shoes, looking green around the edges.

I sidled toward him, keeping my voice low. "You okay?"

He swallowed and nodded, not speaking. Twelve of us

packed the wooden landing, including the guide, but I tried to tug him off to the side as best I could. He didn't move.

PA Janine went first so she could record the rest of us zooming into view (and possibly capture some hilarious footage when some of us got stuck without making it to the other platform or crashed on the other side).

Ed followed, shoving off with a howl of joy. "Look, Ma! *No hands!*"

Justin still hadn't looked up. I nudged him again. When he didn't respond, I grabbed his chin and tilted it upward. "Talk to me. What's wrong?"

"Nothing. I'm fine."

"Really? Because you look like you're about to throw up."

On the other side of the platform, Tammy Rae called my name and gestured toward the lines. I motioned for her to go on ahead, realizing most of our group had left. Only Ryan, who needed to see everyone safely across, and Connor remained, waiting to film the last of us pushing off.

"Justin? Are you afraid of heights?"

"Of course not," he said. "I have no problem with being on high landings or balconies or . . . anywhere I'm not going to fall and die. I'm just not a fan of rickety landings and throwing myself off firm ground into the air for no good reason."

"Why didn't you mention this sooner?"

"I forgot. Florida's mostly flat, remember? No one's invited me to face certain death in a while."

Poor thing. All I wanted was to take him into my arms and tell him everything would be okay, but the cameras were rolling. He might not appreciate me treating him like a child.

I grasped his shoulders and brought him to face me. I focused on Justin, trying to ignore the camera moving in. "Listen. We're going to be okay. The two of us. We're a team, remember? Jen and Justin. And while it can be frustrating to feel like half of a whole sometimes, there is nothing the two of us can't accomplish together. We're going to leave here, zip across, and land on the other side, safe as houses. You hear me?"

He nodded. "You're going to go with me?"

"You'll have to go first," I said. "But I'm right behind you."

"Why don't you go first?"

"Because if I do, you'll climb down the ladder and catch a taxi to the beach."

He chuckled. "You know me too well."

Ryan approached. "You guys okay? I don't mean to push you, but everyone else is waiting on the next platform, and they can't move on until we clear this one."

I held out my hand. "We're coming. Right, Justin?"

He swallowed and nodded, eyes still attached to mine. The love and trust reflected there warmed my heart. Maybe Justin was afraid to zip-line, but "Jen and Justin" embraced the opportunity for a new experience.

"You know, guys," Ryan said. "There are two lines side-by-side. We tend to send newbies one at a time, but you could go together if you wanted."

"You mean we could race?" I asked.

Justin perked up immediately, his competitive spirit awoken.

Our guide shook his head. "It's not much of a race, since the heavier person is nearly always going to win. But sure, you can race. Or you can hold hands and go over together. That works, especially when one of you isn't sure about taking off."

A smile broke across Justin's face. "I like the sound of that."

Finally, with Connor still filming everything, the two of us moved to the other side of the platform and Ryan reminded us how to strap in. I leaned back in the harness, letting it hold my weight, and surveyed the land below. Absolutely beautiful.

Justin reached across the gap between us. His clammy hand enclosed mine. Hopefully, he'd feel better after the first jump, or we'd need a backup plan. I couldn't expose him to this type of fear over and over so I could spend the day with Tammy Rae. Not even if it made for good television.

"You ready?" I asked.

"No," he said. "But I trust you."

"Okay then. Count of three." With a deep breath, I counted, and on "two" I shoved my feet against the platform as hard as I could, pulling Justin with me. He yelped, but I held firm, and a moment later he zoomed past me, taking the lead. Our arms stretched across the distance, a visible reminder of our connection.

Since the harness held me securely, I didn't need to grip the lines. I let my other arm fall free behind us like Ed. My head fell backward, and I laughed as the wind rushed past my face.

Justin twisted in his harness. "This is amazing! It's like we're flying!"

A peal of laughter escaped me at the pure joy on his face. When we signed up for zip-lining, I never dreamed it would be this exhilarating—not only for me, but for both of us.

We hit the platform on the other side with dual thuds, the sound swallowed by the claps and whistles of the rest of our tour group. Ed put two fingers in his mouth and let out a piercing whistle he'd learned from Abram, one of our competitors on *The Fishbowl*.

Beside me, Justin grinned from ear to ear. The second our harnesses released, he scooped me up and spun me around. "That was amazing! Thank you. God, I love you so much."

"I love you, too."

He cupped my face in his hands and kissed me. My arms went around his neck as warmth shot through my body. I parted my lips with a happy sigh. Justin's tongue found mine. Our bodies melded together, and for a moment, we were the only two people in the world. Everyone else on the platform faded away.

This was why we needed to be here. It wasn't all about getting secret recipes and promoting the bakery: we craved time together, as a couple, to enjoy each other.

A thud behind me announced the arrival of Connor on the

platform, bringing us both back to reality. Ryan arrived on the other line, seconds behind him.

Justin's cheeks turned red before he released me. "Sorry, I got carried away."

"You can carry me away any time you want," I said.

Our other guide zoomed down the line to wait for us at the next platform, while everyone else lined up to take the second turn. From the front of the line, Ed called out to Justin. "Want to race, lover boy?"

He turned to me. "Do you mind?"

"Absolutely not." He looked like a kid in a candy store. After how upset he'd been earlier, no way would I take that away from him. "If you win, I'll give you another kiss on the other side."

Justin leaned forward. "I hope you're not kissing either winner, because Ed outweighs me by about twenty pounds. He's solid muscle."

I laughed. "Go."

Once the two of them took off, I found myself in line behind Tammy Rae. With several other people ahead of us, this gave me an excellent chance to talk to her–if only I knew what to say after my first attempt at conversation failed so spectacularly.

Before I could say anything, she turned. "That was amazing, you know. What you did for him."

"It was nothing."

"It wasn't nothing. He was totally freaked, and you talked him down, got him to come along and enjoy the trip, and now he's acting like a different person."

"We complement each other well," I said. "He helps me when I get freaked out, too."

"You're a good team," Tammy Rae said.

"Thanks."

"Maybe I didn't give you enough credit before. I saw the sparks between you two when you were alone, but they also spent a lot of time showing Ariana flirting with him. I bought into all her bullshit about you creating a 'showmance' with Justin to take attention away from her. But you care about each other."

Her words brought a huge, goofy smile to my face. The same one I got whenever thinking about Justin and our future. "We do. It was never about ratings or staying on the show for me. All I wanted was to ignore him and focus on winning the money. But I fell in love with him, even though I kept telling myself not to."

"You're a cute couple," Tammy Rae said as she strapped herself to the line. "Tell you what: I may have been wrong. Give me some time to reconsider. We'll talk more about the recipe tomorrow after dinner. Deal?"

Before I could help myself, a shriek of joy escaped, and Tammy Rae laughed. I clapped my hands over my mouth. "Yes, absolutely deal. Thank you!"

She grinned up at me before taking off. "Thank you for reminding me what it's like to be young and in love."

Young and in love and part of a team. I couldn't wait to tell Justin we'd be getting the recipe after all. Maybe America only noticing each of us as one-half of a whole couple wasn't entirely a bad thing.

After several more thrilling jumps and a mouth-watering lunch, the zip-line company bused us back to the beach. The cruise liner sat in the harbor, awaiting everyone's return, but we didn't have to be there for several hours. As I surveyed the beach, wondering what our options were, Justin tugged my hand.

"Come on."

"Where are we going?"

He pointed away from the others, at a line of small bamboo structures with colorful walls dotting the beach. "Clam shells. Mini ocean huts built for two."

"Mr. Taylor, are you propositioning me?"

"Oh, God, yes. We haven't been alone together in days. Those things have beds inside."

Butterflies fluttered in my belly. Even after more than a year together, I still got excited every time he came near me. Every morning when I woke up, I reached for him, finding only the disappointment of empty air beyond my tiny twin bed. My body craved his touch. I didn't know how I'd be able to stand a week of this.

After two days of sleeping apart and being constantly "on," nothing sounded better than locking myself up in a room alone with my boyfriend. Even one where the walls were just curtains.

"Did you say 'alone'?" I wiggled my eyebrows suggestively, and he laughed.

"I'll race you."

Before I accepted the challenge, he took off down the shore toward the bungalows. Without a thought, I followed. Running in sand wasn't the same as running on the street, and I lacked experience even walking on beaches. Florida-born Justin soon took an impressive lead. Still, I slogged along behind him, determined to catch up before anyone noticed we were gone and tried to stop us.

One word kept me going: *Alone.* I chanted it under my breath.

In five hours, the cruise liner would leave port, and we needed to be on it. But until then, I intended to fall into my boyfriend's arms and experience paradise with him. *Alone.*

ELEVEN

QUEEN KELLY'S VOICE
WELCOME TO MONTEGO BAY, JAMAICA!

Wednesday edition

Montego Bay is well known for its variety of glittering beaches, water so blue it looks like an Instagram filter, and popular golf courses. There's also a protected Marine Park, which allows our cruise-goers to get an up-close look at wildlife on coral reefs. Whether snorkeling or diving is more your speed, there's something to see for everyone.

We're expecting high temperatures in the upper 80s with clear skies and lots of sun on this beautiful November day. Anyone who forgot their sunblock can pick some up at the gift shop before we drop anchor or after we set sail this evening.

Our large ship isn't allowed to enter the main port, so we'll be ferrying passengers from our very own floating dock over to the island. Life jackets will be available onboard and are required for all passengers. We're expecting smooth waters today, but if you're predisposed to seasickness, visit the infirmary after breakfast for a shot to get you through the day. Pills are also available for those who prefer.

Return to the ship after lunch for an introductory ASL lessons taught by *Deaf Teen Mother* Madison at 2 PM in the large theater. *The Fishbowl*'s Ariana will also be on hand to assist.

We'll be leaving the harbor at 5 PM sharp, with the last catamarans heading for the floating dock at 4:50 PM.

Tonight, join all the Reality Stars in the Rocker Lounge for themed drinks and dancing until the sun comes up!

Inside this Edition:

As Justin and I left the dining room after breakfast Wednesday morning, something tickled the back of my mind. We'd signed up for an excursion, in Jamaica. Outside. My waterproof bag held my swimsuit, a towel, cheap plastic watch, and flip-flops to wear on the beach, but something was missing. I halted to rummage through it a second time. Justin stopped short behind me. Rachel stumbled, nearly walking into him.

"What's wrong?" Justin asked.

"I forgot my sunblock," I said.

"No worries. You've got mine in there, right?"

"Your SPF 30? That's about as effective as putting a Band-Aid on a bullet hole. I need mine. Don't worry—I'll run to my cabin for it, and meet you at the floating dock."

"We have to be there in fifteen minutes," Justin said. "Here, give me your key, and I'll go get it."

"No need," Rachel said. "I'm going to swing by our cabin before heading to the casino for a bit. I'll let you in."

"Are you sure?"

He leaned over and kissed me briefly. "We don't have time to discuss it. I'll see you in a few."

The two of them raced down the hall. I texted Danielle to tell her I'd be there soon and started toward the meeting point. Because the ship took up so much room, the Queen Kelly wasn't allowed to pull all the way into the port. Instead, the harbormaster dropped a floating dock and smaller boats carried us across the sea in groups of ten to twenty-five.

Watching the boat rock on the waves, my stomach flip-flopped. Maybe I could wait for Justin on the dock until I didn't want to throw up. Or cancel the trip and go sit on the upper deck, not puking.

"You coming?" A smiling guy about my dad's age stood on the deck, directing people into the boats. His flat-topped white hat identified him as the captain.

"I'm waiting for my boyfriend."

"Wait onboard," he said. "That way, these nice people behind you can take their seats. I'm sure your boyfriend will be here shortly."

With a shrug, I moved into the boat. Another wave hit me, but the nausea was nervousness, not actual seasickness. Once someone reassured me this thing wouldn't sink, I'd be fine. Probably.

Danielle hadn't arrived yet. Neither had Justin, but given his detour, I wasn't surprised. A large group of Latinas who appeared to all know each other occupied most of the other seats. They spoke animatedly in Spanish, paying no attention to me. As I searched for three empty seats together, Janine joined the boat. I smiled and waved. She wore a camera bag slung across her upper body. Before I could ask, the captain whistled to get everyone's attention.

"Okay, before we take off, it's time for roll call! When I say your name, raise your hand."

He went down the list of names, while I kept glancing nervously at the ship. Reid and Taylor would be at the end of the list, but where was Justin?

"J. Reid?"

"Here!" I said, before remembering to raise my hand.

"D. Rossellini?"

That's right. In my nervousness over Justin, I'd completely forgotten Danielle would be joining us. I looked up to wave her over, but before I could, a deep voice answered.

"Here."

Not Danielle. Dominic. What was going on? Did she set me up? Danielle swore she would be on the excursion, which meant Dominic couldn't tag along. I'd been genuinely excited about getting to tour the island with her. And now, Justin and I were stuck with her stupid ex instead. My stupid ex.

Or I was.

"J. Taylor?" The captain said. "Is there a J. Taylor onboard?"

I said, "That's my boyfriend. He'll be here any second."

"Okay. A. Sassani?"

Oh, no. A tremor rolled down my spine. Somehow, when she didn't respond, I wasn't surprised at all. The captain called the last two names again, but only silence answered.

"Okay, then, that's everyone. Have a seat and we'll be ashore in about ten minutes."

I stood. "Excuse me. My boyfriend isn't here yet. We need to wait."

"Sorry, ma'am. It's eight o'clock. We need to take off, whether the boat is full or not. No time to wait for stragglers."

"He's not a straggler. Look, he just went to get my sunblock. He'll be here any second." I moved toward the exit. "If you can't wait, I'll get off the boat and wait for him myself."

"I'm afraid that's not possible."

To my horror, when I reached the side of the boat, the floating dock now sat about ten yards away. Each waved pushed us further from the ship, toward the Jamaican shore.

"I pulled anchor before starting roll call," the captain said. "That was so I could tell the cruise who made it and who didn't. I'm afraid we're headed for shore now."

Justin appeared in the doorway of the ship, where the floating dock now lead to nothing. I waved at him, but a crew member held him in place. He waved back, mouthing something I couldn't see.

"Can he take the next boat?"

The captain looked at the sky. "I'm afraid not. The wind's picking up. By the time we drop you off, it won't be safe for these little boats out here. We'll be staying at the dock until it lets up. These catamarans can't sail in bad weather."

With every word he spoke, my heart sank further. "You mean I can't go back to the ship myself?"

"I'm afraid not. You'll all have to stay safe on dry land for a few hours. Anyone not already on shore will remain on the cruise ship until the weather clears up. It's for safety. But don't worry. Your excursion is on the other side of the island, and I'm told it's clear, calm waters over there."

Great. Clear, calm waters for me to go on a "romantic" horseback ride with my ex-boyfriend while my current boyfriend remained behind with the woman who'd do anything to wreck our relationship.

DOMINIC TOOK the seat next to me, despite the two empty seats on the other side of the tiny vessel. I stood to move, but the boat rocked, and I found myself thrown backward, nearly landing in his lap. After lurching to my feet, my gaze darted to Janine who was, naturally, already filming us. Wonderful.

"Hey, babe."

"Don't call me that. I always hated when you called me that."

"Is there another term of endearment you'd prefer? Schnookums? Sweetie?"

"How about 'Woman I swear never to speak to again'?" Grumbling, I grabbed my bag and jumped up again. This time, I rocked with the boat and managed to stay upright.

A voice blared on the loudspeaker in the corner. "Please stay seated for the duration of the trip. We'll be on land shortly. Thank you."

Great. I couldn't move without falling overboard.

Well, I may be stuck sitting next to Dominic, but I didn't have to talk to him. I turned my entire body toward the young woman on my left. "*¡Hola! ¿Como estás?*"

Her rapid-fire response left me desperately wishing I'd picked up more than about fifty words of Spanish since moving to Miami. Unfortunately, whatever the friendly woman beside me said in reply, it wasn't "Where is the bathroom?" or "*Donald Trump es horrible.*"

I smiled helplessly, wracking my brain for something to say. The only words in my head were, "*Yo soy una margarita.*"

I'm a margarita? Great, Jen. Just shut up.

Over my shoulder, Dominic spoke, addressing the woman in flawless Spanish. She smiled at him and chuckled before turning her attention to the man beside her and the toddler in his lap. Darn it.

I stared at my lap resolutely for about thirty seconds before curiosity got the better of me. "What did you say to her?"

"I apologized for my American sister and said you have a condition that makes it impossible for you to think before you speak."

Rolling my eyes, I returned my gaze to my lap. I shouldn't have asked.

"Hey, since we're stuck with each other, and I'm apparently

the only other person onboard who speaks English, you could try talking to me."

"I have nothing to say to you. Besides, Janine speaks English."

Dominic gestured over his shoulder with one thumb. "That Janine?"

On the other side of the boat, the eager production assistant still held a camera to her eye, pointed at me and Dominic. She didn't seem inclined to pause the video so I could chat with someone other than my ex.

For a moment, I heartily wished I could whip my microphone out into the ocean, never to be seen or heard again. Then chuck the camera, and possibly Dominic, in after it.

But I agreed to do this show. And I didn't want to spend five hundred dollars to replace a wireless mic destroyed in a fit of pique.

Swallowing my frustration, I forced a smile for the benefit of the viewers. "I may be stuck with you, but I don't have to like it. What are you doing here? Where's Danielle?"

"I convinced Danielle to let me take her place. She admits we were a bad couple, and we're both hoping you'll give me another chance."

I looked at him like he'd sprouted a second head. "What are you talking about? Doesn't Danielle have a restraining order against you?"

He chuckled. "Sweet, sweet Jen. That was all part of the plan."

"No way," I said. "Aren't you here with Ariana?"

"We may be on the ship together, but we're not here as a couple. Let's just say Ari and I have a similar agenda. Danielle graciously agreed to help once I waved enough money at her."

He had to be lying. None of what he said made sense. Why would Danielle help her ex-husband lure me away from Justin for the day?

Money's a powerful motivator, a voice inside me said.

But she got a huge settlement, I argued with myself. I didn't want to believe Dominic, but the evidence lay before me: no Justin, no Ariana, no Danielle. Just me and Dominic, alone on a "romantic" excursion with ten other people who physically couldn't talk to me, a representative of the Network, and a video camera.

Bile rose in my throat when I realized all three of them played me. "You're despicable. I can't believe I ever thought I loved you."

He shrugged. "You'll come around. All I need is time to convince you how sorry I am for not telling you about Danielle sooner. Then you'll realize we're meant to be together."

"Are you high?"

"Nope. I'm a determined man in love."

"And I'm a woman in love—with Justin."

He looked around the boat. "Speaking of, where is your darling 'Reality Lover'? If he's so great, why isn't he here with you?"

"I forgot my sunblock. He went to get it," I said. "Something must have delayed him."

"Something or some*one*? Wasn't Ariana with him at the dock?"

My head dropped into my hands. How stupid of me not to predict something like this. "I should've gone with him. I'd much rather be stuck on the boat with Justin than enjoying our excursion without him."

"Well, you're not. And since we're here, we might as well make the most of our day together. Just think, you spend an excruciating, miserable eight hours with me, and when we get to the ship, your golden boy can kiss you and make it all better."

I hated myself for the chuckle that escaped me. Dominic was right, though. I didn't need to make myself miserable all day because Justin wasn't here. I'd always prided myself on being able to make the best of bad situations—before I met Ariana.

Surely I could enjoy one tour of Jamaica and one beach horseback ride, even if my ex happened to be nearby.

"At least let me give you some sunblock," Dominic said. "You burn like crazy."

The last thing I wanted was my ex-boyfriend slathering lotion on my back, leaning forward to whisper seductively in one ear while turning to ensure the cameras captured his good side. Silently, I cursed everyone I knew: myself for forgetting the SPF 100; Justin for going to get it; Rachel for spending the day shopping instead of providing backup on this excursion; Danielle for whatever part she played in this switcheroo; Dominic for taking her spot on the excursion; Ariana for engineering the whole thing; Ed and Connor for planning this cruise in the first place; the Network for casting us all on *The Fishbowl*.

Still, I'd burn to a crisp if I stayed out here much longer, and I couldn't reach my back without extendable arms. "Fine."

A smile that used to be sensual but now made me queasy stretched across Dominic's face. "Great. Turn around and I'll rub your back."

"No need." Stifling my revulsion at the thought of his hands on my flesh, I pulled my waterproof bag off my back and rifled through it before producing Justin's aerosol can of SPF 30. "Spray me?"

His face fell so fast I wanted to laugh, but he took the can. "Turn around. And hand me your bag so you don't have a giant strap mark across it tomorrow."

I turned my back on him, willing the catamaran to travel to shore faster so I could get away from him. Once there, ignoring my ex should get easier. Even in a twelve-person excursion where we didn't know anyone else. Make that a ten-person excursion. Sigh.

With a deep breath, I forced away those thoughts and turned toward the railing, letting myself enjoy the cool mist hitting my face and the dazzling view unfolding in front of me. If it had been Justin standing with me applying the sunblock, my mind would've been racing at the day's possibilities for romance.

Instead, the voice that said, "All finished" was too deep, too rumbly.

"Thanks," I said, putting my hand out for the bottle and my bag.

"No problem." He put the bottle into the bag and zipped it. "You sure you don't want to spend the day with me?"

The boat tooted its horn, signaling our arrival at the main dock. Not a moment too soon. The faster I could get away from Dominic, the better. I gazed out at the shore, already trying to figure out how to keep him from getting on the bus to our excursion.

Men appeared on the dock, pulling the ship in and securing it. When he realized I didn't intend to answer his question, Dominic repeated it.

"Positive," I said. "I'd rather spend it with a snake—of the reptilian variety."

"I'm very sorry to hear that," he said, flinging the strap of my bag over his head. "Especially since you handed me your wallet, which has your key card, and you can't get on the cruise ship without it."

Well…. crap. Stupid. Stupid, stupid, stupid. How could I have handed over my bag? Even to get sunscreen, it wasn't worth it. I should've let myself burn.

Dominic trotted down the gangway toward the bus, leaving me with no choice but to follow him, cursing under my breath. Behind me, Janine followed, her handheld camera never straying from the two of us. It was going to be a very long day.

TWELVE

MORE FROM THE GUPPY GABBER, WEDNESDAY:

Justin: *Karma's a bitch, right? I complain about everyone lumping me and Jen together as a couple, and now I don't get to spend the day with her in Jamaica. I hope she and Danielle are having fun together.*

What do you mean, Danielle's not there, either? Why is she with her ex-boyfriend?

Ariana: *Well, Jen did it again. I was looking forward to Dominic teaching me to do snuba today, which is like a cross between scuba diving and snorkeling. Anyway, she somehow got him to join her excursion instead. I'm trying so hard to be nice to her, but she's making it impossible.*

Danielle: *Oh, my head. My eyes. I'm never going to drink again. Alcohol is evil, kids. I swear I only ordered a couple of drinks last night, but they must've been strong.*

. . . Wait, what time is it? I missed the excursion? Crap. I gotta go find Jen

---

A bus provided by the cruise line sat at the dock, prepared to take us across the island to the stables where we'd get our horses. After boarding, I pretended to ignore Dominic, chin held high, until he patted the seat next to him and held up my bag. He grinned like the cat who swallowed the canary. With a groan of frustration, I fell onto the seat beside him, refusing to look at him.

Thankfully, our bus driver, an extremely upbeat woman named Aimee, kept up a monologue all the way to the excursion site, sparing me the need to talk to Dominic. Or look at him. I prayed most of the sights would appear out the far side of the bus, giving me a valid reason for staring in the opposite direction. Mostly, I saw ocean, which reminded me of the ship, which reminded me of Justin.

We weren't "Jen and Justin" today. I hoped that made him happy. If I'd known we'd be separated, I'd have followed Tammy Rae on her excursion. Even though I felt optimistic about our meeting after dinner, creating more of a bond with her could only help my cause.

Beside me, Dominic leaned closer than necessary to peer out the window, his shoulder brushing mine. A few times, he whispered to me, his lips much closer to my ear than necessary. I kept shoving him away, shifting further toward the far edge of my seat until I essentially squatted in the aisle. I knew exactly what he was doing—trying to catch a shot, a look, a second where I appeared to be flirting with him or enjoying his attention. I'd kiss Ariana before I'd give the Network a chance to make me look unfaithful to Justin. Even if it meant acting like a three-year-old, with crossed arms, lip pout, and all.

By the time we arrived at our destination, I was ready to smack Dominic, cameras be damned. Only my desire never to see the inside of a foreign prison held me in check.

After parking the bus, Aimee directed us to a small, grassy

area outside a stable. A dozen horses stood saddled and ready for us. Not having sat on a horse since getting my Girl Scout Equestrian badge at twelve, I opted for a gorgeous, calm palomino named Plantain. Dominic, having a bit more experience with horses than I did, found himself on a black gelding with more spirit. Hopefully he'd ride on ahead, leaving me to enjoy the scenery in the back, pretending not to notice Janine recording my every move.

No such luck. About thirty seconds after Aimee led the tour group away from the stable down the road, Dominic appeared at my side.

"Don't you want to lead the way with the experienced riders?" I asked.

"And miss the chance to spend quality time with you? Absolutely not!"

I gritted my teeth. "Why are you doing this?"

"You never let me apologize," he said.

"Stalking me and stealing my stuff is a weird apology," I said. "At least give me my bag. It's not like I can turn around and head to the ship at this point. I have no idea where we are."

Plus, although I hated the company, I enjoyed the leisurely ride along the shore. The view took my breath away. Now that I'd come this far, it made sense to appreciate the excursion. After all, when would I ever see Jamaica again?

He thought about it for a minute. "I'll give it back if you give me a kiss."

"Bite me," I said. "Give it back or I'll have Jamaican police arrest you for theft after the excursion."

"You wouldn't."

"Care to test me?"

Perhaps Dominic saw something in the set of my jaw, the furrow of my brow. Or maybe he figured I'd be nicer to him if he handed it over. Either way, he moved his horse closer and held out the bag. Just as my fingers closed around it, Plantain lunged forward, snapping at Dominic's horse. He jerked away, dropping his booty in the process.

Dropping the reins, I lunged for the bag, my fingertips snagging the strap before it hit the ground. Plantain calmed as Dominic moved away, and I hugged her neck for a minute, silently thanking my regular Pilates classes for giving me the core strength not to fall.

"Good girl," I murmured. "Remind me to give you all the apples later."

We stopped while I caught my breath, and Aimee appeared at my side a moment later. She shooed Dominic toward the front of the pack. He apparently recognized the wisdom of not arguing for once.

"Everything okay?" she asked.

I sat up and righted myself before answering, then slung the bag over my shoulders. "Fine. Another horse got too close, and she got territorial with him."

Aimee laughed. "Ah, yes. I forgot to warn you about that. Plantain doesn't like other horses invading her personal space. I'm afraid your friend is going to have to ride up front for a while until she cools off. Maybe you can switch mounts after lunch."

I beamed at her. "That won't be necessary. I'm happy to ride alone, enjoying the view."

With a contented sigh, I nudged Plantain in line behind the others. We moved along, headed south along a road hugging the coast. Even after a week on the water, the spectacular views took my breath away: the beaches, the flawless blue of the water, the sky dotted with clouds. If only Justin had managed to make the boat, this excursion would be absolutely perfect.

After about an hour, Aimee led the group onto a beach and drew her horse to a halt. Dominic hovered nearby, but when Plantain glared at his horse, he moved away. I leaned forward and patted her ear, murmuring promises of treats in the near future.

This tour ended with a swim in the ocean with the horses, one of the main reasons I picked it. How many chances would I get to swim in the ocean with a herd of horses? And to have it paid for by the Network? Just the one. When my whole life went to hell a year and a half ago, I'd sworn to grab life by the reins and live it to the fullest. That meant seizing special opportunities. I could snorkel or shop anywhere.

A small stand with changing rooms sat on the beach where we'd stopped the horses. I dismounted and tied Plantain to a tree as directed so she wouldn't wander away. Then I changed quickly, untied the rope, and remounted, quickly donning a life vest. Following Aimee's lead, I turned my horse toward the water along with the other nine people in the group. A few steps into the saltwater, the horses took off at a run, and suddenly, I felt free.

Clutching the reins, I leaned back and lifted my face to the sun. Warm water cascaded over my legs, and the breeze sent my ponytail flying out behind me. Riding in water was nothing compared to riding on the land. Here, the horse was in control, and she pranced in the water. We flowed through the water until it became too deep to run, and Plantain started to swim.

All too soon, Aimee signaled and turned the horses toward the shore. Even though the end of the swim meant the start of getting back to Justin, a wave of disappointment went through me. Then my stomach growled, reminding me of some of the benefits to be found on the shore.

While we'd been swimming, other members of the tour group set up picnic tables with sandwiches, fried plantains, and soda. They took our horses, and I let Plantain go with a hug and a regretful sigh, making them promise to give her something special.

Once I got my stuff back, the need to be polite to Dominic evaporated. Still, the members of our group gathered around the table, laughing and talking about our experience. Even though I didn't understand a word, their laugher and enthusiasm pulled me in to the interaction. When Dominic began translating for me, I almost forgot I hated him.

After lunch, Aimee gave us fifteen minutes to wander, change, and take pictures before meeting at the tour bus for the return trip. I popped into the restroom to change into my regular clothes. The room was a bit of a hike from the beach. On the way there, I daydreamed about how different things would be if Justin were here, sneaking off with me for some alone time.

I'd just shimmied out of my bottoms when cheers went up in the distance. I wondered what surprise the tour company brought for us. The ocean made my hair crunchy, though, so finding out could wait a minute. I rinsed the saltwater out of my hair in the sink and reapplied sunblock as best I could before returning to the beach.

The empty beach.

What the hell?

My breath came in huge gasps as I stood open-mouthed, looking one way, then the other. At absolutely nothing.

No horses, no bus, no tourists. Just me, the sun, and the sand.

"Hey, Jen?"

And Dominic. Of course.

I whirled on him. "What did you do? Where's the bus? Aimee? The horses?"

He raised his hands. "Don't blame me. You disappeared—I had no idea where you went."

"You didn't think to check the bathroom before the entire group abandoned me?"

He pointed to a small set of outbuildings, about five feet from where we sat, behind where the bus used to be parked. I hadn't noticed them earlier.

"I did check the bathroom," he said.

I pointed down the beach. "I went over there. I didn't see the closer one. What happened?"

"Janine stepped on a jellyfish on the beach. You didn't hear the screaming?"

"I heard people cheering. Thought it was all part of the excursion." Stupid, stupid, stupid. I should've rushed back immediately.

"Definitely not cheers of joy," Dominic said. "Aimee got another tour guide to take her to the hospital to get checked out, and then she hurried everyone else onto the bus. I went to the bathrooms looking for you, and then I headed into the trees, just in case. By the time I got back, they were gone."

How convenient for him. I didn't believe this story for a second. He probably stabbed Janine himself. But arguing wouldn't get me to the ship. "So what do we do now?"

He pulled his phone from a pocket in his shorts. "We've got about five hours to get to the docks. Ready to walk?"

I pulled my phone out of my waterproof bag, but it only showed one bar. The phone dropped my first call, and my second. Not wanting to wait to contact him, I typed out a text to Justin, with no idea if it would send or if he was anywhere to even get it. If he and Ariana hadn't made it to the island, Justin's phone might still be in airplane mode. Or the battery could be dead again. He certainly hadn't tried to call me.

That thought didn't improve my mood. I shoved my phone into the bag and stomped toward the road. "Fine. Let's go."

We walked for what seemed like forever. Without any water, we conserved energy by not speaking. At least, I did. My fury at the situation fueled each step. I couldn't prove it, but I'd have bet Sweet Reality Dominic somehow arranged this to give us time alone together. Janine was also a suspect. Anything for ratings, right? That's what they did.

The bakery. Tammy Rae. I needed to meet her in a few hours. She'd never give me the recipe if I showed up late, disheveled, sunburnt, pissed off, and with another man. I needed to get to the ship—and apologize to Justin—ASAP.

Finally, a car turned into view. I jumped into the road, waving my arms. Dominic pulled me back to the sidewalk. "What are you doing?"

"Trying to get a ride." I snapped at him as the car swerved around me, honking. "They don't exactly have Uber in Jamaica, do they?"

"You can't get into a random car with a stranger."

"No problem. No one I get into a car with will be stranger than you." The joke wasn't funny. He didn't laugh. I sighed. "I want to get back to the ship. This was supposed to be a fun, romantic getaway with my boyfriend, and it's turned into an utter fiasco."

I stalked down the road, determined to flag down another car. Preferably quickly enough to zoom away and leave Dominic eating our dust.

A moment later, my ex jogged up beside me, ruining that plan. "For what it's worth, I really am sorry. This day isn't exactly going how I'd planned, either. I was hoping we could be friends. We'll never rebuild what we once had if you hate me."

"We'll never rebuild what I thought we had, because it wasn't real," I said. "And I don't believe you really want me back, anyway. This is some bit for the ratings. You never liked me this much when we were together. If you want to be my friend, Dom, get me to the docks without any more unfortunate incidents."

"Let me find a taxi service." He pulled out his phone and tapped away on the screen for a moment.

"You have a signal?"

"I got a Caribbean sim card before we left Miami."

What a great idea, not that I'd tell him. Getting a cell phone to use in the Caribbean never occurred to me. My phone flashed "no service." I tapped out a second text to Justin, with no more hope it would go through than the first tries.

The sun moved away from us as we continued our trek. Finally, a Jeep pulled up in front of us and came to a halt. The driver hopped out and opened the rear door. "Someone called for a taxi?"

"Oh, thank god," I muttered.

He handed me a bottle of water, and I slid into the air-conditioned back seat, downing half of it in a single gulp. I didn't care if he'd come to axe-murder us. Anything to get out of the sun and stop walking.

"We need to get to the docks," Dominic said. "We got separated from our tour group."

"The docks?" The driver chuckled and jerked one thumb over his shoulder. "You are walking in the wrong direction! The docks are behind you. About twenty miles."

Of course they were.

With a groan, I leaned back and put my head against the seat. Why wouldn't we have spent hours walking in the wrong direction? I wanted to cry, but was too dehydrated. And too tired. We'd be there soon. Might as well take a quick nap. I let my eyes flutter shut before Dominic finished buckling into the seat next to me.

When the car came to a stop, my eyes flew open. Something soft lay against my cheek. T-shirt soft. Dominic's t-shirt. I jerked away and lunged to my corner of the vehicle, smacking my head on the window in the process.

Ow!

"Good afternoon, beautiful," Dominic said.

"Afternoon? What time is it?" Uneasiness twinged in my stomach. How long had we walked? How long had I been asleep?

He glanced at his watch. "We're fine. It's almost five. We have plenty of time to get to the ship before six."

"Plenty of time? We have to be on the dock at five!" My voice screeched, so high-pitched I barely recognized it. "Driver, can you please hurry? We need to get there as soon as possible."

"No problem, miss. We're almost there."

"What's wrong?" Dominic said. "Ariana told me the ship leaves at six."

"Either she was wrong, or she lied." I had my own opinion as to which was more likely. "The last catamaran to the ship is at five, and the boat sails a few minutes later. I can't believe we're cutting it so close."

The second the Jeep came to a halt, I leapt out and tore across the dock, leaving Dominic to deal with paying. When we first arrived, people swarmed up and down the area. Now, the wooden planks lay mostly deserted. Panic rose in my chest. Screaming and waving my arms, I raced to the place where we'd left the catamaran, but it was too late.

Ahead of me, the final ferryboat moved away from the shore, headed for the ship. My phone read 5:02 p.m. No more boats were headed toward our cruise ship today.

As I stood there trying to figure out whether I could swim to the floating dock, the cruise ship tooted its horn and moved away, leaving me trapped in Jamaica. With Dominic. While Justin sailed away with Ariana.

THIRTEEN

STILL MORE FROM THE GUPPY GABBER, WEDNESDAY:

Justin: *Has anyone seen or heard from Jen? She wasn't in the dining room, my phone's dead, and I can't find Rachel. We were supposed to call my sister before leaving the port. It's not like Jen to forget. I hope she's okay.*

Tammy Rae: *I waited for an hour to meet Jen to talk about my cupcakes. I guess she didn't want my recipe as bad as I thought. What's worse, though, is that her mother isn't going to get an autographed picture now. It's so sad when the fans get hurt because of someone else's thoughtlessness.*

Rachel: *After I got back from shopping, I went up to the deck to lounge in the sun and nap. I had no idea Jen wasn't onboard until Justin showed up looking for her, after dinner. We went to our cabin to check, but she wasn't there. The producers finally told me she missed the deadline to get onboard. I hope she's okay.*

Summoning all of my psychic powers, I narrowed my eyes, held my arms out toward the boat, and willed it to turn around. Shockingly, nothing happened. Eight years as a diver in high school and college turned me into a decent swimmer, but it didn't give me the confidence to throw myself off a pier in pursuit of a floating hotel moving away from me. Or the lack of self-preservation. I needed to stop the ship, see if a speedboat could take me out to catch up.

Cruise ships in some areas worked with pilot ships, meaning captains who lived in the area came out to help the boat in and out of tight harbors. They'd pull right up to an open railing on the eighth or ninth deck and the captains would hop over. I could do the same. If I could find a boat. And someone to open the gate on the railing.

I reached for my phone, realizing too late I'd left my bag in the car. They wouldn't let me on the boat ever, at this rate. Or into America. Suddenly, I couldn't breathe.

Whirling around, I searched for our taxi. Gone. My heart pounded in my ears.

"Jen? Hey, Jen? Hello??" Dominic caught up to me. A wave of relief flooded me when I realized he'd brought my bag. My precious bag.

Before I said anything, he held it out. "Here."

Without looking at him, I yanked the bag out of his grip and stalked away. This was all his fault. Thankfully, my phone found a signal. I refused to think about what this call would cost.

My initial instinct was to call Justin, but he'd have to go find the right people to talk to. It's not like my boyfriend possessed the power to turn the ship around. If he turned his phone on while the ship was in port. Instead, I scrolled through my contacts list until I got to Ed's name. Ed didn't know how to turn his phone off or set it to airplane mode. Even on actual planes.

"Hey, beautiful, where are you? Was the ride amazing?"

"Actually, that's why I'm calling," I said. "Justin missed the boat this morning. I wound up on the ride by myself. And the ship left the port without me. I'm standing on the dock, watching you sail away. Can you get Connor for me?"

"Hold up. Say that again?"

I repeated myself, slower this time. Giggling filled my ear.

"Ed, this is serious! I'm stranded in a foreign country with my ex-boyfriend."

"Oh, honey, I know, I'm sorry. But you have to see the humor. That Ariana is an evil genius."

"Would you believe I'm not quite appreciating your point of view right now?"

"Okay, fine. We'll laugh about this later."

"*Much* later," I said. "I need to talk to Leanna. She can talk to the captain and get me onboard."

"Sure. Connor's at a meet-and-greet, but I'll have him text you her number."

"Now, Ed. This is an emergency. I have nothing but my passport and like ten dollars American. No way to get to Grand Cayman tomorrow. Or home."

"No problem. I'll call you back in ten minutes if we haven't found her."

"Thanks, you're a lifesaver," I said. "And when you're done, can you do me another favor?"

"Yes, I'll talk to Justin for you. Don't worry. Stay safe and get back here as soon as you can."

After he hung up, I paced the dock, refusing to look at Dominic. I had about a billion things to say to him, none of them appropriate to say in public, but I needed to talk to Leanna first. Once I fixed this problem, I'd know exactly how pissed I had a right to be. With any luck, my feet would hit the deck of the Queen Kelly before the late seating in the Simon Dining room.

Nine minutes later, my phone rang, displaying a call from an unfamiliar number.

"Connor?"

"Jen? It's Leanna." She didn't sound happy. "What the fuck happened?"

"Ariana happened."

"Ariana's here on the ship. You're not."

"Yes, she is, but she detained Justin so he couldn't join me on the excursion, then she sent my ex with me in his place, and he made sure I missed the boat. Now we're both stranded in Jamaica. Please help me."

"We can't possibly turn the ship around to come pick you up."

"I know, but can I get a boat to come out and meet the ship? The Network must have some kind of protections in place in case something like this happens. Or the cruise line. What do they normally do when someone misses the sailing time?"

Silence. I pictured her head tilted, tongue sticking out between her teeth while she pondered the best way to use this situation to create more drama. Producers: Helpful, yet evil. No way the Network would let me come out of this unscathed. I'd be lucky if she didn't tell me to make out with Dominic before she'd help.

"Usually, they tell people to get to the next port of call at their expense. You may join the cruise again in Grand Cayman if you can get there."

"Great! How are you going to get me there?"

"How is this my problem, Jennifer?"

My spirits plummeted. The Leanna who'd seemed so cool and helpful during the early days on *The Fishbowl* vanished. We'd been friendly until I'd refused to participate in the last mini-challenge. Not my fault I didn't want to win an in-house dinner with Dominic, who they'd mistakenly called my "serious boyfriend." Nope. I'd been happy to let Justin win a visit with Sarah instead. I'd never dreamed that move would bite me in the ass later.

My mind raced, seeking any way to sway her back on my side. Or to get her begrudging assistance. "Well, let's see: You invited Ariana on the cruise, knowing our history. You let us bring guests. You put me and Justin in separate rooms to drive a wedge between us. You sent me and Dominic out with a production assistant who happened to disappear, which is how we lost the bus in the first place."

"What are you accusing us of, Jen?"

"Oh, come off it. I'm not stupid," I said. "Getting left behind can't have been a coincidence. The Network is footing the bill for this whole week. You're going to make an utter shitload of money off these episodes, especially since Dom's following me around with puppy dog eyes. You'll get sixteen million viewers, easy. But if you ditch me in a foreign county, I'll take my chances violating the nondisclosure clause in my contract."

She didn't respond, so I pressed on.

"But if you help me, I'll play along, do what I can to get the show over twenty million viewers. I'll promote the hell out of it after we get home. Do you want to give up the publicity? There are three days of cruise left. Don't you want to see me confront Ariana? I promise, it's going to be good."

Leanna sighed in my ear. "Okay, fine. There's an airport in Kingston, but you're nowhere near it. I'll see if I can find a captain to bring you over to the next port on a private boat. I'll call you back."

"Thanks, Leanna. You're a peach."

She didn't answer. I didn't expect her to.

Dominic approached as soon as I put my phone away. "So what's the verdict?"

"You were not a part of the conversation." I turned and walked down the pier, knowing he'd catch up to me easily. A moment later, he appeared at my side.

"Where are you going?"

"Away from you."

"Are you going to abandon me in Jamaica?"

"Only if I can't find a way to shove you in the ocean with no one noticing."

He stopped, pulling my arm to bring me to a halt with him.

"C'mon, Jen. I'm sorry. I just wanted to spend more time with you. How can you fault me for that?"

"When you want to spend time with someone, you ask! You don't steal their passport, follow them around a foreign country, and then strand them on a pier. You want to talk, to make up? Not today, Satan! Leave me alone."

To my surprise, he burst out laughing. "God, I've missed you. The way you phrase things. Your smile, your jokes, everything."

I glared at him. He wouldn't be seeing my smile any time soon. Not after all this.

"At least let me buy you dinner," he said. "We haven't eaten in hours, and you don't have any idea when the producers will call you."

"I'm not leaving this pier unless it's on a boat."

He pointed behind me. "There's a bar right over there. You'll feel better once you eat. The second Leanna calls you back, you can ditch me. Scout's honor."

Before I could refuse, my stomach howled. We'd been in the sun all day, riding horses, then we walked at least three miles. I hadn't eaten in more than six hours. Passing out from hunger on the dock wouldn't get me on the Queen Kelly any sooner.

"Fine," I said. "But don't talk to me."

STILL REFUSING to look at him, I stomped to the small restaurant at the end of the deck and took one of the empty seats at the bar. Dominic started to sit on the empty seat next to me, but I put my hand over it.

"Don't. There are plenty of empty seats here. Leave me alone."

He started to argue, but must've seen something in the firm line of my mouth. Or the daggers flying out of my eyes. "I'm going to the bathroom. We'll talk in a minute."

The bartender brought me a menu, but I waved him off, requesting a mai tai and whatever local delicacies they offered. Dinner would probably cost a fortune. Good. Dominic was paying.

Before my drink arrived, a short, stocky guy with cornrows and warm brown eyes slid onto the stool beside me. After an entire day of glaring at Dominic, being rude to strangers felt like too much effort, so I smiled at him. He smiled back, flashing one perfect dimple. He was nice to look at, although at least fifteen years older than me.

"I like your dress," he said.

My dress? In case my outfit changed since walking into the bar, I glanced down at my black capri pants, tank top, and running shoes. Ah, well. "Thank you."

"You are American? My name is Isaac."

"Jen. Yes, American."

"Wonderful. I love America!" He winked at me, which finally tipped me off that this guy was hitting on me. Wonderful. At least Janine wasn't around to film it.

The bartender returned with my drink, and I took a long sip, wondering how to extract myself from the conversation gracefully. Then he said, "Bartender, I will pay for her drink."

"No, thank you. I can't let you do that. I have a boyfriend," I said.

"What kind of boyfriend would let a beautiful woman like you walk around these bars by herself?"

"Well, we kind of got separated. Physically, I mean. But I'll be seeing him soon."

He nodded sagely. "Ah. Sorry for your breakup. Now you drink with me. I'll make it better."

Not wanting to be rude, I raised my glass. "Cheers. But really, I'm fine, thanks."

"Do you like the Foo Fighters? Lots of American women like the Foo Fighters."

I wracked my brain, coming up totally blank. What a random

question to ask a stranger. "That's a band, right? They were popular before I was born, I think, so I'm not very familiar with their oeuvre."

"What a shame. Come home with me. I'll play you Foo Fighters, yes?"

Being polite was not getting me anywhere. I sighed and stirred my drink before meeting his gaze firmly. "I appreciate the offer, but I have a boyfriend, and I'm not interested."

A hand landed on my shoulder, and I jumped. "The lady said she's taken." I never thought I'd be happy to hear Dominic's voice again. To me, he said, "Hi, honey. Sorry I'm late. Are you ready to move to our table?"

Gratefully, I nodded, sliding off the stool. As badly as I wanted to never see or talk to Dominic again for the rest of my life, he momentarily seemed to be the lesser evil.

"Thank you," I said when we sat down. Even though I blamed him for this entire mess, I could be gracious. Sort of.

"No problem. I'm glad you changed your mind about having dinner with me."

I snorted. "You're incorrigible. I'm not having dinner with you."

"Oh, no? You want me to get up, give my seat to your friend over there? What was his name again?"

"Shut up. I appreciate you rescuing me. Even though I hate needing rescue."

"It's a different culture here. You just need to be firm. You're too nice. I should've known better than to leave you alone."

Briefly, I wondered if I was too nice to throw my cocktail in his face. Except, after the long day, I needed the drink.

"Smile," Dominic said. "You're in love with me, remember? The other men in the bar are looking at us."

I showed him my teeth in what probably could not be accurately described as a smile. "Have I mentioned lately that I hate you?"

"Not in so many words, but this seems like the perfect time

for a relationship post mortem, doesn't it? I'm an ass, I treated you horribly, and I deserve to be strung up the nearest flagpole by my testicles."

Laughter burst out of me, filling the room. "Well, I wouldn't go that far, but Danielle may have a different point of view."

"Danielle already got my nuts in the divorce. She can do whatever she wants with them."

"She's wonderful," I said. "How could you cheat on her?"

The bartender delivered a platter of steaming fried plantains to our table. The scent set off my stomach, drowning off any further conversation. Not that I wanted to talk to my ex about our relationship. Or about his marriage. Instead, I dove into the food.

More plates followed. We devoured jerked chicken and rice, some amazing fritters, and something called "ackee and salt fish." Dominic, a firm believer in drinking local beer whenever possible, washed everything down with Red Stripe. I stuck to my mai tais, which probably contained as much water as alcohol. Even after my third, I didn't feel the slightest buzz. Except everything Dominic said seemed hilarious. Like when he offered to go to the bar for more chips and guacamole.

Finally, Leanna called me. The Network arranged for a local boat owner to take us to the Cayman Islands, where we'd rejoin the cruise ship in the morning. I would've preferred to get back immediately and sleep in my tiny bunk bed—after talking to Justin and Tammy Rae, of course—but she said the ship wasn't allowed into the harbor until morning. Even if they were, it wouldn't be safe to open the gangway in the middle of the night. Since she was doing me a huge favor by not making me swim, hitchhike halfway across the island to get to an airport, or pay for my own boat, I didn't argue. Instead, I thanked her politely and disconnected.

Then I sent another text to Justin. No response. What a time for his phone to give him problems.

Dominic paid the bill, and I led the way. Using the directions

Leanna gave me, I found our ride. Either the ship was fairly new, or the owner possessed an awesome sense of humor, because the *Boaty McBoatface* waited for us in the harbor. When Dominic saw the name, he burst out laughing. A genuine smile broke out across my face. Anyone who'd name their vessel *Boaty McBoatface* should be interesting to pass a few hours with. This last stage of our voyage might turn out okay after all.

"Welcome aboard!" The man greeting us stood about six feet tall, with flawless ebony skin, dreadlocks down to his waist, and perfect, gleaming white teeth. My best guess put him a couple of years younger than me. "I'm Ty, and I'll be your guide this evening."

Dominic introduced us, while I steeled myself for another rocky voyage.

"Are you okay?" Ty asked when I settled into a seat in the corner.

"I'm fine thanks," I said. "Just not a big fan of boats."

"You're in Jamaica on a cruise ship, aren't you?" Ty kept a perfectly straight face, but Dominic chuckled behind him. I glared at him over Ty's shoulder.

"Okay, fine, I'm not a big fan of *small* boats," I said. "I always worry about getting seasick."

"Ah, well, then! I have the thing for you. Would you like some of the good ganja?"

The good ganja? *Oh, dear.*

"No, thank you. I don't smoke. Do you have any ginger ale?"

"No problem," he said. "I'll bring you some brownies instead. Special recipe."

Chocolate probably wouldn't settle my stomach, but since my fear of seasickness outweighed any actual nausea about a hundred to one, no reason to say no. I'd never been one to turn down chocolate without a good reason.

Dominic started to say something, but I interrupted him. "That sounds amazing. Thank you, Ty."

Without another glance at Dominic, I pulled a book out of my bag and stared resolutely at the pages. My mind wandered, and my eyes spun uselessly down the page. Hopefully no one would ask me about the book. It didn't matter. I just wanted to ignore my ex until we got back to the Queen Kelly where I could hand-cuff myself to Danielle and avoid him until we got to Miami while simultaneously apologizing to Justin and getting Tammy Rae's secret ingredient.

A moment later, Dominic settled onto the bench beside me. "Did I mention I'm sorry?"

"Did I mention I'm not speaking to you?"

"You just did."

Ty saved me from answering by appearing with a large plate of brownies and a bottle of ginger ale. Although we'd just eaten, my stomach found space at the sight of the thick, chocolate icing. After a horrible day, it looked even more enticing than a coco-chocolate cupcake topped with toasted coconut.

"Thanks," I said. "How much for this?"

"On the house. Or rather, on your Network. They've got you covered," he said. "You can sleep down below. There are two couches and a bed. I'll show you when you're ready."

As nice as it sounded to crawl into bed and lie there until the boat reached the Cayman Islands, I was too on edge after our day to even pretend to sleep. I wanted my brownies and ginger ale.

Twenty minutes later, realizing I didn't feel seasick in the slightest, I got up to explore the boat. This was my first time on a yacht. If I wanted to embellish the details for the viewers in my interview when I returned to the cruise, I should know what a rich person's boat looked like.

Below decks, the ship held a living area larger than some downtown Seattle apartments. Blue couches lined the walls, clean and firm. From what I'd seen on tiny house shows, the cushions probably concealed storage. The door across the room would lead to Ty's bedroom; I left it closed. The kitchenette took up about twenty square feet, most of that taken up with tiny, adorable appliances, but a determined person could cook in there. I spotted a wireless router in the corner and wondered where you got Wi-Fi in a boat. A door next to the kitchen showed the smallest bathroom I'd ever seen–just a showerhead over the toilet and a drain in the floor. How efficient.

Upstairs, benches lined the deck. A covered area in the middle held two sets of chairs. Ty showed me how one converted to tables and the other concealed life jacket storage. I reached immediately for one, but he stopped me.

"This should be a smooth trip. You'll wind up below decks for most of it," Ty said. "I'll let you know if you need a jacket, but for now, just enjoy the trip. Nothing beats an ocean sunset."

He had a point. I tossed back the rest of my brownie and wandered around the deck, looking for a good spot. The sail remained furled for this trip, as we'd use the motor to take us to the Cayman Islands. The view from the front of the ship beat the one from the ship, because this close to the water line, I saw fish playing in the sea.

Although it was early, the sun dipped below the horizon, casting an alien orange light across the water. Or maybe aliens hovered out of sight. Only a UFO could make this day more unreal. I giggled at the thought, glancing up to examine the sky.

The stars were so beautiful. How had I never noticed? I moved toward the railing, into the open air and looked up. The sky swallowed me. Somewhere in the distance, music played. My body swayed to the rocking of the boat, and I tipped my head to the sky, relishing the breeze on my face. It felt like angels brushing me with their wings.

A moment later, Dominic appeared holding out an unopened bottle of water. "You're going to want this."

"Thanks. Look at the sky! The stars are so big! And Tammy Rae was right: the ocean *is* totally vast. I feel so small, you know? So insignificant. Like none of this matters. Why am I being so mean to you? You brought me water! I love water."

Laughing, Dominic leaned against the railing. "So how were those brownies?"

"So good. I love brownies. Are there any left?"

"I think you've had enough."

As we passed another, larger ship, music and laughter drifted across the harbor to us. People stood on the deck, milling around.

Jumping up and down, I waved. "Hiiiiiiiiiiiiiiiiii, people! I'm Jen, and I'm on a reality cruise!"

Someone shouted, but I couldn't make out the words. They were dancing, so I danced, too. They cheered and shouted, so I shouted back. "Yay for new friends!"

Dominic lifted his water bottle and clinked it against mine. "To new friends—and old."

"Man, I feel amazing! Don't you feel amazing?"

"Yeah, I feel pretty good, too. You're funny like this."

"I'm not funny, your face is funny!" I hooked my elbows around the railing to see how far I could bend backward. "I'm so happy. Why do I feel so happy? I don't like you. I miss Justin. I love Justin."

He turned and cupped my face, his eyes searching mine. "Hey, Jen? When Ty said 'special recipe brownies,' you knew what he meant, right?"

"Like his mom's recipe? Some secret ingredient?" The lips of his mouth turned upward, like he struggled not to laugh. "What?"

"Jen, when someone offers you 'special' brownies or 'funny' brownies, they have pot in them. You're totally high right now."

Me, high? No way! No one ever offered the nerdy girl drugs. And I'd never, ever accept them. I needed my brain cells intact. On the other hand, this explained why my soul soared on the ocean breeze while we talked.

Although I wanted to be angry at Dominic's revelation, my brain lost control over my emotions. I burst out laughing. "Why didn't you tell me?"

He shrugged. "I figured you knew."

"How could I possibly know that?"

"How could you possibly *not* know that? You went to college."

"I've spent half the week trying to find out a secret ingredient for a special recipe Sarah and I need for our bakery," I said. "When Ty said special recipe, that's what I thought he meant. Perfect. Now watch, Tammy Rae's secret ingredient is probably pot."

As frustrating as the day had been, it was impossible not to see the humor in the situation. Or the THC had taken over my nervous system. Giggling helplessly, I let my feet slide down until I sat on the deck with a thump. When my bruised butt hit the deck, I gasped.

"What's wrong?" Dominic asked.

"I fell on my ass on the deck yesterday. I've got a bruise the size of Neptune."

"Don't you mean Uranus?" Dominic sat beside me, and the two of us laughed until tears ran down my face and my sides ached.

"Do you want me to take a look at it?"

"No, I don't need you to check out my butt. Thanks, anyway."

"I meant the bruise. I'm a nurse, remember?"

I'd almost forgotten. When we were together, he rarely talked about work, and after I found out about Danielle, I figured he made up the traveling nurse thing to explain his long absences. It never occurred to me that he might possess actual medical knowledge.

"Thanks, but no. I'll be fine."

The mental image of Dominic "examining" my butt set off another fit of giggles. When I calmed, he was watching me.

"What?"

"You," he said. "You're having an awesome time. Admit it,

spending the day with me is not the worst thing that possibly could've happened to you."

"It could be the brownies talking, but you might be right," I said. "This hasn't been a terrible day. But I still never want to see you again."

"Jen, I do feel horrible about the way things ended between us. Danielle and I married too young. I didn't know what love felt like until I met you."

His words sent a pang through me. Before I met Justin, nothing would've made me happier than to hear those words. But it was too late. I'd moved on, and now I understood how a real relationship worked. Justin and I had a partnership, something more than canceled dates, apologies, and stolen moments, always at my place.

"Don't say that, Dominic. It's too late. We've been over for almost two years."

"I'm an idiot. I should've left her the minute I met you."

I shook my head. "It doesn't matter now. Danielle is happily living the single life, and I'm in love with Justin."

"Are you?" he asked.

He scooted closer, so near that the heat of his body enveloped mine. I inched backward until I bumped into a corner of the ship. Ignoring him, I took another drink of water, then turned my attention to the sky.

"Man, the universe is huge up there. Like the ocean! We're such tiny parts of this massive whole. As insignificant as ants. Crawling around on the deck like ants, too. When did I get so deep?"

He chuckled, bringing my attention to him.

We sat very close, our knees almost touching. Our heads mere inches apart. Man, he had a big head. How had I never noticed his big head while we were dating?

That probably *was* the brownies talking.

"What do you mean?" I asked. "Of course I'm in love with Justin."

"You've spent the last ten hours with me. Laughing, joking, drinking. Dancing. We're in this amazing place, on this amazing journey. And where's Justin? On the ship, with Ariana."

"It's not his fault he missed the boat. It's not like he purposely ditched me to hang out with her."

"Of course he didn't. That's why he's been calling you all day."

I forced myself not to reflexively reach for my phone. "His phone stopped working the first day on the ship. The battery won't charge."

"Right. How convenient. Right after you run into Ariana, his phone stops working?"

"I never said it was after we ran into Ariana."

"But it was, right? Didn't they have a thing together on the show?"

"Before the show. A long time ago. It meant nothing." Even to my ears, the words sounded weak. I hated Dominic for pushing at my sore spots. But wasn't this what I'd worried about all along? That Justin would leave me for Ariana? What if he'd somehow arranged to stay behind with her?

No, that was ridiculous. The brownies were making me paranoid.

"Come on, Jen, let this happen," Dominic said. His face was so close to mine, I couldn't see the stars anymore. "Forget Justin. That guy's not good enough for you. I love you, you love me."

"That's ridiculous." I shook my head. "Justin's the best thing that ever happened to me. And I don't l—"

He cut me off, bending forward and pressing his lips against mine. In my shock, I froze. Two things brought me out of my stupor: Dominic's tongue wriggling its way into my mouth, and the unmistakable click of a camera shutter.

FOURTEEN

SHOCKING ENTERTAINMENT NEWS ONLINE

THE FISHBOWL COUPLE TO SPLIT?

Are Jen and Justin experiencing trouble in paradise?
by Talky Ted, Nov. 8

Sources report that Jen, one-half of America's darling "Jen and Justin" spent a romantic day in the Caribbean with her ex-boyfriend instead of her current love. Jen and Dominic rode horses on the beach and swam in the ocean. Rumor says the couple failed to return to the ship before it departed for the next stop. An unavoidable emergency? Or the perfect opportunity for a spontaneous lover's tryst away from prying eyes?

About a mile off the shore of Jamaica, a group of twenty-somethings aboard a party ship report seeing someone matching Jen's description on a smaller vessel nearby, headed in the direction of Grand Cayman. The young woman in question reportedly danced, cheered, waved her shirt around her head, and generally acted as if she were having a marvelous time. Witnesses spotted two men aboard the smaller yacht. One appeared to be steering, but the other matches the description of Jen's ex-boyfriend, Dominic. A moonlit cruise for two? Dancing? How romantic.

The picture painted by our sources creates quite a contrast to the rather unflattering things Jen said about her ex when she appeared on *The Fishbowl*.

From the beginning, viewers touted Jen as the evil genius of the show, taking control whenever team challenges required a bit of brainpower and generally trying to organize votes and alliances among her teammates.

Her reputation for high intelligence and ability to manipulate makes this reporter wonder: Has Jen experienced a change of heart about her ex? Or was she playing Justin—and the American public—for a fool all this time?

Meanwhile, Justin remained on the Queen Kelly with a certain sultry siren who's never made any secret of her designs on him. Is this truly a love boat? Or is this cruise ship secretly a destroyer? More to come.

Related Stories:

Watch Joshua "J-Dawg" Adams react to not being invited on the *Real Ocean: Caribbean*

Where are they now? Catch up with Hot Catches Abram, Mike, and Raj.

Shoving with all my strength, I sent Dominic sliding away from me. Then I lunged forward and slapped him across the face so hard my hand turned red. Without another glance in his direction, I jumped to my feet and raced after Ty. He walked quickly toward the door leading below decks as if he thought there was a place onboard to hide from my wrath.

"Stop!" I called desperately. "At least tell me you got a picture of the slap, too."

Ty stopped and turned, chuckling. "I did not see any slap, ma'am."

"If I give you ten dollars, will you come back? I can hit him again." Nothing would bring me more pleasure, other than waking up in my bunk and finding out this entire day had been a nightmare.

"American dollars?" he asked.

"Yup. Let's make it twenty."

We returned to the spot where Dominic stood, rubbing his cheek. He dropped his hand when we approached. "What's going on?"

I moved toward him, hand raised, but he flinched. I paused, hand hovering. He grabbed my wrist.

"What are you doing?" Dominic asked.

I ignored him. To Ty, I said, "Darn it, I can't hit him. It's one thing to slap someone in the heat of the moment, but the moment's passed."

"Perhaps he could kiss you again?" Our captain suggested. I glared at him. "Or make you angry some other way?"

"I'm very good at that," Dominic said.

"Maybe we could stage it? I could raise my hand, Dominic could throw his head back and you could take the picture? Or I could lift my knee toward his balls."

"That could work, but you won't get the right expression of surprise and pain on his face."

I sighed heavily. This wasn't going to work. Throwing out a self-defense slap was one thing, but I wasn't a fighter. Even to prove to Justin the kiss wasn't my idea, I couldn't attack my ex. No matter how badly he deserved it. My foot tapped against the pavement as I searched for a solution.

"While you two discuss the best way to assault me, I'm

headed to bed," Dominic said. "This has been a great trip and all, but it's been a long, abusive day. I'm not up for getting slapped —or pretend slapped—repeatedly."

I sighed. "I can't hit you. You might as well go. I'll see you in the morning."

Ty lifted his camera. "No slap?"

"I guess not," I grumbled. "Any chance I could convince you to delete the other picture?"

"Not for only ten American dollars." Ty grinned, revealing a row of perfect, gleaming white teeth. "You cannot afford to pay me what I'll get for selling this picture to your tabloid newspapers."

<hr>

ALL NIGHT, I tossed and turned, trying to come up with any way to convince Ty not to sell the picture. Throwing his camera overboard seemed the most obvious option, but he wore the thing around his neck. As much as I'd wanted to throttle Dominic for kissing me, shoving the only witness into the ocean wouldn't help anything.

By the time the ship docked, pink rays peeked through the window. I hadn't slept a wink. Listening to Dominic snoring on the other side of the cramped cabin didn't help. With a sigh, I yanked the blankets from the bed and carried them up on deck to see if moving somewhere quieter would help me sleep.

It didn't.

People milled around the dock, talking excitedly. In the slip to our lift, three men unloaded nets of fish–early catch, apparently. On the other side, a mother tried to corral her two small children into life jackets before setting sail for a family outing.

I wandered around the deck, looking for a place to sleep. A small bench beckoned to me when across the pier, I spotted the Queen Kelly. The gangway wasn't down yet, but maybe I could get close enough to get on their Wi-Fi system and send a message to Justin. Grabbing my bag, I went to find our captain.

He stood on the pier, speaking to two men with their backs to me. The shorter one wore a camera bag strapped around his upper body. The other's lanky form I knew well after being locked in a house with him for eight weeks the prior summer.

"Ed!" My fatigue evaporated. I cheered and jumped to the ground, racing to wrap my arms around my friend. "And Connor! What are you doing here?"

"Leanna sent me to pick you up," Connor said. "She told me to tell you the cost of your transport to the ship is one exclusive interview about your romantic night with Dominic."

"Of course it is." I rolled my eyes.

Ed said, "She doesn't know I came along. I wanted to see you and make sure you're okay."

I pulled him to the side, leaving Connor and Ty to finish whatever they were talking about. In a hushed tone, I filled him in on my day and the evening. His eyes widened, his brow furrowed, then his jaw dropped.

"Oh, snap! Jen, what are you going to say to Justin?"

With a shake of my head, I said, "I have no idea. But I need to get to the ship ASAP before Ariana gets her hooks deeper into him. Especially since Ty over there won't delete the picture. What do I do when Justin sees it? Worse, what if Ariana shows it to him before I can talk to him about it?"

Ed wrapped one arm around my shoulders, and I leaned against him. "Give the interview," he said. "Be honest, but brief. Tell Connor your side of the story while I go wake up your ex. We can be out of here in five minutes."

"Do we have to take him to the ship with us? Can't we send him back to Jamaica with Ty?"

"I'm afraid that's part of the deal. Don't forget, he's a paying guest. The cruise line won't let us ditch him. However, Connor and I will do whatever we can to keep him away from the ship until you find Justin."

"You're a lifesaver." I pulled him close for a moment, happy to have someone on my side.

"Butterscotch," Ed agreed, winking at me. "And you're as refreshingly adorbs as a Chiclet."

He headed over to where Ty and Connor stood, leaving me wondering what the heck to say in my interview. And how to fix my hair. A moment later, Connor approached, camera in hand.

"Do you by any chance have a mirror?" I asked.

"You couldn't get one from Ed?"

"Forgot to ask. How bad do I look?"

Connor took in my appearance before shrugging. "You never know. Maybe looking like you escaped from a rabid bear attack on a frat party will garner some sympathy with the viewers."

"Ugh. Ok, fine. Let's get this done so I can get to Justin."

Ed returned and handed me a mirror. "Dominic will be here in a minute."

The damage was worse than I feared. My hair stuck out in about seventeen different directions. A full day in the sun with only SPF 30 turned my face and neck the color of a ripe strawberry. No wonder every inch of my body hurt. Black circles rimmed my eyes, and a steak of mascara trailed down to my chin.

Sighing, I licked my middle finger and tried to at least erase some of the excess makeup. It didn't help much. "Whatever. Let's do this."

Connor directed me to the edge of the pier, with the water as a backdrop. He lifted the camera, and Ed stepped behind him, out of the view.

"Justin and I planned to spend the day on the beach, horseback riding and touring Jamaica with Danielle, from *Suddenly Single in Seattle.*" I spoke directly into the camera. Nothing to hide here, America.

"That's your boyfriend's ex-wife, yes?"

"Danielle is my *ex-boyfriend's* ex-wife," I said, well aware that all interview responses needed to include the question for the sake of the viewers. "I don't know what happened, but when they called roll aboard the catamaran carrying us to the mainland, Dominic appeared instead of Danielle. The passenger list only showed first initials and last names. No one but me knew something went wrong."

I intentionally didn't mention Ariana's role in the mix-up. My last stint on television taught me the futility of trying to make her look bad when I didn't have any proof. Or, actually, even when I did. Even though we weren't competing for a $250,000 prize this time, I didn't feel any inclination to help her gain fans. Or to make myself look like a jealous asshole. The more people who walked away from this show with a high opinion of me, especially in the Miami area, the better for me and Sweet Reality. I didn't have the luxury of forgetting that my actions didn't only affect me anymore.

As briefly as I could, I outlined the prior day's events, careful to make getting left behind seem like a perfectly understandable glitch that could've happened to anyone. Blaming Dominic for the missed connection wouldn't win me any favor with the fans, either. I wished I could afford to not care what America thought of me. All that mattered was what my boyfriend thought, and I needed to get to him to explain my disappearance.

"One more question," Connor said when I finished with my boarding the *Boaty McBoatface*. His face was inscrutable, but I'd spent enough time on these shows to guess what he wanted to know. "I don't want to ask, but I'll get fired if I don't. Take as long as you need to think before you answer. Did you and Dominic kiss? Are the two of you getting back together?"

My face grew warm. Behind Connor, Ed mimed throttling him, but it wasn't his fault. He'd done a lot to help me so far, but I couldn't ask him to risk his job by intentionally botching the interview. And why bother? As soon as we got to the ship, if he didn't have the answer on tape, one of the other forty or so PAs walking around would be happy to ask.

"Yes, Dominic kissed me last night," I said. "I did not kiss him. I pushed him away and slapped him. The only person I ever want to kiss again is Justin. Can we go now so I can find him?"

"Jen, when you say the only person you want to kiss again is Justin, do you mean forever? Are you talking about the M-word here?"

A vision of myself walking down the aisle in a white gown flashed before my eyes. Justin stood at the end, with Sarah on one side and Ed on the other. Brandon walked ahead of me, the man of honor. I imagined Justin putting a band on my finger and promising to love me forever. In my vision, he leaned forward and kissed me sweetly while all our friends and family clapped. Then I felt my throat closing up, saw myself choking on the ring, spitting into the sink. And I remembered that Justin hadn't even hinted at any type of future since we got on the ship. What if he changed his mind?

My cheeks grew warm, and I looked at the ground before answering. "Marriage is a big step." But I couldn't get what had to be a ridiculous-looking smile off my face. "But, sometimes I think marrying Justin would be the best thing that ever happened to me. I love him."

"Beautiful," Connor said, dropping the camera. "If nothing else convinces him, the look on your face when I asked about marriage should tell him how you feel."

Gratefully, I popped onto my toes to kiss his cheek. "Thank you so much for that."

A golf cart carried the four of us across the docks. Ed gave me the front seat next to Connor. In the back, he kept up a steady stream of banter that probably would've been funny under other circumstances. Instead of listening, I stared out the side of the vehicle, chewing on my lower lip and wondering where every-thing went wrong. What had Justin done while I was gone? Did he spend the day with Ariana? Was he furious with me for not returning to the ship immediately? He'd never answered a single one of my texts, but I didn't know if his phone was on and working. We hadn't used the messaging app all week. Maybe he hadn't seen any of my messages.

When we got to the ship, I alighted from the cart practically before it stopped moving. Dominic stepped out behind me, but Ed called him over for an interview. Good ol' Ed. I raced for the gangway, phone already in hand. Battery dead. I couldn't text Justin until I got to my room to plug the stupid thing in, and but I didn't want any delays before I got to his cabin.

Instead of waiting for the elevator, I raced up the stairs to our deck. On the fourth floor, one of my flip-flops tore, making me stumble. My toe came off the sandal, banging against the step. I yelped.

For a second, I paused to look at the damage. The thin piece of plastic once separating my toes now dangled uselessly above the foam bottom. Stupid two-dollar shoes. How dare they not be sturdy?

Not willing to let poor craftsmanship slow me down, I yanked the other flip-flop off my foot and kept running. I didn't slow until I got to Justin's door. Panting, I rapped on the door once, twice. Then again. What if Dominic somehow beat me here? Maybe he took another staircase or found an empty elevator. My heart pounded in my chest. Glancing up and down the hall, I knocked again, louder.

Finally, the door swung open, and the remaining breath whooshed out of me. Before me stood Ariana.

In Justin's room. Wearing a fluffy, white bathrobe.

FIFTEEN

INSIDE THE GUPPY GABBER, THURSDAY:

Jen, 8:00 AM: *I'm sorry, but I can't right now. Nope. Sorry.*

Tammy Rae: *What? Of course my secret ingredient isn't marijuana! I haven't done drugs during this century. My secret ingredient is completely natural and totally organic, but not, like, illegal.*

Justin: *Jen's back on the ship? Where?*

Dominic: *Bro, she totally dug that kiss. I am IN. The rest of this week is going to be epic. Wait and see.*

My jaw hit the floor. Ariana smirked at me, the same look I'd wanted to slap off her face a thousand times. "Can I help you?"

Stepping backward, I turned to check the names on the card by the door: Morgan, Rossellini, Silva, Taylor. Not Sassani, of course. I hadn't actually met Mr. Morgan yet, but suffered no delusions the Network gave Ariana a fake name and stuck her in the guys' cabin. Nor did I think it was a coincidence, finding her in my boyfriend's room at six o'clock in the morning.

There had to be a reasonable explanation. I struggled to keep my voice even. "Is Justin here?"

"Oh, yeah. He's in the shower. Should be out any minute."

No. Nonononononono.

Then I heard Justin's voice, and my blood ran cold. "Ari? Who's there?"

Ari? So it was Ari now?

This couldn't be happening. I'd been trapped on a boat all day with my ex-boyfriend, a camera-toting production assistant who wouldn't talk to me while filming, and a dozen people I couldn't talk to thanks to a language barrier. I'd been forced to sail away from my boyfriend, leaving him with my least favorite person in the world. Bad weather stopped me from getting to him. I'd been stranded, left to walk hours in the sun with my second least favorite person. Then I got stranded on an island with said SLFP, in a foreign country, without any money or my passport, and had to beg the Network's executives to let me on the ship. The ship captain drugged me, my ex surprised me with a stupid, drooly kiss, and it got captured on camera. On top of having to deal with all that bullshit in less than twenty-four hours (on about two hours sleep, no less), now this.

The double whammy of finding my archenemy in my boyfriend's room after the worst day and night of my life was too much.

My brain balked at any type of confrontation. My mouth opened and closed, but no sound came out. The ability to process information, to reason, went right out of me. I forgot how to word. Couldn't brain. No thinky.

Without uttering a single sound, I let my feet carry me to my cabin. Although part of me wanted to run, I practically crept down the hall, praying Justin would call me. That he'd chase me across just like he followed me down the driveway, apologize, and offer a reasonable explanation for everything. Then I could apologize and fall into his arms. We'd kiss, make up, and go hang out in the giant hammocks advertised by the spa up on the fourteenth deck. A wonderful end to a horrible twenty-four hours.

But it was all a fantasy, a waking dream. When I got to my cabin, I stood outside the door, leaning my forehead against it for what seemed like forever. No footsteps fell on the carpet. No voice called my name. He wasn't coming. He stayed in his cabin with Ariana.

When I finally opened my door, ears still straining for signs of Justin behind me, the lights were out. Rachel's soft snoring, much less intrusive than Dominic's, filled the room. Moving as soundlessly as possible, I crawled into bed, not bothering to undress. With a pillow over my head, I let exhaustion claim me.

Sometime later, a weight landed beside me, shaking me awake. Light now streamed through the curtains.

"Jen! Where were you?" Rachel asked. "I was so worried!"

I couldn't even. I wanted to believe there was a reasonable explanation for finding Ariana in Justin's room, for him calling her *Ari*, but my brain wouldn't work when I was this tired. With a groan, I cracked one eyelid. "I promise to tell you everything later, but I didn't get any sleep last night. Go on without me?"

"You don't want to go snorkeling?" Rachel asked. "Or shopping?"

We'd been planning to go shopping for jewelry. Jewelry reminded me of rings, and rings reminded me of engagements, which took me right back to Connor's question and my perfect wedding vision. The wedding I'd never have now. Tears filled my eyes.

Once I got home and Justin told Sarah I'd cheated on him with my ex, she'd probably fire me. Even if she let me explain, even if she believed I didn't do anything, could I handle the constant reminder of Justin and Ariana every time I turned around? But at the end of the day, I suspected Sarah would take

Justin's side. If he believed I cheated, she'd believe it, and I'd be out of a job. That's what happened when you worked with your boyfriend's sister.

When Justin insisted on putting the buyout clause into our contract, Sarah and I both laughed. Why would we ever need something like that? Now I knew. Score one for the lawyer.

After banning me from the bakery, Sarah would throw me out of her apartment. I'd be where I started twenty months ago, only with the image of Ariana in a bathrobe searing my brain instead of nearly naked Danielle.

Even after the way we met, before I got to know Danielle, I never hated her. Dominic lying about his wife was a betrayal. The English language didn't contain a word appropriate to describe Justin sleeping with Ariana behind my back. Maybe there was one in German. Like *die über-heinous betrayalwurst.*

When I didn't answer, concern overtook Rachel's face. "Are you okay? What happened?"

My face crumpled. I couldn't answer. She sat on the bed, one hand on my shoulder, but I couldn't accept her comfort. Not now.

"Just go," I said.

"I'm not leaving until I know you're going to be all right," she said. "What kind of friend do you think I am?"

"I can't talk about it right now," I said. "Let me sleep. I'll catch up with you at lunchtime. Go. Snorkel, shop. I could use some time alone."

"What do I tell your boyfriend when I see him at breakfast?"

She'd know the answer the second he appeared with Ariana. "Don't tell him anything."

A fresh wave of despair hit, and I pulled the sheet over my head. After a heavy sigh didn't convince me to come out of my cocoon, Rachel kissed my forehead through the blanket. A moment later, the door clicked shut, leaving me alone.

All alone.

No Justin. Forever.

When I woke up again, my mind worked much better. Justin and I had been together for more than a year. He planned an entire proposal, and although I accidentally ruined it, he'd brought the ring on the trip with us. He couldn't be planning to walk away from everything we'd been through now. There had to be some kind of explanation for what I'd seen.

Picking up my phone, I sent Justin a message, keeping it casual.

Hey. I'm back on the ship. Crazy long story.

His first response made me smile.

Glad you're OK. We were all worried about you.

Maybe there was a reasonable explanation for what I saw. Maybe everything would be okay.

However, the second text crushed my budding optimism.

On the bus to the rum factory tour with Ariana. We need to talk later.

"We need to talk." The worst four words in the English language. This couldn't be happening. Not to me and Justin. We were solid. This wasn't like Dominic—Justin and I had a foundation, a history, a life together. But for some reason, he'd decided to throw it all away for a woman who'd done nothing but ruin my life.

He didn't come looking for me in the morning to see if I'd gotten back to the ship. Why didn't he come to the smaller boat with Ed and Connor? Had he noticed I was gone, or were he and *Ari* having too much fun onboard to notice I stayed in Jamaica? Surely Ed would have told him I'd been found and they were leaving to pick me up. So what happened?

With a growl, I hurled my phone at the window. It connected with a satisfying clack before thudding onto the carpet.

Things didn't look much brighter when I woke up the second time. As if the universe understood my mood, black clouds blotted out the light through the window. Great. No need to go sightseeing.

Except Rachel would probably appear and drag me down the gangway if I didn't make an appearance for lunch. Grumbling to myself, I rolled over and grabbed my phone. Still dead. In my shock at finding another woman in my boyfriend's bedroom —*again*—I hadn't thought to plug it in before crawling into bed to hide.

Why did this keep happening to me? Was there something fundamentally wrong with me as a girlfriend? Did I lack the ability to please men? Or were they genetically programmed to lose interest after a certain amount of time?

The clock on the television told me it was ten after noon, ship time. That meant people roaming outdoors on Cayman Islands time would want to eat in less than an hour. As much as I didn't want to get up, hiding in the room wouldn't make me feel any better. And I still needed to find Danielle and ask her what happened. Part of me wanted to believe she was the snake I originally thought and that she colluded with Dominic to give him a day alone with me, but the theory didn't gel with the woman who'd become my friend. I didn't want to believe I'd been so wrong about her. Or about Justin.

Maybe I should've stayed in Jamaica. Or maybe I could stay here, avoid having to watch Ariana gloat all over Justin for the next two days. If only I'd paid to upgrade us to a suite on the first day, I could hide out alone. Except Justin and Ariana would probably be in there together. Sigh.

With a jolt, I realized I did know someone who had a suite— and she didn't like Ariana or Dominic any more than I did. Maybe Danielle would let me crash on her couch until we got to Miami. No idea what I'd do after that, but at least I could avoid all members of the Taylor family until we docked.

Although drinking myself into oblivion until I'd forever blotted the image of Ariana in a bathrobe out of my memory appealed to me, the last thing I wanted to do was tour a rum factory. Unfortunately, Tammy Rae planned to be there. We still needed to establish camaraderie. Getting her stupid secret ingredient might be the only way to save this trip from being an utter disaster. Even if I couldn't use it once Sarah exercised the buyout option in our contract, maybe I could wave it in front of me like some kind of peace offering.

Having a ghost of a plan made me feel a scintilla better. Now I needed to get up and face the day. Before dragging myself into the shower, I found my phone charger so I could message Danielle once I got out.

Dominic's words ran through my head on repeat. Had Danielle been playing me this whole time? Pretended to be my friend just to screw me over? Even though my obligation to Sarah meant I should beeline for Tammy Rae the second I left the cabin, I couldn't think straight before finding Danielle and having a chat.

The cruise line's messaging system only worked while people were connected to the ship's Wi-Fi, so I prayed while sending her a quick message to ask where she was before getting in the shower.

After a day of horseback riding, swimming, and boating in the sun, followed by virtually no sleep and wind-swept hair, hot water turned out to be the best thing since sliced bread. As droplets sluiced down my body, a flood of tears followed. My shoulders shook, and my knees buckled, sending me sliding down to the wet floor. When the water turned cold, I finally pulled myself up, blew my nose, and gave myself another mental pep talk to go out and face the world.

My phone, sitting on the tiny bathroom sink, contained three messages I hadn't heard arrive. Thankfully, all from Danielle.

Finishing a late breakfast on the Lido Deck before I head into town. Where are you?

Are you okay?

Rachel told me you didn't make it back to the ship last night. What happened?

She still could be lying. But my gut told me to talk to her before trusting the word of a proven liar, especially one in cahoots with another proven liar. There had to be some reasonable explanation for why Dominic took her place on the excursion.

I sent a quick reply.

Coming to the Lido Deck. Will explain everything in 10.

Not bothering to dry my hair, I ran a comb through it, grabbed a random sundress out of the closet, and slipped my feet into the first two shoes I found. The blue and green patterned sundress might have been Rachel's, but it didn't matter.

My stomach howled on the walk up the stairs, reminding me I'd missed breakfast and eaten very little the night before after a long day of physical exertion. Not wanting to go off on Danielle because I was hungry, I swung by the buffet for a cup of coffee and a cupcake before confronting her.

The tiny vanilla cake felt like a brick in my hand. Even without biting into it, I knew it wouldn't be as good as Sarah's. Just the reminder of our shop—and Justin—made me queasy. When I found Danielle, I let it plop onto the table and fell into the chair.

"You look like shit," she greeted me. Naturally, she looked as gorgeous as ever, in an emerald green halter top and white capris. How did people wear white pants? If I even thought about wearing white on my lower half, I'd immediately start my period while falling into a mud puddle and spilling coffee in my lap. But Danielle looked amazing, her red hair held off her face by giant sunglasses perched atop her head, and her wide eyes full of concern.

"Thanks," I mumbled. "Rough night."

"So I heard. That can't be your breakfast. Here." She picked up a plate off her tray, covered with scrambled eggs and bacon and scones. "I got this for you."

My stomach emitted a sound like a dying whale, but no way

was I accepting food from the person who'd conspire to stick me with Dominic for the entire day. I pushed the plate away and gulped my coffee instead.

"What happened to you?" I asked. "Why weren't you on the boat to the mainland?"

"Ugh." She wrinkled her nose and grabbed a slice of bacon off the plate she'd handed me. "I feel awful about that. Monday night, I went to the club after dinner. I was drinking and dancing and… next thing I knew, I woke up on Tuesday with a mariachi band playing inside my skull. The excursion completely slipped my mind."

"That's it? You got drunk and forgot about me?" For some reason, that hurt almost as much as if she'd intentionally betrayed me.

"I didn't think I drank very much," she said. "The drinks on this ship are weak, you know? Mostly water. So after I woke up again, feeling like I'd been hit by a dumpster, I went to the club and asked some questions."

She gestured to the man who'd been busing the tables around us since before I sat down. He approached with a big smile and a name tag identifying him as Julio from Mixco, Guatemala. They spoke in Spanish for a moment while I wished I'd spent more time listening to the Rosetta Stone CDs Justin bought me for Christmas.

Finally, Julio turned to me and introduced himself. "I work at the nightclub on Monday evening. I served Ms. Danielle here."

"Yeah?"

"Yes, ma'am. She only ordered two drinks." He held his finger up in a vee. "But this other man, he paid me hundred-dollar tip to keep her glass full. I brought her many drinks throughout the night. Ms. Danielle was dancing, she didn't notice."

My spidey senses tingled. "How many?"

He shrugged. "Nine? Ten?"

My mouth dropped. Nine or ten drinks consumed by someone Danielle's size?

She turned to Julio. "Can you describe this man for us?"

"I'm sorry, ma'am. I never saw him. But I have this note?" Julio pulled a folded piece of paper out of his pocket and offered it to me. My hand shook as I opened it.

The words didn't matter. The writing mattered: the same scrawl I'd seen on half a dozen birthday cards, anniversary cards, and "I miss you notes" mailed while my ex-boyfriend couldn't see me because of his "travels."

"Dominic," I said. Danielle nodded and thanked Julio, who left.

"Well, shit," I said.

She nodded a second time. My appetite returned full force, and I pulled the plate of eggs toward me.

"I'm really sorry, Jen," she said. "I had no idea what he planned. I'm already drafting an angry email to my lawyer."

"That doesn't help me," I said.

Quickly, I filled her in on our day shore side, followed by what I found in Justin's room in the morning. By the time I finished, her eyes resembled saucers.

"There's no way," she said. "No way Justin slept with her. She was probably there looking for Dominic. Aren't they sharing a cabin?"

"Then why didn't he come after me?"

"You'll need to ask him that," she said. "But what are you going to do about Dominic and Ariana?"

I chewed thoughtfully before responding. "I promised Leanna a showdown in exchange for getting me back on the boat. After Tammy Rae gives me her recipe, Ariana's going to get it."

SIXTEEN

MORE FROM THE GUPPY GABBER, THURSDAY:

Ariana: *I don't think Jen ever loved Justin. She wanted him because I liked him, and now that I'm with Dominic, she's tossed Justin aside like garbage so she can once again take my man from me.*

Jen, Noon: *I don't want to talk about Justin and Ariana right now. Today's the day. I'm going to get Tammy Rae's recipe for Sweet Reality or die trying. Preferably the first one. Wish me luck.*

Ah, "reality" television. Where you flat-out lie about how incredible you're feeling until someone starts to believe you. Preferably yourself, but if I could get ten thousand people out in TV Land to think I felt good about my chances of success with Tammy Rae, maybe I'd feel better myself.

After the utter failure of every single thing I tried to do all week, the thought of trying to wheedle a secret out of a near stranger who probably thought I stood her up the night before didn't exactly fill me with excitement.

Even if things with Justin weren't weird, after missing my chance to bond with Tammy Rae on Tuesday night, she might not appreciate me tracking her down on the rum factory tour. I prayed I'd catch up with her before her, um, exuberance over the rum made conversation difficult. Alternatively, I hoped she'd be so drunk she'd spill the entire recipe and not remember.

On the docks, the tour bus had long since left, so I caught a taxi to take me to the factory. Ed and Rachel stood at the end of a line that snaked its way around the parking lot and into the building. I ran to catch up to them.

"There you are!" Rachel said. "Ed filled me in on your day yesterday. What the hell happened this morning? Why did you come to the room instead of grabbing breakfast with Justin?"

"Ariana happened," I said glumly.

"Oh yeah?" She pulled out her phone and tapped a few times, then turned the screen to face me. My image filled the small device, but I wasn't alone. Dominic's lips firmly pressed against mine. Freaking Ty. After getting me high, the least he could've done was not sell the picture.

Unless that was why he got me high. I swallowed a scream of frustration and kicked the ground. Stubbing my toe didn't make me feel any better. "It's not what you think."

"It's not? Enlighten me."

Briefly, I explained about the brownies, the unexpected lip attack, and the slap, none of which had naturally been captured on film. "Do you think Justin saw that?"

Ed nodded. "It's all over the pier, and someone passed it around our bus on the way here. I'm surprised you didn't see it yourself."

"Wait. He's here? I need to find him." Then I remembered Ariana answering the door in his room. Maybe it was too late already. Before he saw the picture, Justin apparently decided he didn't care whether I stayed in Jamaica.

Rachel shook her head. "He and Ariana took off a few minutes we arrived. I don't know where they went, but she didn't look right. Stumbling around like she was already drunk."

Of course. Pain slashed through me. I stared at the ground, willing myself not to cry, but the ground in front of me blurred. What a mess. Somehow, I'd ruined everything.

Rachel wrapped her arms around me, and I buried my face in her shoulder, not caring at all about the cameras or the other people in line. Behind her, Ed cracked jokes at the crowd. "She heard a rumor they're out of rum. It's all good."

Their concern touched my heart, gave me what I needed to pull myself together. Sniffling, I wiped my face on the tissues I'd wisely stuffed into my bag before leaving my cabin.

"Are you okay?" Ed asked.

Rachel said, "You can go back to the ship if you want. We won't mind."

"I love you guys for offering, but I have to find Tammy Rae and explain why I didn't meet her last night. We were supposed to talk about her recipe for Sweet Reality, and I need to find her before she changes her mind."

A few minutes later, we reached the front of the line and entered the building. I spotted Tammy Rae's long blond hair disappearing into one of the tasting rooms a few feet away. With quick hugs and thanks to Ed and Rachel, I took off after her.

At first, I smiled and stood near Tammy Rae, not talking so she could listen to the tour. When she spotted me, she pursed her lips and looked away. My heart sank.

Still, I needed to keep trying. When we got to the tasting room at the end, I pulled up a seat.

"I'm so sorry I couldn't find you last night," I began.

She waved one hand. "I'm over it. At first, I thought, maybe you didn't want the recipe after all."

"No, I absolutely want it! I missed the final catamaran in Jamaica."

"Really." She tilted her head at me. "Wow. That's dumb.

Really dumb. So dumb, it's not quite believable. Weren't you the brains of your season?"

"Smart people do dumb things all the time," I said. "But this wasn't my fault."

Briefly, I explained what happened. By the time I finished my story, she looked a fraction less hostile. I sipped my rum, hoping she'd do the same and she'd feel more gracious toward me.

Ugh. The liquid burned down my throat. Even "good" rum made me want to puke. But I'd have this conversation while snorting rum through my nose if that's what Tammy Rae wanted. I needed her help, especially after yesterday. By sheer willpower, I avoided hacking up a lung while Tammy closed her eyes and sipped from her mug, apparently near ecstasy.

She emptied half the glass before acknowledging me again. "You're lucky to catch up to us."

Not wanting to explain my deal with Leanna, I nodded and sipped from my glass again.

"If you're going to use my secret ingredient, I want everyone to know it," she said. "You have to attach my face."

"You want us to draw your face in icing on each cupcake?" Sarah was a talented baker, and all our baked goods looked pretty, but I didn't know about her portrait skills.

"It doesn't have to be *on* the cupcake." She rolled her eyes at me. "Create a display with my name and a promo shot from the show. Preferably the episode where I won. Then, I want a royalty on all the profits from those cupcakes. Fifty percent."

Half? She wanted half what we made on the cupcakes for telling us one measly ingredient? She wasn't giving up the whole recipe! Besides, what if it turned out to be a "secret" ingredient like the brownies I got in Jamaica were a "special" recipe? Sarah would kill me if I gave up so much of our profits without knowing what we'd be getting in return.

I swallowed, searching for a diplomatic response. "I'll have to speak with my partner before I can agree to that."

"Go. Call her."

"She's in Miami. It would cost me ten dollars a minute to call her from Grand Cayman. If we can get to Wi-Fi, I'll send her a message. But maybe we can reach an agreement on our own. What if I give you a thousand dollars right now for the secret ingredient? You tell me what it is, and we'll work out the percentages on our own."

Paying off former child stars wasn't in the bakery's budget, but I had some money left from *The Fishbowl*, and I'd be getting a per diem from the show for this week. Thirty bucks a day covered almost a quarter of what I offered her. I could afford to match what Sarah and I originally agreed to pay her. If the cupcakes turned out half as well as we hoped, we'd make a profit soon enough.

She tapped her chin with one long, electric blue fingernail. "You'll have to sign something promising never to tell anyone what it is."

"As will you," I said, pulling a piece of paper out of my back pocket. "We can't pay you for a secret ingredient if you're going to turn around and sell the recipe to Betty Crocker."

This move was pure bluff on my part. According to Justin, the Network actually owned all recipes created on their cooking shows. That's why we weren't asking for the entire thing: Tammy Rae needed the producers' consent to sell her award-winning cupcake recipe. Our goal was to get the secret ingredient, come up with something similar enough to the cupcake currently secured in my cabin's refrigerator, and market it at as "inspired by Tammy Rae's *Totally 80s Bake-off* winning cupcakes." We had zero legal right to interfere with the Network's selling it to third parties, so this contract basically meant nothing. Not that Tammy Rae needed to know that.

"You brought a contract?"

I shrugged. "My boyfriend's a lawyer. Or he will be, once he gets his bar exam results on Friday."

Ex-boyfriend, my traitorous brain piped up. I couldn't believe things might be over, not when we'd been on the brink of getting engaged. We had to work things out, right? Except, after what I saw this morning and Justin's "we need to talk" text, I didn't see how making up could be possible. I'd never felt so alone.

"What's wrong?"

If she'd responded with derision or continued talking about how stupid it was to go into business with a friend, I probably could've pulled myself together. But she tilted her head at me, her blue eyes searching mine. Tears prickled my eyelids, and I looked away, blinking furiously. Tammy Rae couldn't see me cry. She seemed more the type to accuse me of emotional blackmail than to say anything helpful. I'd lose all the ground I'd gained with her, and I could kiss my chances of getting the recipe good-bye. Just like the man I loved. *Oh, no.*

When I didn't respond to Tammy Rae's question, she leaned forward and put one hand on my shoulder, like my mom used to do when I was in high school. "Jen? Is everything all right?"

Her sympathy undid my composure. I let out a wail and buried my head in her shoulder. "I think we broke up!"

She signaled a waiter over my head, and a second later, two drinks appeared as if by magic. "Oh, honey. Tell me everything."

The entire story spilled out: Ariana's original quest for Justin, which Tammy Rae had watched on the show; bringing my ex as her "date" purely to drive a wedge between us; getting stranded with Dom in Jamaica; finding Ariana in Justin's room when I got back, and the worst part: that stupid, horrible, fraction of a second kiss I hadn't initiated or responded to.

When I finished, Tammy Rae leaned back and shut her eyes, saying nothing. Great. On top of everything else, now she thought I was some whiny lunatic.

"I'm sorry to hear you and Justin are having problems," Tammy Rae said. "Do you remember what I said to you the other day?"

"I know, I know, I'm an idiot for going into business with my boyfriend's sister. Especially without a ring on my finger. But we have a contract. And once I give Sarah your recipe, I'm hoping she'll forgive me. She still needs my help. For one thing, she can't afford to buy me out yet. But also, she doesn't know anything about marketing or bringing in customers or branding. She needs me for marketing."

"That's not what I meant," Tammy Rae said.

For the life of me, I couldn't figure out what she was talking about. "You want to throw in an autographed picture for my mom? Or buy your CD?"

She reached over and whacked the side of my head with one hand. "Are you drunk? I'm talking about our conversation on Tuesday, while zip-lining."

I wracked my brain through the haze of rum and sadness. Finally, a lightbulb went on. "Oh! You said we were an inspiration."

"Right. Jen and Justin were an inspiration. Not Jen and Justin's twin sister I've never met. Not Jen, all alone. You and Justin, together, are what warmed the cockles of my blackened heart. But you're not some fairy tale romance after all. You're nothing but a showmance, after all. Worse, you're such a poorly executed one you couldn't carry out the farce for another three days."

My mouth dropped open. "You think we faked our whole relationship to get your stupid secret ingredient?"

"No. I think you faked it to win *The Fishbowl*. When that didn't work, you used your popularity to fake it again to try to steal my cupcake recipe. Which wasn't so stupid when you offered me a thousand dollars not two minutes ago." She practically spit the words at me, growing angrier by the second. "But you fucked up by running away to make out with someone else. Then Justin couldn't keep it in his pants until the end of the week, and now you're going home with nothing."

Her words hit home so hard, I flinched. I bit my tongue, because nothing I possibly said in response could fix this moment. Every time I thought things couldn't get any worse, they did. All I wanted was to rewind the last two days and start over.

Before I figured out what to do, someone on the other side of the room said my name. A moan followed. I turned to find Rachel doubled over, heaving. As much as I wanted to convince Tammy Rae she was wrong about us, this wasn't the time.

"Are you okay?" I asked Rachel, hurrying to her side. "Where's Ed?"

"I wandered away while he was talking to Connor," she said. "I think I need to go. I'm so sorry. I don't know where we left the ship. And the world is moving so fast. Can I lie down?"

The poor thing swayed on her feet. A couple of inches in one direction or the other, and the dozen or so bottles she carried from the gift shop would hit the ground. Rachel needed me. And my conversation with Tammy Rae was clearly over, possibly forever. "Yeah, honey. We'll go lie down. Come on."

Taking the cardboard containers carrying the rum from her, I wrapped one of Rachel's arms around my shoulder, and put my right arm around her waist. Luckily, she was only a couple of inches taller than me, and *The Fishbowl*'s three-legged race challenges taught me how to walk awkwardly with someone else. I handed her one of the boxes to carry in her free hand, lifted the other with a grunt, and the two of us staggered away.

"I'm sorry I ruined your day," Rachel moaned. "Did you get the recipe?"

"No, I didn't," I said. She didn't need details right then. "But it's okay. I'll come up a backup plan. Let's get you to bed, okay?"

"That's what she said!" She giggled. "The door's behind us!"

Of course it was. With some effort, I turned the cheerleader around and headed for the door. Tammy Rae stood a couple of feet from where I originally left her, leaning against the bar.

"I'm sorry Justin and I couldn't be your perfect 'fairy tale couple,'" I said to her back. "We're human people, not celebrities, and we've made some mistakes. But our relationship is real. At least it was, before Ariana ruined it."

Tammy Rae didn't move or respond. I had no idea if she heard me. But it didn't matter. Getting Rachel to the ship safely where she could sleep it off mattered. Once we got there, maybe, just maybe, I could sleep away days of frustration and heartache.

SEVENTEEN

STILL MORE FROM THE GUPPY GABBER, THURSDAY:

Justin: *I wanted to tour the Tortuga Rum Factory with the group, but Ari wasn't feeling well, so we left. She's taking the news about Jen and Dominic hard. So am I, I guess. I can't believe she'd cheat on me, after everything we've been through.*

Ed: *Can Rachel and I squeeze in together? Fabulous, thanks. When my friend did this cruise years ago, they bought thirteen bottles of alcohol. Amateurs. We doubled that.*

Rachel: *"Reality TV." Is that a misnomer? Is any of this real? Should we believe everything we see? Or are other forces at work?*

Ed: *Don't mind her.*

Rachel: *Rum makes me so deep, y'all. I like rum. Don't tell, America, but I think Ed may have gotten me drunk. I slept for two hours, and I'm still feeling it.*

Tammy Rae: *Dude, the factory tour rocked. That blonde girl got totally hammered! I guess reality TV contestants can't hold their* *liquor like a former rock star. Of course, I've got a good twenty years of drinking on her. *hiccup**

Rachel promptly passed out once I got her to our room, before I finished tucking her into bed. Not knowing what else to do after a crappy morning followed by a worse afternoon, I climbed into the other bunk bed without undressing and pulled the covers over my head.

Approximately nine minutes later, I realized that wasn't going to help anything. Rachel's snores made it impossible to get a good mope in, and even if they didn't, moping for more than a few minutes wasn't my style. I was a plotter, a planner. The cure to my heartbreak lay in getting up and doing things, not lying here and staring at the bottom of the upper bunk, bored out of my mind.

The ship still sat in the port, so much of the onboard entertainment remained closed, but the running track on the top deck could be accessed any time. Once I admitted to myself that sleep would be impossible, I changed, grabbed my iPod, and headed for the stairs.

In the lobby, I spotted Ed waiting for the elevator. "How's Rachel? I looked up halfway through the tour, and she'd vanished."

"She got *hammered*. She's sleeping it off."

"And you?"

I started to say something upbeat, but my face crumpled. Ed wrapped his arms around me. I buried my face in his shoulder and sobbed.

"It's going to be okay," he said. "Justin loves you. You love him. He has to know you'd never willingly kiss your ex."

"What about Ariana? He called her *Ari!*"

"There has to be a reasonable explanation."

"He regrets picking me?"

"I said reasonable, not utterly ridiculous. He never wanted her, and you know it."

That didn't make me feel any better. Sleeping with someone he didn't like was worse than someone he did. Instead of answering, I pressed my lips together and held my breath, burying my face in his shoulder. Ed rubbed my back until I got control of my breathing.

"Thanks," I said several minutes later. "Sorry to mess up your shirt."

"No problem," he said. "I'll send you the dry cleaning bill."

The elevator dinged, and the doors opened behind us. I'd planned to take the stairs, but since the elevator was here, and so was Ed, I might as well talk to him on the way up. Then I spotted Ariana exiting the open doors, with Justin a few steps behind her. She walked by me, nose in the air, as if I wasn't there at all.

Something slammed into my shoulders. I stumbled forward, through the doors. It took me a second to realize Ed must have pushed me. I put my arms out to catch myself, colliding with Justin's chest. Momentum carried us into the far wall with a thud. In the tight space, our bodies reacted with familiarity, forgetting the events of the past two days. Justin's arms wrapped around me reflexively, and my lips skimmed his ear. He sighed, pulling me closer.

I leaned into him without thinking, feeling every line of his body with mine, taking in his scent. *Mmmmmm.*

When we were on *The Fishbowl* together, everyone smelled like suntan oil and Dreft detergent. Being on the cruise, breathing in the coconut scent overpowering his usual musk and hair gel, reminded me of the days when we first met. How my fingers always itched to touch him, but the cameras and the uncertainty held me back. With a sigh I let myself relax against him before Ariana's outraged shriek penetrated my brain, reminding me of everything we'd been through.

Right. Ariana. Not in the Fishbowl. Not at home, either, where we belonged. On the cruise. Ariana in a bathrobe. In Justin's room, early in the morning. Where she had no business being.

Justin's green eyes gazed at me from the floor where we'd both landed. "Are you okay?"

"Fine." I struggled to my feet and turned toward the front of the elevator. A long brown arm pushed the top floor button before vanishing through the closing doors. "Ed pushed me into you. I'm so sorry."

I reached down to help him up, his warm palm sending tingles up my spine. I gasped and pulled away, hoping he didn't see the effect he had on me. But of course he knew. He'd always known. Ever since our eyes first met at the audition, and my stomach filled with butterflies that had nothing to do with getting onto the show, he'd known exactly how he affected me because he felt the same way.

I loved him so much. And he'd slept with Ariana while I'd been trapped on a boat with my ex-boyfriend. I couldn't begin to think what to say to him. All rational thought left me.

The elevator lurched upward, headed from floor eight to eighteen. *Shit.* I couldn't stay here. I needed to escape, get out of this elevator before he registered my red eyes. Before he realized I wasn't out of breath because of the fall. When I reached to press any other button to stop us earlier, my fingertips brushed the cool metal wall. We were in the express elevator straight to the pool. No escape until the top deck.

Fine. Maybe I couldn't leave in this enclosed space with Justin, but I didn't have to talk to him. Not until he apologized profusely and possibly denounced Ariana as the true devil on national television.

"So you're not speaking to me at all? Is that it?"

I lifted my chin into the air, hoping he couldn't hear my pounding heart. "I'm not sure what there is for either of us to say after last night."

"Maybe you're right, but I feel like more than a year of history shouldn't be thrown away without so much as a conversation."

He was right. I turned to face him, leaving my arms crossed over my chest like they protected my heart from being shattered by whatever he said next. "We definitely should talk. I'd love to know why Ariana spent the night in your room when I'd gone missing, and you didn't have any way of knowing if I was alive or dead."

"I knew you were alive, Jen. I'd have felt it if you weren't." Disbelief filled his eyes. "I meant, I was going to give you a chance to explain why you were making out with your ex-boyfriend in front of the tabloids."

The words and his tone lit a fire in me. I wanted to slap the smug look off his face. How dare he look at me like this was all my fault?

"Me? *You'll* let *me* explain? The ship left without me. I spent a miserable day abandoned in a foreign country with my ex-boyfriend, the first hours of which I spent wondering how or if I'd manage to return to America. When I finally make it to the ship, you've got another woman in your room!" Fury made me spit the words at him. "So, thanks for the opportunity to 'explain,' but I'm not the one who needs to account for their behavior."

"You're not? Well, let's see. You dawdled over breakfast, leaving us to take the last boat to shore. You sent me to your cabin, causing me to miss the catamaran. Instead of turning around and returning to the ship or waiting for me on the dock, you spent the day with your ex, who's been panting after you since the minute we got onboard."

"You offered to get my sunblock! I would've done it myself. Don't put that on me. I had no idea you'd stop to chat with Ariana on your way to join me."

"What are you talking about?"

"I saw you, Justin. On the floating dock. She appeared in the doorway right behind you. What happened? Did she ask you to untangle something else? A knot in her bikini?"

He flinched at the reminder of the first time we almost kissed on the show. Ariana had appeared out of nowhere, naked, to go for a midnight swim. I stormed away after she asked Justin to help get her necklace unstuck from her hair.

"What are you talking about? I went to your cabin, like I said I would. Rachel gave me your sunblock, and I headed down to the floating dock. Halfway there, the staircase was closed. Apparently, the front of the ship is roped off in the mornings for cleaning. I had to go up three flights, run across the eighth level, and head back down to get to you in time." He shook his head. "I didn't see Ari until after the boat pulled away from the floating dock. She got locked out of the stairs, too."

Jealousy stabbed me in the gut every time he said her name like that. "What's up with that? Ari? You two have nicknames now?"

"We spent almost twenty-four hours together after our dates floated away to spend the day together—and never came back. So, yeah, we're friends now. You've always thought the worst of her, but she's actually nice when she's not trying too hard to impress people."

At those words, I saw red. "That's the point. Dominic and I didn't ditch you guys. Or I didn't. I tried to make the catamaran wait, and I asked if I could come straight back instead of going on the excursion. Ask the captain. Or ask the PA, Janine. She saw everything."

"Janine never returned to the ship after Jamaica."

The blood drained from my face. I pondered the implications of his words. "You mean…? Oh, hell. Someone set us up."

"What are you talking about?"

"I used those stairs to get to the floating dock. All the doors were open and unlocked. Janine appeared right behind me. She saw me try to talk the captain of the catamaran into waiting for you or letting me off the boat. She got stung by a jellyfish, *allegedly*, setting off the string of events that led to missing the boat to the ship." Realization dawned on his face. "So, it's very convenient that the only person who could tell you what really happened has mysteriously vanished."

"You think the Network set us up?"

"The Network, or more likely, Ariana set us up. Again. She's been trying to get between us since Day One. Dominic must've closed the stairway behind him on the way to the floating dock. And someone sent Janine away. It's all too perfect."

"Do you have any proof? How is any of this Ariana's fault and not Dominic's or the Network's?"

Damn lawyers and their love of hard evidence. Of course I didn't have proof, and he knew it. "Once upon a time, you'd have taken my word over hers. I know she's behind this. She has to be."

"Ariana didn't do this. I know she didn't. We spent the whole day together."

My eyes filled with tears. "Would you believe her over me, after everything we've been through?"

"It's not about believing or not believing you," he said. "You're guessing. You may hate Ariana because of how she acted on the show, but she's been great all week. Yeah, she made a stupid joke the first day, but she apologized right away. She's been nothing but nice to us ever since. She didn't know her agent was setting up Dominic as her date. I believe Dominic masterminded the whole thing, and maybe his ex-wife helped or maybe it was Leanna trying to boost ratings, but I swear, Ari wouldn't have done this. She really is trying to make amends."

I did a double take. "Why on earth would Danielle help Dominic get me back? She hates him as much as I do."

"She likes fame, though. She likes the show she got after their breakup, which is on the verge of being canceled. She likes the camera time she's getting from the two of you being so buddy-buddy, and she probably thinks your friendship will get her contract renewed. You're too trusting, Jen. Constantly pointing the finger at Ariana, when the real fox in your henhouse is Danielle."

"I talked to Danielle. She produced a waiter who said Dominic paid him to ply her with alcohol all night. He showed me a note in Dominic's handwriting. Danielle had nothing to do with this."

"Then it sounds like the issue is Dominic, not Ari," he said. "I know she was awful before, but she really is turning over a new leaf. You'd know that if you spent some time with her. And Ariana isn't the real issue here. Even if she set the whole thing up, she didn't make you kiss anyone. I noticed you skipped over that part when summarizing your terrible day. Good kiss?"

I flinched. The kiss. That meaningless kiss I ended immediately. I wanted to strangle Dominic.

"I didn't kiss him. Dominic—"

Before I could finish, the elevator ground to a halt. The doors dinged open.

"It doesn't matter who started it, Jen. We're not kids on a playground. I know what I saw." With that, he turned and walked away.

In the lobby, Ariana waited, alone. Ed was nowhere in sight. When Justin approached, Ariana put one hand on his chest, and they spoke in low voices.

Not knowing what else to do, I stood in the elevator, watching helplessly, trying to will him to turn around. Tears blurred my vision. My mouth opened and closed, but my throat wouldn't allow any words to come out. Not even the apology he deserved, the explanation I so desperately wished I could give. How had things gone so horribly wrong? Why didn't we trust each other, after everything we'd been through?

But one thought stuck with me. Maybe he thought I'd done something horrible, but how could he have flown into the arms of my archenemy without talking to me? This mess wasn't entirely my fault. I didn't go have sex with Dominic after finding

Ariana in Justin's room. Or one of the thousand other unattached men on this cruise ship.

My heart lurched. I wanted to say something, anything, to try to make things better. But instead, Ariana said something, her voice low. Then my boyfriend put his arm around her shoulders, and the two of them walked away together. The doors slid shut, leaving me all alone.

EIGHTEEN

QUEEN KELLY'S VOICE
EXPLORE COZUMEL & PLAYA DEL CARMEN, MEXICO

Friday edition

This morning, we cruise into the beautiful port of Cozumel shortly before sunrise. We'll drop anchor at the floating dock and take guests over to the island by catamaran beginning at 7:30 AM.

In Cozumel, a variety of activities await you. On the far side of the island, swim with stingrays, snorkel, scuba-dive, or water-ski with our tour guides. Take a 35-minute ferry ride across the sea to Playa del Carmen, where you can tour Aztec ruins, either on foot or on horseback. Or stay on our island here for some excellent shopping, Mexican food, entertainment, and more!

We set sail sharply at 5:00 PM, so leave yourself plenty of time to return to the dock. Cozumel time is an hour earlier than ship time. We sail on ship time, not local time.

For those staying onboard today, venture into our casino at 9 AM to play poker with your favorite stars. Prizes awarded for both the fan and the reality TV star with the highest score at the end. All participants receive points, which may be redeemed for onboard credit, usable to purchase alcohol, souvenirs, onboard dining, or casino credit.

Don't know how to play? No problem! Start with a brief tutorial from Tammy Rae. Tutorials run every 15 minutes, beginning at 8 AM. Please note: the regular casino will not be accessible while we are in port; all slot machines, cashiers, and non-tournament tables will be closed until 6 PM.

Inside this Edition:

THE SHIP ROCKED. Sirens blared. I struggled to breathe as smoke poured through the room. We were going down! I needed to find Justin. No, wait. Justin didn't want me anymore. Where was Rachel? I needed to get off this ship. The air was so thick, I couldn't move. I clawed and thrashed, getting nowhere.

"Jen. *Jennifer!*" Rachel's voice penetrated my panicked mind. My eyes flew open. Sheets cocooned me, and both my tiny hotel pillows lay on the floor.

"We're sinking. There's a fire. We have to get off the ship, now!"

"No, we're not." She gripped my shoulders, speaking firmly.

Finally, her words penetrated my sleepy brain. "You're having a bad dream. It's okay. We're fine."

Outside the door, a voice spoke continuously on the speakers in the hall. I strained, but couldn't hear the words. "Then what's the announcement? Why are there sirens and alarms? And why are we still rocking so much?"

"There's a rough sea today. The catamarans to the mainland and the far side of the island can't make it. They sent an alert to our phones through the messaging app, and it's on the TV. But that's it. Take a look."

Before reaching for my phone, I peeked out the window beside my bed. Waves covered half of it, creating a moving diagonal line of water. Water pelted the sea from above. Watching it nauseated me. The skies were as gray as my mood, and the water matched. Nothing beautiful or paradise-like outside our window.

Rachel was right: Bad weather woke me. A storm. Not a fire. We weren't sinking. It was a nightmare.

"Thanks, Rach. I'm an idiot."

"No, you're not. The guy doing the announcement said things like 'emergency trips only.' It's easy for your subconscious to distort that. But the important thing is, we're fine. Even if we can't tour the Mayan ruins today."

"No ruins?" I'd signed up for the tour with Justin, so I didn't know whether to be disappointed I wouldn't make it. Better not to see him and Ariana walking around together all day, hand-in-hand. Not that the reality probably looked much worse—or much better—than the torturous images on constant repeat inside my head.

Rachel shook her head. "No, but get up. Since we're stuck onboard, I'm going to enter the poker tournament. Want to join me?"

Usually, I'd enjoy playing cards for a few hours. When we'd been locked up on *The Fishbowl,* I'd made my cards to pass the time. But then I remembered who was hosting the poker tournament.

Ugh. I didn't have the heart to spend another day getting insulted by Tammy Rae. I needed a plan before I approached her again. If only I could talk to Sarah, find out whether the recipe would make a difference if Justin didn't love me anymore. After what happened in the elevator, as much as I wanted to work things out, the future seemed bleak. If I was going to get fired either way, I could go sit at the free bar on the Lido Deck for the rest of the cruise.

With a groan, I flopped onto the mattress, pulling the sheets over my head. "You go on without me. And hand me a pillow?"

Rachel responded with a heavy sigh and her foot tapping against the floor. "Are you planning to mope all day?"

Through the sheets, I said, "Well, the man I love is sleeping with the person who tried to ruin my life and smear me on national television, and I'm stuck on this boat with them both until Sunday. Then, when we dock, I have to find my own ride home, because he won't drive me now, and then I'll have to move out of his sister's apartment and find a new job. So, yes, I plan to mope all day."

A hand fell on the top of my head. "I'm sorry, honey. The two of you just need a few days to think, gain some perspective. You can still work it out. But I'll leave you alone."

The door clicking into place swallowed my "don't count on it." That was fine. Arguing with Rachel, on top of everything else, would only take the cruise from "a total disaster" to "the worst experience of my life." Grumbling under my breath, I grabbed my pillows off the floor, flopped over, and willed the day to pass faster.

Some time later, my phone beeped, waking me. The skies outside were still gray, and the ship still rocked more than usual, so I must not have been out long. I found a message from Ed, sent through the ship's messaging system.

You have to get down here.

Where? Why? I replied.

He said,

I'm in the casino. With Rachel and Tammy Rae. They're facing off against each other.

So?

My stomach growled. Darn Ed for waking me up. Now I'd have to find food before I could go back to sleep. Room service always took at least an hour, which meant I'd have to leave the room now. Unfortunately, visiting the buffet up on the Lido Deck greatly increased the odds of running into people I couldn't stand to see at the moment. Or ever again, in some cases.

Rachel asked Tammy Rae if she wanted to throw in a side bet to make things more interesting. If she wins, Tammy Rae has to give you the secret ingredient.

Suddenly, the room brightened. Even after the way I'd been moping for half the trip, Rachel really made a special bet just to help me? My heart grew three sizes at the thought of anyone doing something so selfless for me after I'd been such a misery. I didn't deserve such a wonderful friend.

My fingers flew over my screen, sending a reply.

That's amazing! Hug her for me before I get there?

I sent another text.

What did Tammy Rae say?

She agreed, but if she wins, Rachel has to shave her head. She's super confident. Get down here to show moral support.

Imagining the expression on Rachel's face at the idea of losing her perfect blond hair made me giggle. In time, it would grow back, but the thoughtfulness of her gesture improved my spirits considerably. Maybe Dominic and Ariana ruined my relationship with Justin and I was going to lose my home and my job, but at least I had some amazing friends who cared about me. That meant a lot. Especially if one of them had a couch for me to sleep on.

I'm on my way. Swinging by the buffet for coffee.

They're on a ten-minute break. Bring me a muffin? And one for Danielle. Thx. :-*

It took less than two minutes to grab a sundress out of the closet, stuff my feet into a pair of flat sandals, and finger-comb my hair into a ponytail. Eight minutes after I read Ed's last message, I arrived in the casino carrying a cup of coffee, a plateful of baked goods, and a lighter heart than I'd carried since Tuesday morning.

The casino was the one part of the ship I hadn't visited at all yet. Ringing slot machines gave me a headache, and the Network wasn't funding anyone's gambling habits. If I wanted to come in here and play games instead of being out in the world, creating drama for the viewers, it would be on my dime. And while I loved board games, card games, and puzzles, I didn't love watching my money spin away from me and down the drain.

The room took up the entire port side of the ship. Rows of slot machines ran along the near wall. Plush carpet with colorful swirls covered the floor. As the boat rocked, the motion and pattern started to hypnotize me until I dragged my eyes away. About a dozen poker tables filled the center of the room, with more slot machines behind the tables farthest from me. A cloud of smoke rose from that section. On the far side of the room, the one feature distinguishing this casino from others I'd seen was a lounge area with a row of windows. I'd never seen a casino where people had any way of gauging when time passed.

Tammy Rae held court at the center table, signing autographs for fans during the break. Rumor said she used to be a high roller at the top of her fame. It made sense when my mom told me Tammy Rae would appear on *Celebrity Poker Matchup*, but I hadn't thought about any of it after she dropped out at the last minute. At the end of the season, her replacement came in eighteenth out of twenty.

Now, I wondered why Rachel thought she could beat someone who'd been playing high stakes tables in Vegas since practically before she was born. We'd played a little while on the show, but Rachel never came across as a card sharp. She mostly played for the social interaction, or so it seemed. I prayed she had better luck this trip than I did.

Across from Tammy Rae sat Rachel, chatting with Ed. The crowd parted when I started toward them, creating a path straight to Rachel's side. "Hey, you don't have to do this," I said.

"I know," she said. "But you're having a terrible week, and you need something to take your mind off everything. Besides, I've got the bone structure to pull off a bald head."

Leaning forward, I kissed her on the cheek. "You're an amazing friend. But try to win, okay?"

"I always win, remember? Cheerleading champion, hog-tying champion, winner of *The Fishbowl*?"

"Good point. She destroyed me in the finale," Ed said.

"Exactly. I can handle a poker game. More importantly, I can handle Tammy Rae."

At the front of the room, Leanna blew a whistle. I hadn't noticed her standing there holding a microphone. "Okay, everyone! Break's over. It's time for the final round. Tammy Rae versus Rachel, heads-up. Now, this is a friendly tournament, so both start the final table with twenty-five thousand in chips. Blinds double every five minutes, starting at fifty and one hundred dollars."

My mouth went dry, and my heart pounded as the dealer dealt the first two cards. On my left, Ed gripped my hand. Danielle made her way through the crowd, moving to my right. With the two of them flanking me, my breathing evened out.

After looking at her cards, Tammy Rae checked, meaning she passed the bet to Rachel without adding anything. Rachel threw a red chip toward the center of the table.

"That's a thousand," Ed whispered to me.

A thousand dollars? On the first hand? What was she doing? She only had twenty-five thousand in chips to spend! Tammy Rae raised the bet to three thousand. I silently begged Rachel to drop out, but she called, and the dealer laid three cards down in the center of the table.

Ace of diamonds. Ten of diamonds. Ace of spades. Everyone had a pair of aces. Not a bad start. Tammy Rae checked to Rachel again, who bet ten thousand. My mouth fell open. Beside me, Danielle squeezed my hand.

"Try not to move or react," she whispered in my ear. "You don't know what cards Rach has. You don't know what Tammy Rae has. If Rachel is bluffing, you don't want to give her away by mistake."

Hoping I seemed nonchalant, I sipped my coffee while Tammy Rae called the bet. The fourth card flipped face-up onto the table. Three of Clubs. Tammy Rae checked, and Rachel stood. "I'm all-in."

The crowd gasped. Spots danced in front of my eyes. All the air evaporated from the room.

All-in on the first hand? With a pair of aces on the table? What was she doing? Ed stepped closer, bolstering me with his shoulder. Danielle stood ramrod straight, not moving or reacting, just like she advised me to do.

Tammy Rae tapped one finger against her mouth for a long moment. I held my breath. Finally, she set her cards down and shoved her chips toward the center. "I'm all-in, too."

She also stood, and the crowd shoved in around them. The front of the table dug into my ribs, but I already couldn't breathe, so it didn't matter. The dealer flipped Rachel's cards over first. Ace of Hearts, Ace of Clubs.

"Four of a kind," the dealer announced. Four aces! What an awesome hand! Then he flipped Tammy Rae's cards, revealing a king and a jack. "Pair of aces."

To Danielle, I whispered. "Why did she go all-in if she only had the pair of aces showing on the table? Bluffing?"

She shook her head, then pulled out her phone and started typing. A moment later, mine buzzed with a message.

She's got the king and jack of Diamonds. She's chasing a

straight, a flush, or a straight flush. She needs the queen of Diamonds, but any queen or diamond gives her a good hand. She probably thinks Rachel is chasing, too, but Tammy Rae's got the king, which would give her a better hand if they both get a flush.

The dealer looked from Rachel to Tammy Rae and back, drawing out the tension. A bead of sweat appeared on Tammy Rae's brow. Rachel tossed her head and winked at me, appearing no more stressed than if she waited in line to pick up takeout.

The final card moved onto the table, face down. I gripped Ed's and Danielle's hands so tightly, Danielle winced. The final card flipped. The crowd gasped. Ed let out a strangled sound. My heart plummeted straight down into the sea.

Queen of Diamonds.

We lost.

* * *

To her credit, Rachel didn't seem at all disappointed when the dealer revealed the final card. She tossed her hair, raked one hand through her blond curls, and grinned at me. "I'd been meaning to get a trim, anyway."

"Me, too." I squeezed her hand. "Let's go up to the salon."

"You? You don't have to hold my hand."

"I'm not coming for moral support. I can't let you do this alone."

"Don't be ridiculous," Rachel said, hands on her hips. "This was my bet. Not yours."

"Your bet, trying to do something nice for me? Trying to save my business and my relationship with Justin's sister? You're right, this bet had nothing to do with me."

She grinned at me. "You get one last chance to change your mind before I'm going to give in."

"It's beyond your control. I'm doing this. Cabinmate solidarity. Besides, who do I need to look good for?"

Ed jumped, clapping his hands. "Me, too! Me, too!"

On my other side, Danielle slammed the rest of her drink. "You're all nuts. No way I'm shaving my head, but I'll come along for support."

Rachel blinked several times, then waved a hand in front of her face. "You guys! I love you both so much."

Without so much as a glance at Tammy Rae, the four of us marched out of the casino, holding hands, with our heads held high.

The salon attendants didn't seem fazed by three people walking in and asking to have their heads shaved, not when Connor appeared to video us. Naturally, the producers weren't going to let us experience this moment in private.

We took side-by-side-by-side chairs, and Danielle went to the gift shop to buy matching hats. Ed, of course, suggested she find one with his picture on the front.

Moments later, the stylist got started. Rachel's gorgeous blond curls hit the floor first, followed by Ed's short black hair, then my stick-straight brown locks. We didn't speak until the stylist finished brushing final bits of hair off my shoulders. Then we all turned to face the mirrors at once.

My bald head looked like the top of a lamppost. Round, smooth, and gleaming white. I started to stay something, but at least my face and scalp matched.

Rachel may have possessed perfect bone structure, but her fake tan hadn't been applied to her scalp, giving her a white line across her forehead. She wailed at her reflection. "I look like one of those things from *Charlie and the Chocolate Factory!*"

I started to reply, but Ed hooted. "Oompa loompa doompety dee. If you are wise, you'll listen to me!"

Rachel glared at him, lips clamped together, but when her shoulders started shaking, a giggle escaped me. The stylist broke down, too, which only made everyone else laugh harder. When the unflappable Connor cracked a smile from behind the camera,

I stopped fighting the urge to laugh. Beautiful features aside, Rachel really did look ridiculous.

Every time my eyes met hers in the mirror, I heard the Oompa Loompa song running through my head, and a fresh wave of laughter hit. Finally, I stopped and sat up. "Thanks, Ed. I needed that."

"No problem. And Rach, we'll get you an awesome hat." He leaned into the mirror, turning his head slowly from side to side. "Meanwhile, I look fabulous."

Unlike me and Rachel, Ed seemed more attractive than ever without hair. Or maybe I'd forgotten how hot he was. That's how I could tell what good friends we'd become: he'd morphed into Ed, the guy I turned to for laughs and comfort rather than Ed, the hottest guy I'd ever seen in real life. Even with a newly shaved head.

After the week I'd had, the sadness I felt staring at the mixed pile of hair on the tiles surprised me.

Ed squeezed my hand. "It's only hair. It'll grow back."

"I know," I said, swiping at my nose. "This is stupid. It's not about the hair."

"Everything's going to be okay, Jen," he said.

"Really? How?"

"I don't know. I was going for supportive."

"Don't listen to him," Rachel said. Her scalp gleamed, creating a white cap atop her tanned face. "All you and Justin need is to sit down and talk about your relationship."

"What could he possibly say about sleeping with the enemy?" I asked.

"Come on," Rachel said. "There's no way he actually slept with her. And you'd know that if you'd swallow your pride, tell him the truth about Dominic, and *ask him*."

"She's right," Ed said.

If only I shared their certainty that this whole fiasco was nothing but a misunderstanding. Seeing Justin and Ariana together, over and over, made me wonder how I could have misinterpreted things. What possible explanation could he have for a naked "Ari" in his room? Did I want to hear it? How could I forgive him?

Thinking something happened between me and Dominic didn't give him a free pass to sleep with whoever he wanted. Especially not the one person he knew would hurt me the most.

"If he had an explanation, why didn't he tell me when we talked in the elevator? He had plenty of time to say, 'Look, nothing happened,' and he didn't."

"Maybe he doesn't know what you thought you saw," Ed said.

"Yeah. Did you see Justin, or did you just take off?"

"I ran," I admitted. "But he heard me knock. He asked who was at the door."

"And Ariana probably told him it was housekeeping or room service at the wrong cabin," Ed said. "You've got to talk to him."

"I don't know. He was awfully quick to assume the worst about me. And to take his revenge."

"That's the whole point," Rachel said. "You don't know if he actually did anything. Maybe he's sitting around, crying on Ariana's shoulder and wondering why you haven't explained yet if nothing happened."

I didn't know he slept with her, but I felt it deep down. Especially when I saw him and Ariana everywhere. The stabbing pain in my guts couldn't be all a figment of my imagination. I shook my head. "Maybe we weren't meant to be, Rach. It's not like couples who meet on reality shows usually work out long-term. Look at all the failed relationships on those dating shows. Maybe we were destined to be a statistic."

"Don't think that way," she said. "You need to talk to him."

I'd tried to give him a chance. Instead of explaining, he'd attacked. But I'd done the same. What a mess.

The three of us left the salon and squeezed into an elevator with the ever-present, never-speaking Connor and his camera. Rachel hit the button for the fourth floor, where we would meet

Danielle at the gift shop. I prayed we wouldn't pass Justin on the way. Or Ariana. Or Dominic. Or any combination of the three.

We didn't see them, but as we exited the elevator and walked past the casino, Tammy Rae whistled, stopping me in my tracks. "Jen! Love the new look."

Curling my lip, I kept my gaze focused firmly ahead of me. The last thing I needed at the moment was to deal with her gloating. According to Danielle, Rachel played her hand perfectly. She just got unlucky. I didn't see any reason to relive the game.

Then Tammy Rae spoke again, softer. "Come on, Jen. I want to talk to you."

I couldn't imagine what we had to talk about after everything. She'd decided my relationship was fake, cruelly twisting the knife as I watched the world around me crumble. She never let me explain what really happened, believing the worst about me, like Justin. Like all of America did, back when Danielle called me a home wrecker on national TV, and I almost got voted off *The Fishbowl* because of it.

Still, something in her tone made me pause. Maybe she wasn't just planning to laugh at me, after all. And if she was, I *did* promise Leanna a showdown. It didn't have to be with Ariana.

Ahead of me, Ed turned back. "You okay? Want us to wait?"

"No, it's fine." I shifted from one foot to the other, wishing I knew what Tammy Rae wanted.

"I don't bite," she said. "I promise. Come on, five minutes of your time. What do you have to lose?"

She had a point. I waved Ed and Rachel on.

"I'll buy you a hat," Ed said.

"I'll make sure it doesn't have a whale tail on it," Rachel added. She mouthed, "Good luck" behind Ed's back, where Tammy Rae couldn't see her.

After wavering from me to Ed and Rachel and back for a moment, Connor locked eyes with a cameraman standing just inside the door to the casino. He lifted his eyebrows, which must have meant something, because the other guy nodded. With a thumbs up, Connor turned and jogged after my friends.

"That was a cool thing you did for your friend," Tammy Rae said.

Rubbing my head self-consciously, I approached like a fish nudging past a sleeping shark. "It's nothing compared to what she did for me."

"Still, you're not so bad."

"Thanks, I guess."

"How's the blond doing?"

"Rachel's fine. You saw her; she still looks great. The three of us were on our way to pick out matching hats for the rest of the cruise."

"Adorable. Those two a couple?"

"No." I didn't elaborate. If she'd paid as much attention to the show as she'd made it seem when claiming I faked my relationship, she'd know pretty girls didn't catch Ed's attention.

"Too bad. They look good together," she said. "Come with me. Let's talk."

She hadn't bitten yet, so I followed Tammy Rae to a small seating area on the far side of the casino. I still wasn't sure I wanted to hear whatever she planned to say, but this week couldn't get any worse. As if by magic, a waiter appeared when we sat. Maybe she was still a high roller. Since it was only ten o'clock in the morning, I ordered a hot chocolate with extra whipped cream.

"I heard what you said at the rum factory, you know," Tammy Rae told me. "I've been thinking a lot the past day or so. You were right. You and Justin are normal people, same as me. I mean, totally not as famous or talented as me—and you're a terrible singer." She winked at me.

My face grew warm. "Sorry for butchering your song like that."

"It's not the first time. Won't be the last. Anyway, like I was saying, I can't hold you two to impossibly high standards. The other day, you gave me a glimpse of true love. I can't expect you to never hit a rough patch. And I can't let whether I help you depend on things that are none of my business."

"Does this mean you're going to give me the recipe?" My hopes skyrocketed, but a lot of noise surrounded us. My ears rang already; maybe I misheard her.

She nodded. "You're good people, Jen. Good people constantly get screwed by the world. Watching the four of you leave the casino, I realized I didn't want you to be one of them."

"Thank you," I said, genuinely touched.

"Also, your friend Rachel? Before the tournament, she offered me five thousand dollars to tell you. Sober and everything."

My mouth dropped. Sarah and I could never repay her generosity. Even offering a thousand dollars had been a stretch. Five thousand meant taking almost two months' living expenses out of my *Fishbowl* winnings.

"I thought playing for it would be more fun," Tammy Rae said. "But then I saw you come down to support your friend, how you sat with her throughout the game. I love the kind of loyalty you inspire in your friends."

"Rachel's a wonderful person and a good friend. It's easy to be loyal to her."

"Maybe, but don't sell yourself short. You didn't have to come watch the game. You didn't have to rescue her at the rum factory. And you didn't have to shave your head because she did it. It wasn't your bet."

I started to disagree, but there was no point in trying to talk Tammy Rae out of having positive feelings toward me. Not when it sounded like she might be giving me exactly what I needed. Instead, I asked, "Speaking of the bet, why did you go along with the bet if you were going to tell me the secret either way?"

She shrugged. "I wasn't going to. It's a woman's prerogative to change her mind, you know."

"Thank you so much. You have no idea how much this means to me."

"I don't want anyone to overhear, so I'll text it to you," Tammy Rae said. "You're on the cruise line messaging system?"

I nodded, afraid to breathe in case she changed her mind. She began tapping, and I pulled out my phone, ready to pounce the second the notification arrived.

An excruciating five seconds later, the device buzzed in my hand. The message popped up, containing only two words. Words that so confused me, I blinked and rubbed my eyes before reading them again.

Breast milk.

NINETEEN

INSIDE THE GUPPY GABBER, FRIDAY:

Rachel: *Ok, so I've been planning to donate my hair to Locks of Love for a while now. Sure, I wasn't thinking I'd shave the whole thing, but it's only hair. It'll grow back. I'm just bummed I lost. Jen really wants Tammy Rae's secret ingredient.*

Ed: *The hair does not make the man. And I think my man likes my new smoothness. I may keep this look. What do you think of this hat?*

Jen: *Oh my god, oh my god, oh my god. Ew. Oh my god. I'm gonna puke. Get out of my way. Sorry.*

Danielle: *Maybe I should shave my head, too. Show my support for Jen? No, wait. No way.*

My mouth opened and closed soundlessly for what felt like an eternity. "Did autocorrect change this? Is the first word supposed to be . . . goat? Or maybe soy?"

Please, please, please tell me this is a joke.

We couldn't put breast milk into food we were serving to humans. The health department would shut us down in a heartbeat. Even if they didn't, no one would eat at our bakery once word got out. Even with other products, they'd always wonder what other bodily fluids made their way into our food. I shuddered at the thought.

She checked her phone. "No, that's right."

I wracked my brain. "Where do you even get breast milk? Aren't your kids in their twenties?"

"Oh, honey, a woman can keep producing breast milk forever as long as she's got the stimulation. Now I'm nursing my grand babies."

This conversation kept moving further down a road I never, ever wanted to take. It took every ounce of self-control I possessed not to gag.

"Don't look so grossed out," she said. "It's totally natural. And you promised not to tell anyone my secret ingredient. You share, I sue."

"There are cameras everywhere," I said. "You think none of them picked up this conversation? Maybe they didn't get the text, but I can almost guarantee there are microphones around."

"Not my problem. You share, I sue."

"I'm not talking. What would be the point? We can't use this recipe now. Not with breast milk in it."

"Sure you can. All you need is the right stimulation. You could actually buy a pump, and you and Sarah could produce your own. It takes time, but—"

She kept talking, but my ears actually shut down out of self-preservation. I heard nothing but the pulse beating in my forehead, threatening to explode. So this is what hysterical deafness felt like. I wanted to run away, but my legs wouldn't move.

The waiter brought our hot chocolate, which I grasped like a life raft. After a couple of deep gulps, I managed to speak. "I'm not sure my partner and I can afford to be tied to breast pumps while starting a business."

"Okay, fine, I get it if you're not up for that. I'm not far from Florida. We'll work something out. I can have the product delivered to you if you don't have a wet nurse."

Unwilling to believe what I heard, I surreptitiously gripped the skin under my right arm with my left arm and forefinger and squeezed. A flash of pain ran through me, but this nightmare, apparently, wouldn't end.

"Thanks so much," I said, struggling for the right way to explain that she completely missed the point. "But I don't think it's legal to use human byproducts in food products sold to the public."

"Why wouldn't it be? It's all natural!"

I opened my mouth, but immediately closed it. Pointing out that marijuana was all natural but also didn't belong in food—and so were a million other things, like dog shit and henna—might not help at this exact moment. I still needed a recipe to bring to Sarah, and maybe Tammy Rae could tell me something else of use.

"Have you ever tried a substitute? Coconut milk? Soy?"

"Nope. It's gotta be breast milk to get the texture right. Plus, there's this unique, subtle flavor to it." She shrugged. "Look. Use it or don't. You swore not to tell anyone. And I still want the five hundred dollars you promised me first."

I didn't have the energy to argue. A lead balloon filled me. I'd lost everything trying to get a recipe I couldn't even use. Leaning to one side, I withdrew five folded bills from my pocket and held them out. "Here."

Tammy Rae took the money and shoved it into her bra. "Thanks, Jen. It was a pleasure doing business with you."

In response, I forced the corners of my lips upward. I couldn't manage any other reaction. Trying not to let my disappointment show, I stuck the phone back in my pocket.

Total cruise fail. Total relationship fail. Total life fail.

AFTER TAMMY RAE LEFT, I stayed on the couch, trying to figure out what on earth to do next. What a waste of a week. I should've stayed home, researched recipes on the Internet, and watched reality shows for more ways to tie our products to other stars. I should've known better than to come on this stupid cruise. There was never any chance Ariana wouldn't ruin it.

"Here." A voice spoke nearby, but I didn't recognize it, so I kept studying my shoes.

A piece of paper entered my field of vision. Unfolding it, I found a copy of the itinerary that appeared in our cabin every morning. Finally, I looked up to find Madison smiling down at me, her interpreter off to the left.

Just what I needed. A friend of Ariana's to come . . . what? Gloat over my misery? Tell me how happy Justin was now?

"Hi." Realizing she couldn't hear me, so I waved. Then, I flushed, as her interpreter passed on my greeting. Of course I could speak normally. That's why she had an interpreter.

To cover my embarrassment, I tried spelling out her name using the ASL alphabet I'd learned in Girl Scouts as a kid, but I wasn't sure about some of the letters.

After a minute, Madison laughed and put her hands over mine. Her hands flew through the air. "You don't have to sign. We can use our phones to chat privately for a minute, if you don't mind?"

I nodded and pulled out my phone. Madison signed something to the interpreter, who moved a few feet away and turned around. A real private chat. Surely, interpreters were governed by some kind of code. What could Madison want to talk to about that even the interpreter couldn't know about?

My phone showed a friend request from Mother Madison, which I accepted.

Hi, Madison. How can I help you? How's the baby?

She gestured to the corner where a young girl with dark, spiky hair sat next to the stroller. I'd seen her around, so I waved. She waved back.

My friend Kat is sitting with Noah for now. He'll be fine for a few minutes. Thank you for returning his bear.

It was nothing.

She pointed at the piece of paper still sitting in my lap.

I brought something for you.

What, this? The itinerary? I have one.

Flip it over.

Since we were in port all day, the itinerary didn't include much of a list of onboard events for the day. I flipped the document over, revealing an unprinted page filled with rows of neat, precise letters in blue ink:

2 medium, ripe bananas

2 eggs

1 cup sugar

1/2 cup oil

Hardly daring to believe, I dropped the paper in my lap and picked up my phone again.

You've brought me a recipe?

I can read lips, sort of. I saw your conversation with Tammy Rae from over there. Parts of it, anyway. Tammy Rae's had so many collagen injections, her lips don't move when she speaks. But I got the gist from you.

I giggled, resisting the urge to cover my mouth with one hand. It never occurred to me that Madison might be able to read lips. Deaf people always did it in books on TV, but I thought that was more about laziness than accuracy.

I had no idea you can read lips.

Very little. It's not easy. Anyway, you can't use her recipe, right? Unless you substitute baby formula?

My fingers flew over the tiny keypad.

Not in this lifetime. Even if we could find a workable substitute, if word got out what the secret ingredient should have been, it would be a PR nightmare. No one would believe we didn't use breast milk. We'd get sued. The health department would shut us down while they investigated, and we'd lose all our customers if we reopened.

I shook my head miserably.

My partner's going to kill me. If I still have a partner.

Madison stared at me sympathetically before she started typing again. A moment later, my phone buzzed.

Use this. It won the bake-off, right? There's some cachet for you. It's my grandmother's specialty: chocolate cupcakes with roasted banana centers and peanut butter frosting. No bodily fluids included.

I chuckled at the last bit. A second later, another message popped up on my screen.

What could be better? You don't have to pay me a royalty, although I want my picture next to the display.

My taste buds sang at the reminder of the cupcakes Madison presented at the bake-off. Suddenly everything looked brighter. Caramelized bananas as a secret ingredient beat the hell out of breast milk. Maybe I could get something good out of this cruise, after all. If Sarah didn't fire me. I typed,

You mean it? You'll let us use the recipe? Why? You don't know me.

1. Putting breast milk in people food is effing gross. You can't use that shit.

2. You've been through a lot the past year. I know a bit about bullies. You think it's easy to be pregnant at sixteen? Switching to the hearing high school because it's got free day care and being the only deaf girl around? Trust me, I know assholes. Consider this your reward for putting up with Ariana.

3. You chased me across half the deck when my son dropped a toy. You didn't have to do that.

I blinked at her reply several times before responding. After deleting a couple of false starts, I sent a message.

You saw the show? Then why are you hanging around with Ariana? Aren't you friends?

She shook her head.

She's just practicing her ASL. It's not so great, but it's nice to have someone make the effort. Besides, she doesn't know I read lips. At the bake-off, I saw her telling Braden she's only being nice to me to make her seem more likable to the viewers.

Textbook Ariana. Of course.

That sucks. I'm sorry.

No problem. I'm used to it.

Nibbling my lower lip, I studied her. For someone so young, Madison had been through a lot. I wanted to hug her, but didn't know how the gesture would go over. Still, my heart went out to her.

Shaking my head, I offered the paper to her before picking my phone up again.

Thanks, but it's too late. Justin's with Ariana now. My partner is his twin sister; there's no way she's going to let me keep working there. She'll buy me out as soon as I get home.

She stood and stuffed her hands in her pockets, not taking the recipe. She tapped the interpreter on the shoulder to rejoin us. Madison said, "Things aren't as bad as you think."

Not as bad as I thought? I didn't have the energy to go into it. With a groan, I leaned against the chair and closed my eyes. "It's worse."

"Cheer up, lady." A hand touched my knee briefly before she walked away.

My phone buzzed again. Madison again.

Open your eyes. Look around.

What the hell?

Then, behind me, I heard the voice I'd been yearning for all week. The low tone that sent chills down my spine, that filled me with desire, and that knew how to make me laugh better than anyone I'd never met.

"Hey."

At first, I didn't dare look up for fear I imagined him. When Justin's well-worn tennis shoes appeared in the place where I glared at the floor, my heart skipped a beat.

"Hey," I said softly.

He settled onto the chair beside mine. "We need to talk."

Every time I heard those four little words, I hated them more. Finally, I met his gaze. To my surprise, he looked as bad as I felt. Dark circles ringed his eyes. His hair tousled like when he'd spent four days studying and not bothered to shower. The wrinkles in his clothes might be permanent.

"What happened to your hair?" Justin asked.

"That's what you want to talk about? My hair?" The icing on the cake of this hideous week came in the form of the guy I'd thought I'd be spending the rest of my life with telling me he hated my newly bald head.

"Just humor me for a second. Why did you shave your head?"

Briefly, I filled him in on the poker tournament. As I spoke, his face became less guarded. By the time I got to the final card, he wore a real smile. Maybe discussing my horrible luck broke the ice for us.

My more optimistic side suggested that maybe he was just glad we were talking again, about anything. I certainly was. I missed him like crazy. Every time I woke up in the night and didn't find him an arm's length or a text away, my heart ached.

"I didn't have sex with Ariana," he said when I finished. "And I know nothing happened with you and Dominic."

Hope leapt inside me, lodging in my throat and making it difficult to speak.

"He told you the truth?"

"Nah. When he showed up on Wednesday, I told him I'd

punch him if I ever saw him again. He left without a word. I think he's been hiding in his new cabin. The producers moved him—they'll push us pretty far, but they don't want actual violence. I wish I'd thought to threaten him on Day One, then had Ed swap rooms with you. None of this would've happened."

My mouth fell open. "Then how do you know I didn't cheat on you?"

"It's Saturday," he said, as if that explained everything.

"And on Saturdays, you have more faith in me than other days?"

A ghost of a smile crossed his lips, but it faded almost as if it never existed. "It was never about faith in you. I let my insecurities take over when I saw that picture. I'm an ass. I'm so sorry for doubting you."

His three-sixty spun my head a little. The part of me that had taken a real beating this week spoke up in my brain. What was going on? Had the Network set up this conversation? I hadn't forgotten I still owed Leanna a showdown with Ariana, and she most likely hadn't, either. She was definitely evil enough to send Justin in to shake things up when I didn't confront Ariana right away.

But then my optimistic side took over: No, he wouldn't set me up, no matter what the Network promised. No matter what happened between us, we still had real history, real emotions. This was my Justin, apologizing because he loved me. I trusted him.

"Thank you. You're not an ass. I know how easy it is to jump to conclusions. But what does Saturday have to do with anything?"

Justin said, "The bar results were posted online yesterday. With everything that happened, I forgot to check, but this morning, I convinced the producers to give me fifteen minutes of Internet time so I could look up my results."

"Oh, yeah! How'd you do?" Not for a second did I doubt

he'd done well, but I didn't want to steal the thunder of his announcement by saying it first.

He broke into a real smile, and his entire face lit up. My heart lurched. He hadn't looked at me like that since we left the Bahamas. "I passed!"

"That's amazing! I'm so happy for you!"

Without thinking, I jumped up to kiss him, celebrating in the way we would've under normal circumstances. His stiffened when my lips hit his, which reminded me we still had a lot to talk about before falling into our old habits. Still, when I pulled back, the air between us crackled. I flushed, looking at the ground before settling back onto the couch.

"Did you get to talk to Sarah? How's your mom?"

"They're both fine. I let them know you were worried about them."

"Thanks. Did you . . . ?" I didn't even know how to finish that sentence, so I didn't bother. *Did you tell them you dumped me? Did you tell them how much this cruise sucks? Did you tell them you're in love with Ariana now?*

"Calls cost like three dollars a minute. I asked how Mom was doing and sent your love. They don't need to know anything else before the show airs," he said. "But that's not the point. I also got emails from Google Voice with all your texts, and I found a message from Ty."

"The guy who ferried us over from Jamaica?"

"Yeah. He told me Dominic kissed you out of nowhere, and you smacked the hell out of him for doing it." He raked one hand through his hair, shaking his head. "I'm so sorry. I never should've doubted you. I've been so nervous about all the other stuff, I let my insecurities make me act like an asshole."

"You weren't the only one with insecurities," I said. "Nor were you the only one who acted like an asshole. I should've stayed, charged past Ariana into your room and let you explain before jumping to conclusions."

"Yes, you should have. You know me better than that, Jen."

"I'm so sorry. She does this to me every time. I know better, but when she's nearby, my internal doubt monster takes over."

"Don't let it. You have nothing to worry about. I spent that whole night worrying that you'd been injured, that you were trapped in Jamaica, planning to get off the ship in the Caymans and go find you."

The love in his eyes made me feel even worse for not trusting him. All I wanted was to be worthy of the way he felt about me. Still, I had to know. "I wouldn't have blamed you for thinking something happened with Dominic. Especially after you saw the picture. But why was Ariana in your room when I showed up the next morning?"

"She came in looking for Dominic while I was in the shower. He must've given her his key card. And she was in a robe because they'd booked a couple's massage at the spa." He met my gaze squarely. His face wore an open expression. "I swear, she couldn't have been in the room more than two minutes before you knocked. She was about to leave. It was crappy timing."

Maybe love turned me into a fool, but I believed him. "Why didn't you come after me that morning?"

"Because I'm a dumbass. I was mad at you for going off with Dominic, especially when you didn't come back to the ship after the excursion. And then when I saw that picture . . ." He shook his head. "It doesn't matter. I screwed up. I should've thrown myself into the water back in Jamaica to be with you. Once I knew you were back onboard, I should've gone tearing after you, made sure you were okay, and kissed every inch of your body."

His words warmed my heart, made me want to jump into his lap right there in the casino. I forced myself to keep my response light. "In front of Rachel? That might have been overkill."

He chuckled. "She could've left. Can you ever forgive me? I love you."

"I love you, too."

This time, when I leaned in, he met me halfway. He reached up with one hand to cup my face, and before I knew what happened, I found myself in his lap, putting every ounce of emotion into the kiss. His lips parted beneath mine, and a low moan escaped me. I'd missed him so much. His hands moved down to my hips, and I ran my fingers through the blond hair at the nape of his neck. Feeling him shift beneath me, hearing him, touching him, left no further doubt about the depth of our emotions.

Lights flashed around us: tourists, probably, but I didn't care. All that mattered was Justin. Not just "Jen and Justin," the couple, but Justin, the man, who loved me and trusted me and made me feel things I never imagined, inside and out.

Finally, I pulled back, resting my forehead against his. "I'm so sorry. This trip has been a nightmare."

"It's not your fault," he said.

"True. I guess we should've known the Network would throw some curveballs at us."

"You don't think they were behind *all* this?"

I shrugged. "Reality TV's about drama, right? We've got plenty of that. Inviting the two of us plus Ariana wasn't a coincidence, and I bet they drooled at the thought of Dominic joining us. From the moment Danielle showed up, I knew the Network was up to something. Imagine how much worse it could've been if she hadn't refused to play along. I'm glad she's just here to get a tan and relax."

"And we let them feed on our insecurities."

"Yup."

"We're so stupid," Justin said.

"I think listing us as one person for everything was intentional. They saw the first day how surprised you were that all the pictures to sign were of both of us. Trying to make us share a chair during the bake-off wasn't an accident. They were poking the sleeping tiger. They don't care about us or our relationship, and why would they?"

"Well, luckily, I do. Let's make a pact never to let television or D-list fame, or any of this crap come between us again. We're a team. We might be Jen and Justin, but only we get to decide what that means for us."

I nuzzled against him. It felt so good to melt into his arms. "Right now, what do you say being Team Jen and Justin means I kick Rachel out of our room for about an hour?"

"I've got a better idea." He pulled a key card out of his pocket. "I booked a balcony suite for the night."

"Oh yeah? Cocky, aren't we?" My playful tone took the bite out of my words.

"Not cocky, hopeful. I planned to use all of my lawyerly negotiation skills, plus some groveling." He kissed me again. "Lots of groveling."

"I'm sorry I missed that."

"Don't be. I'm not pretty when I cry." He held the card out to me. "What do you say? King-sized bed. Private ocean view. Care to join me?"

"Nothing in the world could make me happier right now."

TWENTY

QUEEN KELLY'S VOICE
OUR FINAL DAY AT SEA

Saturday edition

Well, it's been a wonderful week for the cast of *Real Ocean: Caribbean,* but we're afraid it's time to head on back to the good ol' U.S. of A. The ship will dock at 10:00 PM, with disembarkation beginning first thing in the morning. Passengers who have flights scheduled prior to 11:00 AM should contact the purser's desk as soon as possible to ensure early disembarkation. See inside for more information and to find out your scheduled meeting time.

Meanwhile, we've got a full day of activities to ensure your final day at sea is every bit as enjoyable as the rest of this week.

Meet *The Fishbowl*'s Rachel up on the Lido Deck at 10:00 AM for a poolside calf-roping demonstration. Then head down to the rear deck at 11:00, where her co-star Ed will give a mixology lecture before lunch.

The casino closes for the rest of the voyage at 6:00 PM, so this is your last chance to test your luck against *Totally 80s Bake-off* winner Tammy Rae. She'll be playing heads-up Texas Hold 'em with the fans all day.

After dinner, join us up on the Lido Deck to watch *The Fishbowl*'s Ariana Sassani star in *Killer Octopuses from Outer Space 2*. Stick around after the show while America's favorite brunette answers questions and signs autographs. Don't forget to pick up posters and other promotional items in the gift shop.

Inside this Edition:

JUSTIN and I spent the remainder of the evening exploring each other. We talked and laughed and drank wine and made love before falling asleep in each other's arms. What a perfect day. We spent the entire next morning in bed, indulging in room service —and each other. Finally, we got to experience the perfect cruise we would've been having all along, if Ariana and Dominic hadn't interfered.

Contented and happy, I snuggled up against Justin after lunch, and his heartbeat lulled me to sleep.

Slanted rays peeked through the slats of the blinds when I woke again. Beside me, I found sheets cool to the touch and a note from Justin that he'd gone to the gym, but he'd see me in time for dinner. Signed with a heart. I held it to my lips with a smile. Finally, things were moving in the right direction. When we got home, we could go back to the way we were, stronger than ever. Not to give Ariana too much credit, but her efforts to drive us apart brought us closer together. I was doubly grateful to Madison for giving me her recipe now that I'd be able to use it.

Most of the day passed while Justin and I became reacquainted. Not knowing how long he'd been gone, I hurried through a shower so my hair could air dry before dinner. Pulling on a robe, I moved outside to bask in the ocean breeze and enjoy the view from our private patio. We hadn't made it to the balcony the night before, spilling into the room and barely landing on the bed. Well, landing on the floor, the couch, the shower, and then the bed. The memory sent warm tingly feelings through me.

Two chairs sat on the balcony beside an end table. I expected everything to be bolted down, but they weren't. Maybe no one expected winds to carry furniture over the four-foot high wall separating the sitting area from the open sea.

On either side of me, walls separated our patio from the guests in the adjacent rooms. The walls stretched to the ceiling on the wall leading inside, but tapered down to the balcony wall, so we theoretically could speak to people staying in those other rooms. Doors in the partitions connected us. That must be what a "semi-private" balcony meant. Good thing Justin and I hadn't stumbled out here, too caught up in each other to notice if people on either side of us peeked around the low edge of the wall. Or to care.

A door creaked open. I turned to look for Justin, but our door remained firmly shut. Then a voice carried over from the patio next to ours.

"Were you throwing up again?"

My ears perked up. Why was Dominic in the suite next to ours?

"Yeah. God, this sucks."

Holy shit. Ariana. Dominic and Ariana were in the suite next to ours. Maybe she'd say something I could use to show Justin she'd set up everything that went wrong all week.

Except Tammy Rae's cupcakes. I didn't see her managing to mastermind that disaster. But all the problems between me and Justin? Easy peasy for someone as devious as her to engineer our issues.

Don't do it, Jen, my inner angel warned me, perched upon my right shoulder.

At least not without proof, argued bad Jennifer from my left shoulder.

Remember how Justin reacted last time you accused her without proof? Good Jen argued.

While we were on *The Fishbowl,* the producers had taken all our electronics. When I'd overheard Ariana admitting to Mike that she felt nothing whatsoever for Justin whatsoever and fabricated the love triangle so viewers would keep her around, I couldn't get any proof. But we weren't on a TV set anymore. My cell phone sat in my pocket, and while I didn't have 3G out here at sea, the video camera worked.

Unwilling to go without a fight, bad Jennifer raised her head. *What about your promise to Leanna? Confronting Ariana with a video will get you twenty million viewers, easy.*

"I'm so tired of feeling like crap," Ariana said. "When will it end?"

She groaned, and a chair squeaked as if absorbing her weight. Holding my breath that they wouldn't hear me, I crept to the barrier between the balconies. The seal between the doors left no gaps, and since I wasn't in a 1950s film noir, no handy-dandy keyhole provided me with a view.

Practically laying against the barrier, I moved toward the far wall. I didn't dare stick my head over the top, but I pulled out my phone and hit Record on the video camera. Then I turned the lens to peek over the wall and slowly raised it.

My heart pounded. What if they saw it? But their suite sat on a corner. As the two of them came into view on my phone's screen, I discovered they sat in beach chairs looking out over the ocean, away from me. Finally, a bit of good luck. Now I could see *and* hear everything I needed to show Justin once and for all who she really was.

Dominic said quietly, "Do you want it to end so soon?"

Ariana sighed. "No, I guess not. I'm so sick of being miserable. Puking all the time, no energy to do anything, can't eat anything."

Why was she puking? Was she seasick? Then a thought hit me like a lightning bolt. I knew one very good reason a woman in otherwise perfect health might find herself throwing up every day.

"We shouldn't have come," Dominic said. "I know you thought the sea air would do your appetite some good, but all we've done is stress you out. You've lost a dangerous amount of weight. Being around these people isn't good for you right now."

"I wanted them to like me," she whined. "I thought if I could get Justin on my side, Jen would get over herself and things would work out."

Get over myself? She tried to stop me and Justin from getting together. She told everyone in America I tried to steal her boyfriend. She spent the trip monopolizing his attention whenever possible. How was any of this my fault? Who could possibly blame me for not liking her?

Since I couldn't hear anything over the rage boiling in my blood, I forced myself to take a deep breath and focus on the conversation. Why did she care if I forgave her? Was she doing some kind of twelve-step program? Assholes Anonymous?

"You were half right," Dominic said. "Justin seems to have forgiven you."

"Do you think he'll come to the service?"

They were getting married? My worst enemy was marrying my ex-boyfriend? Then why the hell had they spent all week trying to break me and Justin up? For fun? These people were fucked in the head.

"I don't know," Dominic said. "But I'll talk to him when the time comes. I promise."

"Thanks. You're the best."

On the video screen, Ariana leaned her head on Dominic's shoulder, and he put his arm around her. If they had been any other couple in the world, the scene would've made me smile. The tenderness between them was palpable.

Why was I spying on them? Would showing Justin this video change anything?

I sighed and leaned forward, placing my head against the wall. What was I doing anymore? Time to turn off the camera and go inside. I wasn't going to find out anything out here, and it didn't matter if I did. Justin and I were together again. Once we got home, he'd stop feeling like only half of a whole, and everything would be fine again. Better than fine; we could resume being deliriously in love.

Unbidden, the vision I'd had when Connor asked me about marriage swam before my eyes. Ariana almost ruined my dream once. I couldn't let my desire for revenge against her take it away a second time. Even if the dream might not ever become a reality, I wasn't about to throw it away. Leanna would have to get over my not staging a confrontation, after all. What was she going to do, sue me?

Just as I'd convinced myself to give up this fool's errand and go inside, Ariana sighed loudly. With good Jen and bad Jennifer still warring on my shoulders about the wisdom of my actions, I waited.

Ariana said, "I don't know why I care. Justin's such a frustrating goody-goody. You know he wants to use his law degree to help people? He turned down a position billing five hundred dollars an hour to work in the firm's pro bono department, representing poor tenants in housing disputes."

"Then why do you care what he thinks of you?"

"I don't, really. I love watching the way it messes with Jen's head when I talk to him. I guess I don't like losing. It kills me that he picked someone else over me."

"Weren't you sleeping with one of the other contestants?"

"Well, sure, but Justin didn't know that. Not even when Jen told him." She cackled, then sighed. "God, I was such an asshole last year."

"No you weren't," Dominic said. "You were doing what you needed to do to win. That's human nature. Now circumstances have changed. You don't need public approval, and you don't have to suck up to people you hate. After this cruise, you'll never see them again. Who cares what they think?"

"I guess I don't," she said. "I just wanted people to have nice things to say about me."

"And they will. Plenty of people love you. You've got a caring family and lots of friends. You don't need these guys."

"You're right. I'm sorry. Feeling so crappy all the time must be messing with my head."

"Here," Dominic said, his voice low. "I can make you feel better. Lean back and spread your legs."

Ariana moaned. "You're the best. I don't know how I managed before I met you."

Oh, no. The last thing I needed to hear was my ex-boyfriend performing oral sex on my archenemy. If I hadn't already decided to confront her, this horrifying moment would've cemented it. I'd caught enough on tape already. Squeezing my eyes shut, I stabbed at my phone, praying I'd shut off the recording. Then I tiptoed inside with my hands over my ears.

As soon as the door shut safely behind me, I sent a message to Ed.

You won't believe what I just witnessed.

Attaching the video, I hit Send and waited for his response. He didn't make me wait long.

This is amazing. What do you want me to do with it?

In a totally fair world, I'd broadcast it on the Lido Deck after dinner for the world to see.

The television screen overlooking the pool provided the perfect location for an exposé. Not just because that's where most people tended to hang out on nice nights, but also because the producers obtained a copy of *Killer Octopuses from Outer Space* 2, which would start playing at 8 o'clock. But no matter how badly I wanted to see Ariana get what she deserved, I couldn't do it. Revenge fantasies were fun, but I couldn't sink to her level.

The phone showed that Ed had seen my response, but he hadn't replied yet. Quickly, I sent a follow-up.

Kidding! I'm going to show it to Justin and see what he wants to do.

The logo next to Ed's name turned gray, then vanished, indicating he'd signed off the app. Oh, no. What if he hadn't seen my last message?

Ed! You know I was joking, right? Please confirm that you're not going to broadcast the video on the Lido Deck.

No response. My heart pounded. Oh, this was bad. So, so bad.

EDUARDO GABRIEL PEREZ SILVA, GET BACK HERE AND REPLY TO ME RIGHT NOW.

Justin would never forgive me if I exposed Ariana to the world, even if she deserved it. Ed had to know that. What the hell was he doing? Why wasn't he answering me?

Leaning my head back against the door, I forced myself to think rationally. Ed would never screw me. He'd have double and triple and quadruple checked I was sure before doing anything. He probably signed off to spend time with his boyfriend. People sucked at saying goodbye these days.

I'd almost convinced myself when my phone buzzed again.

After unlocking the screen, I spotted another message. Not from Ed, from Connor.

This is Ed. Get to Lido Deck STAT. We found Janine, were talking to her when I got your video. She stole my phone. THIS IS NOT A DRILL.

TWENTY-ONE

JENNIFER IN THE GUPPY GABBER, SATURDAY:

Crap. Crap crap crap crap. I need to find Janine. Sure, I was pissed at Ariana, but I wasn't really going to broadcast that video. Aren't there children on the Lido Deck? Part of me wants to show it to Justin, since he was asking for proof, but . . . does it even matter anymore? We've finally worked things out. Why beat a dead horse?

All I really want is for Ariana to know I have the video as insurance, so she leaves us alone. Leanna will still get her showdown. As soon as I get Ed's phone back from Janine. And with that? I gotta go. Thanks for ambushing me, guys. Now let me out of here.

Fuck. Fucking fuckity fuck fuck. What the hell was I supposed to do now?

My phone buzzed again.

Jen, are you there?

Yeah. Dying. Pleaz find her. I'm on my way.

I didn't bother to fix the typo before sending.

My mind raced. Warn Ariana. Find Justin. Text Justin, then warn Ariana. Find Janine. Stop Janine. Steal Ed's phone back. Get to the Lido Deck. There wasn't time to do everything at once.

Would Ariana believe me? If I knocked on her door, in the middle of sex, when I wasn't supposed to know where she was staying, would she thank me? Or would she call me a stalker and tell America I was trying to ruin her "big moment" by keeping her from watching her movie with everyone else?

She wouldn't listen to me, but she might listen to Justin. My fingers flew over the keyboard of my phone, asking him to meet me in our cabin ASAP. Across the room, Justin's phone buzzed, sitting on the desk. Lovely.

I sent another message.

Never mind. Going to the Lido Deck. Whatever happens, I didn't want this. I'm sorry.

Thudding inside the wall told me the pipes had been engaged in the cabin beside us. Ariana and Dominic must be in the shower. Hopefully, that gave me time to find Janine before she aired the video. Would she wait for me and Ariana to appear on deck to make the drama complete? How much time did I have?

Taking the stairs two at a time, I raced up to the Lido Deck, silently congratulating myself for all the exercise I'd been getting onboard. Seven floors up felt like nothing. At the top of the stairs, a couple of staff members pulled me aside and insisted I give an interview. Clearly, they knew what was up. There was no way to get away from them until I said a few words. The second they gave me an opening, though, I dashed away.

Cruise staff had already arranged the deck chairs to face the large screen, which hung on the back of the spa on the sixteenth floor. I scanned the area. Tammy Rae sat on the other side of the pool, reading, but I ignored her. Danielle waved, and I flashed her a brief smile, wondering if she could possibly help in any way. Janine, Ed, and Connor were nowhere in sight. I hoped that meant they were off somewhere, stopping her from handing over the phone, but I didn't want to put too much faith in my luck this week.

How did the screen work? I'd thought there was a projector, but didn't see anything like that out here. I raced for the stairs again, making it up to the sixteenth deck in seconds. But then I realized there wasn't any way to get to the screen itself. A railing separated me from it, and there was no walkway in front of where the movies aired. The whole thing must be controlled remotely. That's where I needed to be.

"Nice try, Jen, but you're too late."

I spun around at the familiar voice to find myself face-to-face with Janine. "I thought you left the ship in Jamaica after you got stung by a jellyfish."

"That's what everyone thought," she said. "No one really looks at the producers, did you ever notice that? No one but you, anyway. After the tour group left the beach, I took a cab back to the port. Bought one of those stupid, racist I Love Jamaica hats with dreadlocks, and got in line with a bunch of tourists. No one talked to me. Leanna gave me a couple of days off for a job well done. And a big bonus. Thanks for that kiss. It was beautiful."

"You're disgusting. Give me Ed's phone."

"Sure thing." The metal device flew through the air. In my surprise, I nearly ducked, but managed to catch it at the last second. "Of course, I've already forwarded the video to Leanna. She's improving the resolution and the lighting as we speak."

"She won't be able to play it. I'll stand here and stop her."

Janine laughed. "Do you think they've got a Blu-ray player up here or something? This screen's controlled by the media room, deep in the belly of the ship. Even if I were going to tell you where it is—which I won't—it's too late."

"You don't have to tell me. I'll talk to Connor."

"I wouldn't do that if I were you. Leanna said if he interferes with the show again, he's fired. How would your best friend feel if you got his boyfriend fired? They live in a pretty nice house. I'm not sure they could afford it on Ed's out-of-work comedian income alone."

She was distracting me. I didn't have time to tell her that Ed and Connor would be just fine. But I also didn't have any idea how to get to the media room, or where to find Connor (who was probably in the media room at that moment, anyway), and the deck below me was filling up with people. I had to do something, anything, but time was running out.

Janine laughed at the expression on my face.

"Why are you doing this?" I asked.

"It's not personal, Jen. We're in the business of making an entertaining show. Watching you guys bake and zip-line and hang out wasn't that exciting. We weren't going to get the ratings we need to beat *The Bachelor*. And if the show doesn't do well, we're all out of jobs."

"So my life is just a thing for you to play with?"

"It's not your life anymore, Jen! You signed it over. This is our story, and we're allowed to do whatever we want with it," she said. "But come on, this is the best part. We've watched Ariana beat you, over and over and over. Finally, you're about to get your revenge! Aren't you excited? Don't you want this?"

I shook my head. "I wanted people to know the truth. But not like this. What you're doing is wrong, and if you had any kind of a soul, you'd know it."

"People with souls don't go far in Los Angeles, kid. When we get back, I'm getting a huge promotion. The next new show, I'm running it."

Across the open space below, the sound of high heels clacking on wood caught my attention. Ariana entered the pool area, wearing a glittering evening gown that seemed a bit much for the Lido Deck, with her long, black hair artfully arranged on top of her head. She could've been ready to walk the red carpet. Some people applauded when she appeared, and she beamed. I swallowed my rising nausea. Dominic trailed a few steps behind her, dressed much more appropriately for the occasion in a pair of khakis, a green linen shirt, and sandals.

They stood with their back to the screen, which had begun moving. The start of the video was quiet; she must not have heard her own voice above the crowd. Since there was nothing I could do to stop the video, I raced down the stairs to warn her.

When Ariana spotted me, she flinched as if slapped and jumped back with a shriek. I stopped dead in my tracks, afraid to get any closer. Yet afraid not to.

"What the hell happened to your head? Did Justin tell you? Are you making fun of me?"

Telling Ariana all about my recipe woes sat high on the list of things I'd get around to right after Hell froze over. "Making fun of what? Your perfect hair? By shaving my head?"

She planted her hands on her hips and tossed her head. "Whatever. Never mind. What are you doing here?"

"We have to talk, Ariana. Now. It's important."

"Of course now is the moment you'd want to talk. When all the attention is on me," Ariana said.

All the attention *would* stay on her for at least the next five minutes, but not in the way anyone wanted.

"That's not it, I promise. But you need to come with me, and we need to talk away over there."

"Anything you can say to me, you can say here."

Above her head, the video screen flickered. Ariana's face moved, but no sound came out. The screen paused. I tried not to smirk at the realization that Janine's attempts to ruin my life were being hindered by technical difficulties. The image on the screen didn't have movie clarity. Shadows covered much of the screen, but the chairs, table, and ocean in the background clearly established that she was somewhere on the cruise ship.

The doors leading to the elevator bank parted, and Justin appeared. For the first time all cruise, I wished he'd been as far away from me as possible. I didn't want him to see this, especially when I couldn't get to him to explain first. He came and stood beside me, kissing my cheek. "Is everything okay? I got a weird message from you."

"No, it's not okay. I made a video and the producers stole it and I can't make it stop. We need to get Ariana off this deck now."

"What the hell are you talking about?" Ariana asked.

At the same time, Justin said, "Slow down. Start over from the beginning."

But there was no time. Gasps echoed around the deck when the video started to play again, this time with sound. Whispers buzzed all around us. The audience had grown while we were talking. People were catching on that this video wasn't part of the scheduled entertainment.

Helplessly, I pointed at the screen. The color drained from Justin's face. In front of me, the much smaller Ariana whirled around to see everyone watching her and Dominic on the big screen. When she turned back, rage contorted her face. "How dare you? You had no right to spy on me. You had no right to air my personal business to everyone."

"I didn't! I mean, yeah, I made the tape, but I only ever meant to show it to you. I was going to tell you that, if you tried to get between us again, I'd tell him that you only brought Dominic on the cruise to break us up."

"That's not why Dominic's here." A tear trickled down her face, but she didn't wipe it away. She'd probably taught herself to cry on command. "Obviously, you know the truth, since you were watching us."

Her voice cracked, and for the first time since we met, I believed she was showing true emotion. A wave of pity hit me. "Yeah, I saw you with my ex-boyfriend. Thanks for the visual."

She sniffled. "This was never about you. It was about me."

Something in her tone set my hackles up. "Really? Trying to break up me and my boyfriend wasn't about me?"

Justin stood horrified a few feet away, eyes swiveling from

the show on the screen, now replaying from the beginning, to me and back. Other people's eyes remained riveted to the screen as if I hadn't spoken, so I turned to my foe.

"You had your shot with Justin, Ariana, on the show. You lost. He picked me. You had a chance to figure out a way to deal with it and move on. Instead, you set out to ruin my cruise. I didn't want it to happen this way, and I'm sorry for that. But I'm not sorry that finally, people will see who you really are."

Instead of watching the screen, I watched the Ariana in front of me as the video continued to play. Her jaw dropped, but no sound came out. Over her shoulder, Justin's face moved as he watched the film. When his mouth dropped open in horror, I knew he'd gotten to the part where Dominic kneeled between her legs.

Ariana's face turned white. With one hand over her mouth, eyes glistening, she turned and raced inside.

Before I could follow her, Justin and Dominic appeared at my side.

Not surprisingly, Justin's wide eyes and clenched jaw told me he was furious. My heart sank. I'd wanted him to see who she really was when the cameras weren't on her, but not like this. No one deserved this type of public humiliation.

"What the hell did you just do?" He asked.

"I'm so sorry, Justin. I tried to stop it. I just wanted her to leave us alone." I summarized what Ed told me and my conversation with Janine.

He shook his head, his entire body practically shaking. "You don't know what you've got there. Dominic, tell her."

My ex's face turned red, and he stared at the ground. "You know I can't. I'm sorry, man."

"What's going on?" I asked.

"He can't tell you because of medical privacy laws," Justin said.

I blinked at him a few times, but those words didn't start to make any more sense. "Dominic's here as Ariana's date. They're sleeping together. She's pregnant, and they're getting married. Medical privacy laws don't stop him from talking about his own baby. Besides, it's all on the video."

"No, it's not," Dominic said. "Jen, think about it. What do I do for a living?"

The missing pieces of this puzzle started to click into place. "You're a traveling nurse?"

"Exactly."

Lightbulbs started flashing: almost running into Ariana in the infirmary the first day; the weight loss; the fact that she'd brought my ex here in the first place. Rachel saying she was stumbling and looking ill at the rum factory tour. The reason both she and Justin had such a negative reaction to my newly shaved head, at least until Justin got the full story.

"Is Ariana sick?" I asked, feeling like the world's biggest asshole.

Dominic avoided my gaze, which gave me all the answer I needed. Thanks, HIPAA.

Justin pressed his lips together in a firm line. "She's got about three months to live, Jen."

TWENTY-TWO

MORE FROM THE GUPPY GABBER, SATURDAY:

Tammy Rae: *Damn. If I'd known, I probably would've asked the cheerleader to do something else when she lost the bet.*

Ed: *Oh, shit. That blows. I wish I'd thought to leave the room before watching the video Jen sent me. But Janine was apologizing for messing everything up back in Jamaica, and I bought it. I'm an idiot.*

Rachel enters the confessional wearing a baseball hat, sits down, opens her mouth, leaves. A moment later, she enters again. She opens and closes her mouth, leans back, blinks, removes her hat, rubs her head, then walks out a second time.

Oh, my god.

My heart pounded in my ears. My head swiveled from Justin to Dominic and back, waiting for someone to tell me this was the least funny joke ever. When no one replied, my eyes filled with tears. Poor Ariana. She was so young. Too young to have the next forty years snatched away from her. I couldn't even imagine what it would be like, being given my expiration date at such a young age.

I sniffled. "I'm sorry. I don't know what to say. I feel terrible for her."

"That's why we were so surprised to see your shaved head." Justin said. "I wondered if you'd figured out she's been wearing a wig all week. The treatments made her hair fall out."

Well, didn't that make me feel like the world's biggest asshole. "Oh, shit. I had no idea."

He said, "The 'service' she and Dominic were talking about is her funeral, not a wedding. And she's so thin because the medication makes her sick. She can't keep anything down."

"Why would she tell you all this when she was keeping it secret from everyone else?" I asked.

"Remember when I got hit by the golf ball?"

How could I forget? Ignoring the growing queasiness in my stomach, I nodded.

"I went to the infirmary. On my way out, I overheard her talking to one of the doctors. She didn't know I was there. In fact, when she came out and saw me standing there, she looked horrified."

"When you saw me hugging her on the balcony, that was about comfort, not sex," Dominic said. "Sometimes, she needs a shoulder to cry on."

That all made sense, but one thing still bothered me. "Then why were you kneeling between her legs?"

"Pain killers," Justin said. "She needs shots, and only a nurse can give them. But she didn't want anyone to see the track marks, so she gets them in her upper thigh. We spent all day Wednesday talking while you two were in Jamaica. That morning in our room, she came in looking for Dominic because he hadn't arrived at her suite to give the shot. That's why she was wearing a robe."

"You said they had a couples' massage planned."

"I couldn't tell you the truth then, but now the cat's out of the bag."

My mind flashed to Monday, during the bake-off. I'd wondered why she went tanning in a knee-length skirt. And now I knew. All the air rushed out of me. "Oh, no."

"Yeah, that about sums it up," Dominic said.

Ignoring him, I turned to Justin. "Did you give her the shot while we were in Jamaica?'

"No way. She went to the infirmary."

The growing pit in my stomach turned into a chasm. "I'm such as ass. Can you ever forgive me?"

He swallowed. "I know how miserable she made you in the house. Made both of us. She never made any secret about hating you. And her joke about the baby on Sunday was in horribly bad taste. She shouldn't have done that. I get why you don't like her."

"Don't like" was a massive understatement, but I didn't correct him. It didn't matter anymore, anyway.

"Still, I've spent a lot of time with her this week, and she's sorry for the way she behaved, both in the house and on Sunday. She's trying to make amends. Can you say the same?"

My face grew warm. "I never should've sunk to her level. Or what I thought was her level. After we made up, I should've left well enough alone. I'm so sorry, Justin."

"I get it. You didn't know. But I'm not the one you need to apologize to. Go find Ari."

Biting my lip, I nodded. "I will. I have to make this right."

MY FEET POUNDED against the deck, but Ariana had at least a five-minute head start. I raced to the elevators, hoping she was still waiting. No one stood in the foyer when I got there. The eleva-tors on this ship moved at the speed of drunk turtles, so I went for the stairs, praying I could race down and catch her before she exited.

At each landing, I paused, listening for a telltale ding. No luck at the fourteenth, thirteenth, and twelfth floors. When I got to the eleventh floor, the doors of the middle elevator opened to reveal an elderly couple, probably en route to their cabin: this floor contained nothing in the way of entertainment. No one else stood in the tiny space.

Maybe she'd taken the bank of elevators at the far end of the ship instead. Not knowing what else to do, I raced across the ship to see if she was over there. A sign for the gym and spa sent me dashing up three flights, but to no avail. She was gone, and I had no idea where to find her. It would take the rest of the cruise to search the ship end to end.

For the first time all week, not a single member of the production staff stood within my sight. Of course not. They were probably all in the control room, laughing their asses off and celebrating what a great show this would make. Under my breath, I cursed my luck. Then I spotted a couple of passing members of the cruise staff, wheeling a cart full of linens toward the elevator.

"Have you seen a tall, very thin woman with dark skin and long black hair come this way?" I asked, desperate. One of them was Julio, from the buffet. The other wore a tag identifying him as Hamid from Tehran. I hoped he spoke English. "Impossibly beautiful?"

"No, but I wish I had," Hamid said.

"Come on," Julio said, "you'd never get a woman like that in a million years. Me, on the other hand—"

"So you haven't seen her?" I didn't have time to listen to their banter, witty as they thought they were. "Ariana? One of the reality show contestants? She was on *The Fishbowl* with me."

They both stared blankly at me. I was about to leave when

Hamid spoke again. "I'm afraid we don't get a lot of time to watch television while we're working, ma'am. There are no televisions in our cabins."

Her cabin. Duh. I knew how to get to Ariana's cabin now. Why had I wasted time searching half the ship for her? To think they called me the smart one. If I ran from the Lido Deck sobbing after being humiliated on national television, hiding in my room made a lot more sense than slinking to the back of the theater or something.

No one responded when I knocked, but that didn't mean she wasn't in there. Besides, there was more than one way to get her to talk to me: what were adjoining balconies for if not stalking the archenemy you inadvertently destroyed? Using my key card, I slipped through the dark room Justin and I occupied earlier and out onto the deck.

Sure enough, quiet sobbing reached my ears. Shame washed over me. "Ariana?"

No response.

"Look, I'm sorry. Dominic and Justin told me everything."

"Go away!" She yelled over the partition. "I hate you. You've ruined everything."

Going away was not part of the plan, not after I spent half an hour tracking her down. And not after I'd realized what an insufferable asshole I'd be. There may be no excuse for my behavior, but I needed to try to make things right.

The adjoining door between balconies, not surprisingly, was locked. But if I were extremely careful, I could climb around the partition. As long as she didn't shove me off into the ocean. The lowest end of the wall came up to my ribcage. Hoisting myself onto it would be doable, but if I slipped, I'd find myself plummeting face first toward open water. That wouldn't work at all. If accidentally killing myself would make Ariana forgive me, I didn't want to know.

A flash of inspiration struck, and I dragged one of the deck chairs up against the partition, placing the back against the wall separating me from the sea. Standing on the chair gave me a full view of the balcony next to ours. My breath caught in my throat.

Ariana was on the balcony, as expected. However, instead of standing on firm ground or sitting safely in one of the chairs, she sat on top of the wall, gazing out over the water.

"What are you doing?" I said slowly. The last thing I wanted was to make any sudden moves or sounds that might send her toppling forward.

"I said, 'go away.' Or do you suck at following directions as much as everything else you do?"

I bit back a sarcastic reply. She didn't mean it. Okay, well, she probably did, but I still couldn't leave until I knew she was okay.

"I'm afraid I can't do that. Not until you come down off that ledge."

"Whatever," she said. "I can't believe Justin and Dominic told you. I should sue Dominic, or report his ass."

"He didn't really say anything. It was mostly Justin. Ariana, I had no idea. I'm so sor—"

"Don't." She lifted one hand, cutting me off. "Just don't. Let's not pretend we're friends now. You never liked me."

"Nope. And you never liked me. But I don't want you to die. And I certainly don't want you to kill yourself. You've still got three months left to live your life. Please come onto the balcony."

Moving slowly so I wouldn't scare her, I swung my left leg over the wall, leaving me straddling the partition between the balconies, my back to the ocean. The wind shoved me toward the ship, leaving me hugging the dividing wall, and I sent up a prayer of gratitude that it wasn't blowing in the opposite direction.

The good news: I couldn't see the drop. The bad news: Short of falling onto my ass, I also didn't see a good way to get to the ground from here. I'd have to kind of stretch for the deck and hope for some long-overdue good luck.

While Ariana's attention was on the ocean rather than on me,

I slid to the ground, bringing my right leg around the wall and landing with a hard thud on the deck.

Thanks to my death grip on the wall, I stayed upright. There. At least we could talk while on the same patio. And I was safe, but Ariana still needed to move out of the wind before it shifted or the boat changed direction.

She sat, still as a statue, staring at me with her face in a perfect mask. Only her red eyes betrayed how she felt.

"Ariana, please come down from there."

"Why bother? Are you worried if I jump, everyone will think you pushed me?" She let out a peal of laughter. "Oh, that would be perfect, wouldn't it? If I'm going to die either way, at least I could take you down when I go. Or maybe I could grab you and we could go over the edge together."

We stood on the eighth floor of the ship. Other than the main levels, the ceilings here weren't quite as high as a normal house, so a fall wouldn't exactly be as bad as jumping off a skyscraper. A person might survive the drop, but I didn't want to find out what it felt like to hit water at this distance.

Using another chair for balance, I slowly climbed onto the wall to sit next to her. Not too close, since I still didn't trust her as far as I could throw her. But close enough that we could talk without screaming over the wind. I prayed the boat wouldn't sway or turn.

"Ariana, listen," I said. "No, we're not friends. But you have friends who care about you. Friends like Dominic."

"Dominic isn't my friend. He's being paid to hang out with me."

"Maybe that's how it started, but he definitely cares now. I see it in his eyes."

"Whatever. He's only here as part of the show," she said. "I know you don't believe me, but I didn't know he was coming in advance, When the Network invited me on the show, I was in the hospital. My agent told them I'd need a caregiver, and they set it up. I didn't know who he was to you until we ran into his ex-wife at the purser's desk while getting upgraded to this suite."

I didn't want to believe her, but she gained nothing at this point from lying. And I certainly wouldn't put it past the show to invite people on the cruise purely to create drama. "Either way, he likes you now. Madison cares about you, too. Rachel. Even Justin."

"Oh, yeah? Where are they? Why aren't they here, trying to talk me down off this ledge? Whose brilliant idea was it to send you?"

I forced myself not to roll my eyes. Voluntarily talking to Ariana was like a sleeping bear inviting a stick to poke it. "I asked them to let me come apologize. I feel horrible for what I did. I misinterpreted everything in the video. I didn't have a clue that you were sick. But honestly, if I'd known I'd find you sitting on this wall, I'd have sent someone you don't hate to talk you down."

"I don't want your pity," she said.

"It's not pity. It's empathy. Twenty-three is too young to die, and even though I'll probably never like you, I didn't want any of this."

She turned her head away from me, white knuckles clutching the top of the wall. Good. Maybe she didn't want to die, after all. "All I ever wanted was to be famous, you know? I thought my good looks would get me acting jobs, but there are lots of pretty girls out there. Then I thought Daddy's money could help. And it did, a little: a few bit parts in a few crappy movies."

"I watched all of those movies," I said. "To see you."

"Oh, yeah? They sucked." She was right, so I didn't respond. "I suck. I'm a terrible actress. I'm not good at anything."

"I don't know about that," I said. "You make an excellent reality TV villain. Much better than J-Dawg."

The one thing almost everyone on *The Fishbowl* agreed on was that Joshua made a complete fool of himself trying to act like the bad guy. My words had their intended effect on her.

Ariana grinned at me before responding in a perfect imitation. "Whaddup, losers? The J-Dawg is here to stay, so all the imposters gotta play!"

Any other time, her impression would've cracked me up. I was too tense to laugh. Still, her joke seemed like a good sign. Maybe I could get her to turn around and come inside with me after all.

"I really didn't know you were sick," I said. "And I know I shouldn't have sent that video to Ed, but he never would have displayed it. No one's seen Janine since that day in Jamaica. I had no idea he and Connor finally tracked her down, at the worst possible moment."

"I believe you. I guess it's just not my year." She paused. "You probably won't believe me now, but I really did come to the cruise to make amends. Kind of like a twelve-step program for the dying."

Since she perched on the edge of the wall, I didn't want to piss her off, so I chose my next words carefully. "You have a strange way of showing it."

"I'm such a mess," she said. "The thing in the hall with the baby? That was a joke. A bad joke, but yeah . . . for some reason, whenever I'm near you, I see red. My brain takes a vacation. You're so smart and pretty and everyone likes you and no one ever likes me. All I want is to bring you down, and I don't care what it takes."

"If it makes you feel any better," I said. "The feeling is one hundred percent mutual. For a second, I really wanted to share that video. If I hadn't been tempted, none of this would have happened."

"Don't feel too bad," she said. "If I had something like that, I'd have shared it in a heartbeat."

"That doesn't surprise me even a little bit."

"Best enemies forever?"

"I guess so."

She sighed, running one hand over her hair before yanking it off her head. I'd almost forgotten Justin said she was wearing a wig. "I hate this thing, you know. Screw it. Let's all be bald together."

When she chucked it off the side of the ship, I burst out laughing. Never in a million years would I have guessed Ariana Sassani would voluntarily walk around bald in public, especially in front of TV cameras.

"You're still one of the most beautiful women I've ever seen," I said. "Hair or no hair."

"Thanks. I know."

The ship lurched.

Voices shouted overhead, and I turned to see Justin and Dominic waving from the deck a few floors above us. I couldn't make out their voices over the wind, but I'm smart enough to guess they said something like, "Don't be stupid. Get your asses off that wall and come inside where it's safe."

I pointed and waved. "See? All your friends are on the deck, waiting to have a drink with you and watch a movie under the stars and make some memories. What do you say we go find them?"

"Will you be there?"

I sighed, but it wasn't like I wanted to hang out with her, anyway. All I wanted was to go home. "Not if you don't want me to be."

She thought for a second. "I guess you can stay, as long as you and Justin aren't playing kissy face."

"I think we can manage that." I didn't move, holding my breath, waiting for her to turn around before I climbed down myself.

Before she could decide, the ship lurched, throwing us both off balance. Ariana put one hand over her mouth and heaved. Vomit poured through her fingers, into her lap. She swayed and fell to one side. She caught herself on the wall, but then heaved forward, sending another wave of vomit into the wind.

Above us, a scream split the air.

My blood ran cold, and the world slowed. If she went over the edge, it would be my fault. And as much as I loathed her, I didn't want to see her dead. Not now, and not in a few months. Poor Ariana. The past year with Justin's mother had really given me a newfound respect for living life to the fullest, but Ariana would never get that chance. Especially not if she fell overboard.

The ship lurched again. Ariana rolled forward, toward the open water. Without thinking, I lunged for her. At the same instant, she caught herself. The ship rocked backward. Ariana rolled off the wall, into the room. My fingers brushed the fabric of her shirt as I flew past her. My fists closed on absolutely nothing. And then I realized my mistake in trying to grab her without grounding myself first.

Sitting on the edge of the balcony wall, my momentum propelled my upper body away from the ship. My ass came up off the wall. Too late, I tried to pull myself back. My arms scrambled, seeking anything to grab, but my fingers closed only on the open air in front of me. With nothing to hold onto, I tumbled over the side of the railing, hurtling toward the open sea below.

TWENTY-THREE

STILL MORE FROM THE GUPPY GABBER, SATURDAY:

Justin: *When Jen went over the side, my heart stopped. Security stopped me from jumping after her. Sure, I was upset about what she did to Ariana, but I get why she did it. I love Jen with all my heart. I don't want to live without her.*

Rachel: *Oh my god, oh my god, oh my god. Those were the only words going through my mind. I can't even. Jen! *incoherent sobs**

Ariana: *What? Of course I didn't push her! Maybe I never liked her, or most of the rest of them, but I'm not a killer. Besides, Jen and I have come to an understanding.*

The moment my fingertips brushed open air, my old training took over, and my mind started to race. An Olympic diving platform stood ten meters off the water. About a fifth of the distance between the eighth deck balcony and the water. In about ten seconds, I'd slam into the ocean. About as soft as a sheet of glass. No way to stop it. No way to slow down. *Think, Jen.* Nine seconds.

Platform divers jumped. They weren't pushed, but the basic principles of diving should apply. Eight seconds.

There wasn't any time to spare. Instinctively, my body folded into the pike position. I rotated one end over the other. The edges of the ship flew through my peripheral vision. As the water neared, I unfolded, pointing my fingertips at the water while twisting my body to face away from the ship. My eyes shut. I inhaled deeply and braced for the impact.

The water stung, but not as badly as if I'd belly-flopped from so high up. My body curled into a ball, allowing me to roll over, toward the surface. I swam away from the ship, seeking not to get caught in the water and other stuff churning from the bottom.

A cheer went up when I broke the surface. Treading water, I waved my arms overhead to let them know I was okay. Halfway up the ship, a tiny blond figure jumped up and down, then disappeared. Justin. He must've gone for help. I cupped my hands and yelled toward him, but the wind whipped my words in the opposite direction. He didn't reappear, so I let my hands drop. Better to save my energy for getting back on the ship. Once I caught up to it.

Surely, the ship's crew would send someone to rescue me once they realized a passenger fell overboard. I couldn't let the ship get too far away, but I wouldn't have to scale the sides or anything.

My mind racing, I egg-beatered my legs, eyes scanning for a rescue boat. Thankfully, there were plenty of witnesses to my fall, so I didn't have to wonder if Ariana cared enough to call for my rescue. Breathing in and out, I forced myself to remain calm and not wonder if sharks lived in the water off Cozumel. Sting rays. Jelly fish. Manatees.

Okay, Jen. Chill. One thing at a time. Step one, don't drown. Keep on swimming.

Something brushed against my foot, and I screamed. In the dusky light, it was impossible to see what lurked below the surface, and I probably didn't want to.

Finally, a siren split the air, and the boat stopped moving away from me. Floodlights lit up the area. The waves flickered around me as fish swam for the safety of the darkness, and my breathing came a bit easier. These were good signs.

Someone shouted instructions from the upper deck using a megaphone. I couldn't hear much over the roaring in my ears, but it sounded a lot like, "Don't move!"

As if I might go for a leisurely swim across shark-infested waters for the thrill of it. A moment later, something white flew high into the air, landing in the water between me and the ship. A life preserver. Awesome.

Feeling better already, I swam toward it. The light guided me to my destination. Swimming in the ocean took a lot more energy than swimming in a pool. Between my argument, my unexpected dive, treading water, and the swim, my arms felt like overcooked rigatoni by the time I wrapped them around the white circle floating on the water. I prayed they wouldn't expect me to hold on while they towed me to safety. What a ridiculous thought; exhaustion was clearly affecting my mind.

Toward the rear of the starboard side of the ship, three lifeboats began to lower. Oh, good. Climbing into a lifeboat sounded much better than hauling myself up the side of an ocean liner. I continued to tread water, trying not to think about what else floated around out there with me. Finally, the orange rafts drew near enough for me to hear one of the occupants call out to me. With graying hair at his temples, a dark tan, and deep-set eyes, the man reminded me of my father. For a moment, I thought I was hallucinating. I blinked water out of my eyes and shook my head, revealing that he looked like most of the other officers on the crew, down to the white uniform, but a couple of decades older.

When he spoke, his unusually deep voice dissipated any lingering resemblance to my father. "Hello there! Are you okay?"

"Just swell," I said. Trying to sound blasé helped me stave off panic. "You should offer balcony diving as a group activity for guests."

The man chuckled. "Hold on another sec. I'm Frank. Let me pull this thing up next to you, and then my friend Raoul and I will haul you aboard."

"No worries. I could float here all night." My voice shook, revealing the lie.

Two hands reached out to me, one tanned, the other dark brown. I stared at them, not wanting to relax my death grip on the life preserver.

"It's okay," Frank said. "Grab my hand first, then Raoul's. We've got you. You're going to be fine."

As scared as I was, getting pulled into a lifeboat sounded better than continuing to tread water indefinitely. I took a deep breath and reached out with my left hand. Once Raoul's warm hand gripped mine, I reached out with my right arm. He and Frank hauled me aboard.

It wasn't graceful. If the cameras reached this far out to sea, I'd go viral on YouTube within a couple of weeks. But I was safe. I lay on the bottom of the boat for a long moment, panting until Frank helped me up.

Once I settled onto a bench inside the raft, Raoul wrapped me in one of those thin emergency kit blankets that looked like aluminum foil and handed me a stainless steel beverage container.

"Coffee," he said.

"Got anything stronger?"

He winked at me. "How about you wait until we get back to the ship for that?"

Frank asked, "You okay, miss? Your name is Jennifer, right? I'd hate to think we saved the wrong damsel in distress."

"Jen," I said automatically. "And I'm the right damsel. Ariana was about to fall overboard, and . . . I miscalculated a little."

"Don't talk now," Frank said. "And don't move too much. Once we get onboard, I need to take you to the infirmary, and then the captain's going to want to take a statement."

"Did you hit your head when you fell, miss?" Raoul asked.

Shaking my head, I sipped from the Thermos. Hot, bitter coffee seared all the way down to my belly. I'd never tasted anything so satisfying.

Finally, our raft reached the side of the *Queen Kelly*. I'd expected a ladder or something, but instead Frank pulled up next to wire hooks dangling from the side of the boat. He attached them to large metal rings at either end of our raft and tugged on the lines sharply. Then he whistled twice, and we jerked upward.

"Is this safe?" Landing in the ocean two times in one night did not sound like twice the fun.

"Much safer than diving over a railing." Frank winked at me.

Someone called my name. Looking up, I spotted Justin only a few decks above us, waving frantically. I waved and blew him a kiss, trying not to create any motion that might capsize us in mid-air. Finally, after what felt like hours, we came to a stop next to an opening in the railing. Raoul went over first, then Frank lifted me up like a child and handed me to him.

My eyes went straight to Justin, who seemed to have aged about ten years. I stepped toward him, but Frank stopped me.

"I'm sorry, but we need to get you checked out by the ship's doctor before you go anywhere. We brought a wheelchair for you."

The idea of not being allowed to walk twenty feet to the elevator and then another few steps to the infirmary made me want to laugh, but the cruise line was probably already peeing their pants worrying I'd sue. They didn't know what was in the waiver the Network made me sign before coming on the trip. I couldn't sue if the captain tried to execute me on live television for the ratings. Still, I let a member of the staff transport me to the infirmary so a medical professional could confirm I hadn't broken anything in the fall.

Also, my legs buckled as soon as Raoul let go of me. He helped me into the wheelchair. I thanked him and turned to Frank.

"Can my boyfriend come with me? He won't be in the way, I promise."

Frank studied our faces for a moment before nodding. I wanted to throw myself into Justin's arms, but I settled for grasping his hand while Frank wheeled me down the hall to the elevator.

Justin gripped my fingers until they turned white, but I couldn't protest. I fully understood wanting to hold on to him and never let go, and I hadn't watched him nearly die. If I'd doubted how he felt after our conversation, the look on his face when he spotted me in the lifeboat cemented my trust in him. In us.

In the infirmary, Frank lifted me onto a paper-covered cot before leaving me and Justin alone. The door hadn't finished closing before Justin pulled me to him, crushing me against his chest. He rained kisses down my face before our lips met hungrily. His hands were everywhere, as if he wanted to examine me for injuries personally. I clutched at him desperately, never wanting to let go. When we finally parted, my breath came as fast as when I'd come up from my dive.

"Sweet Jesus. Don't you ever scare me like that again," he said. "I thought you—"

"Shh." I leaned forward and kissed him again, lightly. Tears streaked his face. "But I didn't. I'm okay, really."

"When you went over the edge, those were the longest seconds of my life. It felt like eons before you broke the surface."

"I'm glad the girls' high school diving coach was such a cutie. Otherwise, I might never have joined the team."

He relaxed the tiniest fraction at my bad joke. My heart still beat frantically in my chest. Before he could reply, the ship's doctor entered.

Fifteen minutes later, the Chief of Security arrived to ask me some questions about what happened. He assured me that the ship's therapist talked to Ariana, and she would be fine. She and Dominic would be moved to a room without a balcony, just in case.

I gave a quick statement, and he handed me a sheaf of papers trying to make me swear not to sue. Justin would never forgive me if I signed a waiver without consulting him. With a polite smile, I declined to take a pen about four times before the doctor let me walk out of the room under my own power, papers still in hand.

When I finally emerged, Justin leaned against the wall, staring at his hands. "What did he say?"

"I should be okay. They want me to stay awake for twenty-four hours in case I have a concussion. And I need to make an appointment with my doctor when we get home. Also, they want me to sign this waiver."

He pulled me into another long hug before dropping the papers into a nearby trash can. "I'll spend the entire night with you, keeping you awake, if that's what it takes."

"I suspect I'm going to enjoy that."

"Oh trust me, you will."

"I love you."

"I love you, too. I can't believe I almost lost you." After one last kiss, he pulled me toward the elevator. "Come on."

"Where are we going?"

"Up to the Lido Deck. We're having an impromptu party in your honor. Ed and Connor are in charge of drinks, and Rachel's making sure we have some food. Danielle's already got the chairs reserved for us. I'm not the only one who needs to see you in one piece." He paused. "Ariana and Dominic are there, too. But I can make them leave if you want."

A rush of love for my friends passed through me. Even considering the horrible start to this cruise, I was the luckiest woman in the world.

"No, it's fine. Let's all enjoy the rest of our last night onboard."

AFTER A QUICK TRIP to my cabin to change into dry clothes, I found my friends at the bar on the back of the Lido Deck. Everyone *oohed* and *ahhed* over me. Danielle complimented my dive, giving me a score of six out of six. Ed suggested I thank Tammy Rae for my new aerodynamic scalp.

"Hey!" Rachel said. "That was *my* idea."

Everyone laughed.

Ariana approached cautiously. I smiled at her, unsure what to say. Luckily, she spoke first. "So, um, I'd already forgiven you. No need to steal the show by almost dying."

"Well, that fall wasn't really part of the plan," I said. "But somewhere in this vast disclaimer they're making me sign, I'm going to make sure they agree not to air the video of you and Dominic. There must be plenty of other footage of us fighting to explain the fall."

For the first time I could remember, Ariana's smile reached her eyes. "I can pretty much guarantee it. Anyway, thanks. I officially promise never to bother you and Justin again."

"I officially promise to say nice things about you at the funeral, if I'm invited."

"Awesome." She eyed me. "We don't need to hug, do we?"

"Better not. I could have a concussion."

Instead I offered her a hand, which she took. A few minutes later, after saying goodbye to Justin, she and Dominic left the deck. With the ship returning to Miami the next day, I wondered if I'd ever see either of them again, other than on TV.

Under the stars, my friends and I ate and drank and talked and joked like I hadn't just almost died. The earlier horror of the evening evaporated. Other than the addition of Danielle and no Birdie or Abram, it felt like being in the Fishbowl. I never wanted the evening to end.

After eating three cupcakes from the ship's bakery (which were nothing compared to Madison's recipe) and draining my second hot cocoa with Kahlua, I leaned against my lounge chair with a happy sigh.

"Looks like I got my perfect final evening on the cruise after all," I said. Ed raised his eyebrows at me. "I mean, sure, I fell into the ocean, but now I've got an awesome story to tell when I get home. People will come into the bakery purely to ask me about it."

"That's my girl," Justin said. "Always looking at the bright side. I'm just glad this chapter of our story didn't turn into a tearjerker."

"Also, I'm surrounded by some of the most important people in my life. I love you all."

"I love the way you look at things," Rachel said. She and Justin exchanged a look. "But I wouldn't say the evening is perfect. Not yet."

"It's awesome for me," Ed said. "The truth has come out about Ariana, so we can all process it and decide how to deal. The three of us are rocking the new 'do. The Network is going to give me and Connor a suite for the evening as a thank you for the awesome drama we provided. Jen and Justin are together and happy, as they should be. Plus, Jen got to show off some bad-ass Olympic diving skills."

I chuckled. "I'm far from Olympic quality. I never even made it to the state championships in college."

"Hush," Ed said. "We're celebrating you. Smile, nod, and take a drink."

"State Championships or no, you're a survivor," Justin said. "That's part of your indomitable spirit, and I love you."

Squeezing his hand, I said, "I love you, too."

Rachel cleared her throat.

"Now?" Justin asked.

She nodded. "What are you waiting for?"

Ed shrugged at my questioning look. "I have no idea what they're talking about."

Before I said anything else, Justin stood, raising his glass. "I'd like to propose a toast. All I wanted for this trip was to spend some time alone with my girlfriend and have a nice, quiet, romantic voyage. Clearly, that was never going to happen." We all chuckled. Of course the Network would throw some wrenches into our plans for a nice, relaxing vacation. We never should've expected anything less.

"But through it all, we managed to come out closer than ever. We're lucky to be surrounded by all our friends." Justin swallowed and continued, speaking only to me, despite the crowd. "First I wanted to do this before we left, but with the other store opening and Sarah burning the cupcakes, it didn't pan out. I wanted to do it in the Bahamas, but I let worries about losing our identities get in the way. Then I wanted to do it in Jamaica on the beach, but I missed the boat. Literally."

I bit my lip to keep from squealing. Was this it? Did he have the ring with him? A balloon of hope started to form in my chest. Was he doing what I thought he might be doing? No. It wasn't possible.

"I missed you so much all week. I hate fighting with you, and I don't ever want to be apart that long again. The moment you kissed me in the casino, it reaffirmed that you're the one for me. I should've asked right there, but I wasn't ready. I'm an idiot for waiting so long. I thought I needed the perfect timing or the perfect thing to say. I don't. All I need is you, because you're what matters."

"*We're* what matters," I corrected him.

"Shhh," he said. "I'm kind of in the middle of something important here."

Oops. "Right. Sorry. Please continue."

"I finally realized: what could be better or more perfect than this moment right here, right now when we're surrounded by old and new friends? Better than sharing our love and happiness with all the viewers who've been with us for every major step of our relationship?"

My heart pounded in my throat, preventing me from saying anything. Tears prickled the backs of my eyes. To my horror, my nose started running. But nothing could ruin this moment for us.

Justin knelt in front of me and produced a box from the pocket of his shorts. My eyes widened. After an entire week of wondering and waiting, our moment finally arrived. He was going to do it.

My breath caught when the box creaked open. The world blurred. Inside the box lay the most beautiful ring I'd ever seen. A dazzling diamond nestled between two triangular sapphires sat in a platinum band.

Justin's eyes met mine, shining with love. Was he crying, too? "Jennifer?"

My ears perked up. This had to be the real thing. He never called me by my full name. No one did.

"Yes?"

"The past sixteen months have been the best time of my life," Justin said. "Ever since I saw you at the audition for *The Fishbowl*, I knew you were someone special. But I never dreamed I would care about anyone as much as I love you.

"I know we've had some ups and downs, but being down with you is better than being up with anyone else. Life with you promises to be challenging, exciting, and full of surprises. Nothing excites me more than the thought of us sharing that life. Jen, I love you."

I barely registered the words. Before he finished speaking, I started nodding and babbling, "Yes!" over and over. He could have been saying anything, and I would have agreed to it.

"He hasn't actually asked you anything yet," Ed said helpfully. Rachel elbowed him in the ribs before I got the chance to tell him to shut up.

To Justin, I said, "I love you, too. More every day."

"Will you marry me?"

Those words, the sweetest I'd ever heard in my life, I heard very clearly.

"YES! Absolutely! Of course I will." My nose flowed freely by then, and I was babbling, but I didn't care.

Tears of joy streamed down my face. Justin gave me a long, lingering kiss, full of tenderness. He pulled me against him, holding me like he never wanted to let go.

All around us, the cameras rolled. Behind me, I heard clapping. Someone whooped. Probably Ed. I'd almost forgotten everyone else surrounded us. Justin and I kissed again before I pulled away to accept his gift. Justin slipped the platinum circle over my left ring finger. It fit perfectly.

We turned to the growing crowd and raised our clasped hands. "Guess what, everyone? We're getting married!"

A roared went up around the deck. Cameras flashed. I beamed and hugged Justin again. Then, he pressed his lips to mine, and the rest of the world fell away. This was what mattered. The two of us, and the way we felt about each other. Nothing else.

"No more cameras, Jen," he whispered. "Just you and me. Forever."

"Forever." I agreed.

No more being on display. We were done with television. And we were going to live happily ever after.

TWENTY-FOUR

SHOCKING ENTERTAINMENT NEWS ONLINE

HE WENT DOWN ON ONE KNEE, AND YOU WON'T BELIEVE WHAT HAPPENED NEXT

The Fishbowl *Couple Betrothed?*

by Talky Ted, Nov. 10

Inside sources tell me Justin Taylor was spotted onboard the *Queen Kelly* on bended knee, talking to a visibly flustered Jen Reid. Are wedding bells on the horizon? Official sources for the show declined to comment. Ms. Reid and Mr. Taylor are at this moment still onboard, leaving this reporter anxiously awaiting communication from anyone in the know.

Still, two thousand people aren't known for their group secret-keeping abilities. If Jen and Justin are headed down the aisle, the news should break before they disembark. The Network may be regretting their choice not to air this show live, after viewers saw with their own eyes what happens when Double J gets together.

Jen's ex-boyfriend Dominic replied to an email seeking comment, quashing any rumors of a shotgun wedding. "Jen was drinking heavily on the cruise," he said. "No way she's pregnant. But based on what I saw, there's no way Justin proposed to anyone onboard. Ariana told me Justin and Jen are done. Mark my words, Jen will come back to me any day now."

This turn of events opens the door to multiple questions:

Will the Network televise the wedding?

Foot the bill?

Will they make Jen pick Ariana for a bridesmaid? Does this mean Birdie will return to television?

What drugs did Dominic pick up ashore that he thinks Jen wants him back?

Click here for rest of article.

Related Stories:

Get the inside scoop on the most amazing reality-show reunion of all time.

Leaked footage shows *The Fishbowl/Real Ocean: Caribbean* **star Jen Reid falling overboard. Real or Staged?**

Deaf Teen Mother **Madison leaks major news; Tammy Rae's upcoming memoir canceled.**

The Fishbowl's **Carrie "Birdie" O'Brien announces pregnancy.**

TWENTY-FIVE

THE MIAMI BEAT

SIGN ME UP FOR ANOTHER SEASON OF SWEET REALITY!

Reality show–themed bakery a breakaway hit
By Beth Schumann, Dec. 2

Ever since the premier of *Real Ocean: Caribbean*, this reporter has eagerly awaited the opening of Sweet Reality in downtown Miami. After all, what could be better than combining my two greatest addictions: baked goods and bad television?

The shop's interior delivers on its name's promise. From the glittering floors to the portraits of America's favorite reality TV stars decorating the walls, this place is utterly adorbs. Jen and Sarah know their target demographic. The elegance of Patty's Cakes might pull in Miami's older crowd, but Millennials created a line 'round the block leading into Sweet Reality. (A gentleman to the core and the brother/boyfriend of the co-owners, Justin Taylor stood outside, handing cups of water to those tapping our feet against the sidewalk. (No confirmation yet on the engagement rumors, but I'm ready for the *Real Ocean: Caribbean* finale on Dec. 23.)

Anyway, I digress. What matters at a bakery is the food, right? Sweet Reality does not disappoint. The names may be a bit odd to anyone who's not familiar with Jen's history, but then so might the decor. Either way, everything tasted delicious. The fishbowl-shaped cookies were thick and buttery, with a creamy vanilla frosting that's making me drool a bit as I write. Not very hungry? Enjoy a "sneak preview"— mini-cupcakes and bite-sized cookies or brownies. Or get a shot of icing called the "commercial break."

The Jen Cupcake slides into first place, a yellow cake with chocolate frosting and a cookie dough center. Despite the name making no sense, the cake tasted delicious, and I love that they also sell the "Cruise Jen," a "bald" cupcake (i.e., no frosting). Unfortunately, the Cruise Jen sold out before I made it to the counter, but 50% of the profits from those cakes are being donated to cancer research, so chow down, Miami! The Madison, an amazing chocolate, banana, and peanut butter creation, also ranks an honorable mention.

Cardboard cutouts of Jen and Justin stand in the corners for patrons who want pictures taken with the "stars." Alas, no Sarah cutout to be found. Where's the love? Call me, Sarah!

Sorry, I got distracted. Whether you're a reality TV fan or not, Sweet Reality is worth a peek. Personally, I'll be binge(-watch)ing there on a regular basis. Hope to see you! 5 spatulas.

Related Stories:
   Patty's Cakes: Too big, too fast?

ACKNOWLEDGMENTS

I have jokingly said that this book is actually about the love between me and cupcakes, but my husband is my one true love and the perfect partner for me. Thank you so much, darling, for everything. Thank you to Stephanie Thornton again for inspiring this series and for being an amazing best friend. No matter where we are in the world, it's like you're right beside me. I would cross an ocean for you (or with you!).

Thank you again to my wonderful agent, Michelle Richter. I hope to thank you in many, many acknowledgments to come. Thank you to the entire Kensington team, especially Wendy McCurdy, Norma Perez-Hernandez, Michelle Forde, and Lauren Jernigan.

Carey O'Connor, K.D. Proctor, and Elizabeth Newmann, thank you so much for your valuable feedback. Thank you to the #17Scribes critique group for help with my first chapter. Marty Mayberry and Kara Reynolds, thank you both for not only reading the book and providing insight, but for holding my hand through countless hours of brainstorming sessions. (Also, you're both rock stars for reading *America's Next Reality Star* just to give me feedback on *Sweet Reality*.) Laura Brown, thank you for all your help with the entire book, but especially with Madison's character. You did your best to steer me in the right direction, and I hope I stayed the course. Any mistakes are 100% my fault, and I apologize to you, my readers, and the Deaf community for them,

Deana Anker, thank you for always being available to meet me at Starbucks and listen to me rant about everything wrong with my books . . . er, I mean, and "write." Thank you to Kellye Garrett for creating the #17Scribes, and for generally being awesome. Thank you to all the #17Scribes and Pitch Wars mentors for your love and support.

Finally, I'd like to thank Carly Rae Jepsen for providing the soundtrack for this book. When life events had me feeling less than cheerful, your songs always put me in the right mood to keep going. Call me, maybe?

I hope you enjoyed SWEET REALITY. I enjoyed writing it even more than the first book, and I didn't think that was possible. The best thing for a writer is to know when readers liked their book. If you did, please consider leaving an honest review on Amazon or Goodreads. A recommendation is the greatest support a reader can give a writer. You can also find me on Twitter @LH_Writes or at www.facebook.com/lauraheffernananbooks.

IN LOVE WITH JEN AND JUSTIN?

Read on for a preview of

REALITY WEDDING

the stunning finale of the *Reality Star* series

Chapter 1

Unlike most brides, nearly every milestone of my relationship with my future husband, Justin, had been captured on video and broadcast to America as part of season one of *The Fishbowl*: our growing attraction, our first fight, our first kiss, the proposal. So I shouldn't have been surprised when I answered my phone in the middle of a lull at work to find my favorite reality show producer asking if we wanted to get married on TV.

Shouldn't have been surprised, but Connor's question stopped me in my tracks. I stared at my phone, watching the timer tick upward. Five seconds seemed an eternity. Then ten seconds passed. The bustle of the bakery continued around me, but all I saw was my phone. That timer ticking.

"Jen?" His voice sounded tinny. Far away. With effort, I returned the phone to my ear and found my voice.

"Hold on," I said, ducking through the kitchen and out the back door for some privacy. I didn't want anyone to overhear this conversation. "You want us to get married in Los Angeles? On what, a special episode of *The Fishbowl*, season three?"

"No, no, no. That season doesn't start filming until July. We want to give you your own show. *Jen & Justin's Reality Wedding. J&J's Big Day. Becoming Mrs. Taylor.* The title's still a work in progress," he said. "Anyway, we'll film everything: cake tastings, dress fittings, meetings with the officiant. Then we'll film the ceremony in a two-hour special. The viewers will eat it up, and it'll be a great lead-in for *The Fishbowl*'s new season."

While theoretically, having your own reality show sounded awesome, this wasn't my first rodeo. I wasn't sure how I felt about having every last detail of my wedding broadcast to the world. This seemed more personal than solving puzzles or taking a cruise. The stakes were higher. I didn't want the Network interfering in my relationship again.

"Being on TV last time almost broke us up."

"And being on TV the first time brought you together," he said. "You'd never have met if not for the show."

That was true, but when Justin proposed, we both swore to leave the reality TV community behind forever. No more pop-up appearances. No more reality fun runs. Maybe a fundraiser or two for the right charity, but absolutely, positively No More TV Shows.

"I'm sorry, Connor, but we can't. Justin and I have retired our reality show personas."

"Are you sure?"

"I'm afraid so. But I appreciate the thought. And you and Ed better still come to the wedding when we have it." My best friend Ed, *The Fishbowl*'s official runner-up, lived with Connor in Los Angeles, where he'd built a successful stand-up career after our appearances on two reality shows.

"We wouldn't miss it for anything. You sure I can't get you to change your mind?"

"If you want, I can ask Justin to be sure, but I'm guessing the answer is no. I'm sorry."

"What if we offer to pay for everything?"

My ears perked up. "Everything?"

"Including the honeymoon."

Now that was tempting. Sweet Reality, the bakery I co-owned with Justin's sister, Sarah, was doing fine, but we wouldn't be able to afford a real vacation any time soon. People thought we had loads of money because we'd done a reality show, but that couldn't be further from the truth. Most of my *Fishbowl* winnings went into launching the business. The second show we did, *Real Ocean: Caribbean*, was only a week. We made almost nothing beyond the free vacation.

Justin was still a first-year associate at his law firm, and we'd spent most of our incomes in the past year on his parents' medical bills and paying down his student loans. To call our wedding budget a shoestring stretched the bounds of the English language. We were on a dental-floss budget, unless we wanted to wait three years to get married. And we could. We could wait for the big, fancy wedding. Or we could have a small ceremony now, and a big, fat vow renewal on our tenth or twenty-fifth anniversary. There were many options. The world was our oyster.

Then another thought struck me. "Wait a sec. The honeymoon? I mean, you're not asking to film the honeymoon, right? Because that would be a hard no."

He laughed. "No, of course not. But we will send you on a two-week tour of Europe, all expenses paid, if that's what you want."

The balloon of hope that had been growing inside me deflated as the reality of those words sank in. "Unless you're also paying someone to run Sweet Reality for me while I'm gone, that could never happen."

It had been bad enough when I'd ducked out for a week to film *Real Ocean* right before our opening last year, though I'd made it back for the big day. Now, the bakery was thriving, but until we hired a full-time manager, I couldn't disappear for several weeks to film a show and then take a luxurious honeymoon.

Sarah needed me. Sweet Reality needed me. I couldn't walk away from my business less than a year after it opened. Not when we were starting to turn a profit.

Connor sighed heavily into the phone. "Okay, look. I'm not supposed to tell you this. Promise you won't mention it?"

"Mention what?"

"I'm in a bind here. Remember Braden from the cruise?"

"Sure." Braden had come in third in a baking competition Justin and I helped judge on the show. He'd starred in some dating reality show where he'd winnowed a pack of beautiful women down to one bride, who I hadn't met. We weren't exactly friends, but he'd seemed nice enough.

"Well, this was supposed to be *his* wedding," Connor said. "The Network has already scheduled everything, and most of it's paid for. He and Amanda broke up last week, so now there's a hole in the TV schedule. I need someone for a wedding-themed reality show, and I haven't been able to come up with anyone else. Besides, you and Justin are perfect. You're reality stars, and you met and got engaged on Network shows. The public has followed your relationship since the beginning."

"I appreciate that, but that's exactly why we'd like some privacy now. We want to start our life together as a married couple away from the public eye."

"I completely understand, Jen, absolutely." He took a deep breath. "But *Braden & Amanda's Big Day* was my shot at being first associate producer instead of a cameraman or assistant. This is my show. All eyes are on me. If I can't come up with another couple, I'm fired."

A pang of guilt hit me. I didn't want to ruin a friend's career any more than I wanted to ruin my own life. Connor had been a good friend over the past couple of years, but I wasn't sure if his career needs were more important than the health of my relationship. Then a thought hit me. Justin and I weren't the only couple that hooked up on *The Fishbowl* and stayed together.

"Why don't you and Ed get married? You've been dating as long as me and Justin. Longer, actually, since we never snuck away on the show to make out. And America loves Ed. He's hilarious."

Connor sighed. "I wish. The first gay couple getting married on live TV? It would be amazing. I pitched it, but Leanna shot me down hard."

"Leanna's running this show?" My voice moved toward a range only dogs could hear. "When were you going to mention that?"

He must be desperate to ask me to get involved with that woman again, after she arranged for me to miss the cruise ship from Jamaica, leaving me stranded with my ex-boyfriend while Justin sailed away with my archrival. She only agreed to bring me back aboard after I promised to create more drama. Drama that nearly broke up me and Justin for good.

"After you agreed," he said sheepishly. "But, I swear, I will be your only contact with the network. We've set up the whole thing. You won't see or talk to her at all. She's the show runner, meaning she'll be in the background the entire time, but she'll be dealing with everyone else."

"Right. Of course she will. Let's go back to you and Ed. Are you guys getting married?" Nothing would make me happier than seeing my friend and twice costar make a lifetime commitment to the man who cherished him and had encouraged him to follow his dreams. After moving to LA, Ed rode the fast track to stardom, becoming the most famous (only famous?) former member of *The Fishbowl*.

"Eventually. When the show said no, I decided to take time to plan the type of proposal he deserves," Connor said. "So, back to you. We're going to film the show over ten days, so you won't have to be gone from the bakery for too long."

"The Network pays for everything?"

"Everything. Picture the dream wedding you always wanted."

Unbidden, an image of Kate Middleton, Duchess of Cambridge, swam before my eyes, pulling up to the church in a horse-drawn carriage. Walking down the aisle in that gorgeous white dress. Not puffy or overwhelming, classy. A simple veil down her back. Carrying a bouquet of white flowers before driving off with her prince while the crowd cheered. I'd watched the entire wedding with my mom, and we'd gone through half a box of tissues.

Some small part of me wanted that. I never would have thought myself the type. I always figured I'd have a fairly low-key wedding. On a beach, at sunset. A simple, lacy sundress. Flowers braided into my hair.

Or no flowers, since I shaved my head on the cruise after losing a bet. Six months later, my hair was still pretty short.

Extensions weren't exactly in our budget, but the Network had much more to spend than me and Justin. My excitement started to grow. I never thought I wanted a princess wedding until Connor said I could have anything.

Reality burst my bubble as I pictured the producers at my wedding, interfering. I shook my head. Justin and I didn't need a fancy wedding. It didn't matter whether I had long hair, short hair, or no hair. All we needed was each other, a marriage license, witnesses, and someone ordained by the state of Florida.

Connor must have recognized my silence as indecision. His words tempted me, although I wished they didn't. "Please think about it?"

"When do I have to decide?"

"Tomorrow. No pressure."

A bark of laughter choked me. "Right. No pressure at all. One more thing: if I do this, I am under no circumstances consuming any food I did not physically see being prepared, unless it comes from Ed. Neither is Justin."

"You think we're going to drug you?"

"I don't know. I didn't expect anyone to give me pot brownies while filming *Real Ocean*, did I? Or cupcakes with breast milk in them?"

"Fair point," he said. "Deal. I'll get Ed to move into the house with you for the duration. He can be your personal chef."

"In that case, yes, I'll think about it. Let me talk to Justin."

"Thanks, Jen. You're the best." He hung up.

Leaning against the brick wall of the building, I nibbled one thumbnail while I debated whether to call my fiancé before heading back inside. I should say no. We didn't need to get married on national television. Sure, it would be nice not to go into debt to fund our wedding, but we were never going to do that. When we first got engaged, Justin's mother had been suffering from cancer, so we'd expected to have a short, quick ceremony, possibly at her bedside. The plan never had been to spend a lot of money, and that was fine with us.

My future mother-in-law had miraculously gone into remission in January, so she could now join us anywhere we tied the knot. But did we want to get married in Los Angeles? And not needing to get married quickly didn't automatically translate to spending a lot of money. Did we *want* a big, fancy wedding? The poufy white dress, a dozen attendants, all that jazz?

My phone buzzed with a text. An image filled the screen. The same picture of the Duchess of Cambridge I'd already formed in my head. A smile spread across my face as I pictured myself in that gown. Connor knew exactly how to tug my heartstrings.

Aw, man. I did want *My Beautiful Princess Wedding*. Or whatever they decided to call it.

Sure, we didn't need a big wedding. But we could also let the Network pay for it. We could have everything we ever wanted, now. If his mother's cancer returned, she'd have the joy of watching us get married before she got sick. Possibly over and over, watching us get married On Demand. Every mother's dream, right? My mother would certainly be overjoyed.

My phone buzzed again with another image. This one of Kate with her sister/bridesmaid, both in their white dresses. The text came seconds later. *You and Sarah? You and Rachel? We'll fly in whoever you want.*

I promise, I'll talk to Justin. We'll call you tonight, I replied.

The phone went back into my apron pocket as I went inside and dove back into the bustle of the bakery. The rest of the morning flew, but as lunchtime approached, I thought more and more about Connor's offer. Finally, about twenty minutes before my lunch break, I pulled Sarah aside.

Her mouth dropped when I explained the offer. "Holy crap, that's huge. They're going to pay for everything? Like, including my maid-of-honor dress?"

"I told you, you don't have to buy an expensive dress."

"Of course I do. Especially if the Network's buying." She winked at me.

"We can afford to close for a week while you come out, right?"

"I don't need an entire week. You know me and reality TV. I'll just come out for the wedding." Her response came as no surprise. Sarah and I met during my audition for *The Fishbowl*, when I found her crying in the bathroom because Justin talked her into trying out for the show with him. She'd never wanted to be on TV, even after seeing how the experience changed my life.

"But you'll still be in the wedding, right? Even though it's televised?"

"I wouldn't miss it for the world." She held my gaze, strong and steady. "Does this mean you're considering it?"

"Depends. Can you make it for a couple of weeks without me?"

At the front of the store, a cashier took and filled orders for a growing line of customers. If anyone else walked in, she'd need to grow a second set of hands. Back in the kitchen, Sarah's assistant iced cupcakes. Someone needed to mop and sweep the floors, and a stack of phone orders waited for Sarah by the back sink. Running the bakery wasn't a one-person job.

"We'll be fine," she said. "It may be time to promote Betsy to assistant manager and find someone new to cover the front. I've been stalling because I have trouble trusting other people to get the work done when we're not here, but you have to cut the cord eventually."

"You're serious? You don't mind?"

"Of course I don't mind! Hiring more people means we can both take regular days off. Besides, your fame is half the draw of this place! Actually, you're most of the draw."

"That's not true. People come for your cupcakes."

"There are a thousand cupcake places in Florida. We get Internet orders from Fort Lauderdale and Atlanta because of you." She gestured at the walls, which were adorned with reality TV stills, mostly me and Justin and other friends from *The Fishbowl*. "Go. Be famous. Talk up the bakery. Sales will skyrocket, both when they announce the show and when it airs. I don't mind leaving Betsy in charge for a couple of days while I fly out for the ceremony. It'll be a good test to see if she can handle the job full time. When are you leaving?"

"If all goes well, the end of the week."

"That's so exciting!" She threw her arms around me. "Why aren't you ecstatic about this?"

I hesitated. "Because I still have to talk to Justin."

"Oh, right. Justin."

Right. The man who swore on his grandmother's antique engagement ring that we were done with reality television forever. He wasn't going to be happy that I was considering another show.

"I'm going to go to the courthouse for lunch." Justin and I had a standing Wednesday lunch date when he had to appear in court, which was more often than not. The walk would give me time to figure out what I wanted to say to him.

"Hold on a sec." Sarah stuffed a white cardboard box into my hand. "Lemon meringue cupcakes. You might need 'em."

"Thanks."

CONTINUE READING

WRITTEN AS ADA BELL

Welcome to Shady Grove...

Aly doesn't believe in psychics. Too bad she just had a vision.

Future scientists don't have visions. Aly's got enough on her plate, with finishing her degree and taking care of her nephew and starting her new job at the antique store while drooling over the owner's gorgeous son. No visions.

Alas, the universe doesn't care what Aly believes. When she turns 21, she starts to feel psychic impressions left on objects. A disorienting power for someone surrounded by antiques. Then cranky customer Earl is killed, and Aly's new boss Olive is the prime suspect. Who hated Earl enough to kill? Police would rather make a quick arrest than investigate, so it's up to Aly to clear Olive's name.

Shady Grove is reeling from the first murder in decades. If Aly can get her hands on the murder weapon, she should be able to solve the crime. Can she learn to control her visions before the killer sets their sights on her?

Mystic Pieces

The Scry's the Limit

Sight Seering

Seer Today, Gone Tomorrow

www.ingramcontent.com/pod-product-compliance
Lightning Source LLC
Chambersburg PA
CBHW050830190726
48286CB00007B/2033